DOWN LOW, DOUBLE LIFE

Other books by D.L. Smith

Handling the Truth
The Dangers of Dysfunction
Handling the Truth II: Brothers and White Women
Divorce Him, Marry Me (First Edition)
Divorce Him, Marry Me (Second Edition)

Coming Soon!

Bitter (The sequel to Divorce Him, Marry Me)
Visit the author's website at www.dlsmith.net

DOWN LOW, DOUBLE LIFE

A Novel by D.L. Smith

iUniverse, Inc.

New York Lincoln Shanghai

Down Low, Double Life

iUniverse, Inc.

For information address:
iUniverse, Inc.
2021 Pine Lake Road, Suite 100
Lincoln, NE 68512
www.iuniverse.com

ISBN: 0-595-31323-X

Printed in the United States of America

C ONTENTS

▼

Thank You
I would like to thank God for allowing me to complete another project.
As always I want to send a shout out to Leslie Swanson.
Sean Garrison, you have been my frat/flight/brother since 92. Peace.
I would like to say hi to all the guys from the block (and the girls).
I want to say thanks to Katrina Robertson, my #1 fan.

Hugs and Kisses to: The Smith Family, The Lowery Family, My former colleagues in social services, my agent, the publisher, the city of Chicago, V103, WGCI, Power 92, Melanie Palmer, Nicole Logan, Farrah Ellison, Loretta Carter, Kim Hesser, Pia Green, Myrtle Rycraw-Jackson, Joy Johnson-Jackson, Mr. Kelly Williams, My team at Hull House, My classmates from NLU, and you the readers…I am nothing without your support!

I would like to give a hug to Amanda (Big Mandy) Good, Amy Douglas, Cortaiga (Country) Johnson, Trina Spiff, Beth Yaney, and my former team at NTN.

Mad Props to: Eric Jerome Dickey, Travis Hunter, E. Lynn Harris, Michael Baisden, Lisa Raye, Syleena Johnson, Terisa Griffin, R. Kelly, The Brat, Twista, and all the Hair Salons in the Chi.
Mad props to Meechie and the guys at Imperial Kutz in Calumet City. Thanks for keeping my fade tight.

CHAPTER 1

▼

BLACKGROUND

Jamie was sweating profusely in the recreation room of his best friend's suburban home. Out front he could hear all of his closest friends laughing and telling jokes. Many of them were celebrating as if they were the one getting married. Jamie was nervous and shaking. He didn't know what to do with himself. In just under an hour, he was scheduled to drive south on Torrence Avenue, to be married to his girlfriend of several years, Mia. Jamie sat and rocked on his bed trying to figure out what he was going to do.

After minutes of torturing himself, Mike Carter walked in the door. Mike was Jamie's best friend and best man. Mike stood six feet four inches and looked every bit like Maven of the WWE with a fade rather than a bald head. He had a Caramel colored complexion and was muscular like a model in a fitness magazine. He took one look at the lost expression on his boy's face and knew immediately what was up.

"Are you all right kid?" He asked.

"Man, Mike I don't think that I can do this."

"It's a little late in the game to be saying that player. So what's the problem?"

"I don't know. I hate to admit it but I am scared as hell."

Jamie stood six feet three inches tall. He was buff like a professional wrestler from all those years playing football at NLU, and the two years that he played for the Chicago Bandits as a wide receiver. He was a handsome brother that looked like *Eric Benet*. He was a fine specimen of a man.

Mike thought to himself that it was hard to imagine Jamie Kennedy being afraid of anything. Still, here he was in his tuxedo running his hands through his dreadlocks to the point that he might straighten his own kinky hair.

Mike asked, "So why is it that you feel you can no longer go through with this?"

Jamie said, "I don't know. I guess I have had too much time on my hands to think. I mean fifty percent of marriages end in divorce."

"So what makes you think that you and Mia are going to end up divorced?"

"I don't…but we might, ya know?"

Mike thought long and hard about his response.

"Look, I am fairly sure that you and Mia are not like everyone else…"

Jamie interrupted, "That's part of the problem. We are exactly like everyone else. We argue, we fight, and just like everyone else we are slaves to our jobs. We are just like everyone else. Mia and I are just *average*."

Mike said, "Jamie, you all are not just average. I have seen the two of you together. You all have something special. In regard to what others go through, you just can't think about that. The *average* person out here trades in their part-ners like they trade in their cars. The average person bails when times get hard or when they become bored. People just don't seem to fight to make their relation-ships work anymore. The average couple out here needs to go back to the old school way of doing things. If you and Mia still fight, that's a good thing. At least you are talking to one another when you disagree. Many of today's couples don't talk at all. They ignore one another, concede to one another as opposed to com-promise, or they say fuck it and bail out. I think if you all are fighting and argu-ing but you can still make love to one another at the end of the night, then what you have is special and worth fighting for. From the outside looking in, you like the ideal couple to me. I'm telling you, it's going to work out."

Jamie said, "This, from a twice divorced man?"

Jamie's words stung. He didn't mean to hurt his friend and that message was clear in his eyes. It was also clear that Jamie needed some answers, and though the words hurt, Mike needed to look beyond the words and be there for his friend.

By looking at Jamie you could tell that he didn't want to say what he said, but it was one of those necessary evils between friends. After what seemed like an eternity between the two men, Mike spoke again.

"Dawg, you can't look at me as the example, but you can learn from my mistakes. My first marriage ended because of poor communication between me and Loretta and my own shortcomings. The second marriage ended because I married a woman that was not into me, but a woman that was with me for what I could do for her. Both flaws in my marriages are not things that you have to worry about in your relationship."

Jamie said, "But you and Loretta, I love you guys. It hurts me to see two people that love each other so much, be away from one another. You guys were the ideal couple once upon a time. You guys had what Mia and I are striving for, and the two of you are divorced."

Mike was again hurt by his friend's words. Not a day passes that he doesn't think about the fact that he has a failed marriage. Mike and Loretta love one another, but their problems seem to be bigger than love these days. Mike works as the Deputy Mayor of Calumet City. His daily responsibilities pulled him in many different directions, including away from his wife. He was often out of town and often working on putting out fires for the Mayor. Mike has political aspirations; these aspirations seem to suggest that he be a single man all his life. It is such a position however that he *needs a woman in his life* to help him deal with the everyday chaos.

He and Loretta still meet for breakfast at IHOP every Saturday and they occasionally go out on a date, but in reference to the healing that needs to happen between them, they are worlds apart.

Still, Mike saw something special when he looked at Jamie and Mia. There was something about the two of them that reminded him of his relationship with Loretta, and he very much wanted that to prosper. Because of that, he decided to simply speak from the heart.

"Jamie, do you love her?"

"Of course I do."

"Then go with that. Love is too hard to come by these days. A good woman is equally hard to come by. If you have a woman that you love, that has your back, hold on to her as long as you can, even if it's just for a little while."

"It's that little while part that scares me." Jamie said.

"Well a little while is better than nothing."

"You think so?"

"Hell yeah. Look, you have a good sister on your hands, you had better hold on to her. I listen day in and day out at city hall to all these younger sisters out there and trust me, you don't want to be out there on the dating scene again."

"Are you sure about that? I mean there are some fine ass women out there."

"Yeah they may be fine, but a lot of these heifers don't have two nickels to rub together. What's worse is some of the stuff that these young sisters let walk out of their mouths these days. Many of them want you to look a certain way, have so much in the bank, and drive a certain type of car and they ain't bringing shit to the table but a big butt and a smile, and you know what BBD said about that back in the day."

"Preach on it" Jamie said, egging his long time friend on.

"All I am saying is a lot of women out here have got the game twisted. If you ever do go back on the market again, you have to hunt really hard to find a black woman out here that has some common sense, decent looks and a good head on their shoulders. Otherwise you will have to date an older sister because they seem to be the only ones with any sense these days."

"Really?"

"Really. These younger women act like you are supposed to do things for them. They act like you owe them something. They don't even say thank you when you hold a door open for them or say thank you for a pleasant evening at the end of a date. They seem ungrateful, mean spirited, and a great deal of them are conceited."

Jamie was surprised at his boy's response to today's dating scene, but Mike would know better than anyone else because he was out there. Jamie hadn't seriously looked at another woman since Mia, and that was several years ago. Mike continued on with his tirade.

"I have been out there for a minute Dawg. Since Loretta and I split, I have tried everything under the sun to find happiness again and it just doesn't seem to be out there. Here I am a Deputy Mayor, with three degrees, and sisters treat me like a damned leper. Some trip because the car I drive is an Oldsmobile. Some are just too damned dominant and bitter with men that they forget how to interact with a man. Others are so busy being independent, that they forget how to be a lady. Then there are those fighting their true urges and are secretly lesbian, and other women that can't make up their mind so they are bi-sexual, and then there are the Jesus freaks, gold diggers, and professional women."

Jamie said, "First of all, the term Jesus freak is blasphemous, secondly what's wrong with the professional women?"

Mike said, "Professional sisters are so busy working on *their careers* that they don't have time for relationships. Those sisters have flipped the script and now they don't want anything but booty calls. They call you, fuck you and then dismiss you."

Jamie started laughing at his friends remarks. He said, "Mike, you are bullshitting me."

"The hell I am!" Mike said seriously. "Just the other day I was at a conference in Washington. I met up with a fine ass congresswoman from New York. She was this light skinned honey with long brown hair, an ass to die for and perfect breasts. She had these Sade lips on her that should be the mascot for Revlon or something. Man, this woman had legs out of this world, and a sharp ass mind. The girl was tight! She was so tight that I had forgotten completely about Loretta and was trying to figure out how to keep this woman for my own. Anyway, after the conference we exchanged a few words, and agreed to meet in her hotel lobby for a night on the town. She and I kicked it to a reggae spot on the north side, we hit this jazz spot out east, and then took one of those long romantic strolls along the coast. To make a long story short, I took her back to her room and tapped that ass. I tapped that ass for old and new until she curled up in the fetal position to get some sleep."

"Sounds like you had a good night" Jamie said.

"Naw, not quite. Just as I was about to lie down, this broad tells me to not get comfortable and to let myself out within the next ten minutes. I was like 'what?' She was like, "let yourself out in ten minutes, I have to get up in the morning." Man I got up washed up in the bathroom and left. On the way out I heard her say "Thanks.""

Jamie broke out laughing. "Damn dawg, she did you like that?"

"Yeah. Would you believe the next day I went to exchange numbers, you know, home numbers, and the sister told me that she didn't want to try a long distance thing but if she was ever in Chicago, she would look me up."

"Well at least that's something" Jamie said.

"Man, whatever. I felt used when that broad told me to get up and leave."

"Well, that's no different than what we have been doing to them for years."

"That's my point, that's what's out there now…drama. Look dawg, if you love Mia I say go for it. There is nothing else out here to save yourself for. Mia is fine and although there *might be* prettier women out there, all they will want an ex pro athlete like you for, is what you can do for them. They will set your ass up faster than that broad that set up our boy in Colorado."

Jamie looked at his boy and nodded his head in agreement. He had a beautiful woman waiting on him that was waiting patiently to pledge the rest of her life to him. For that fact alone, he should be grateful.

"You're right Mike, I can do this."

"Damn right you can do this. I put off a meeting with the Governor to be here." The two men laughed and hugged.

Jamie got up and turned his boy's CD stereo on. He hunted through the 3000 CDs on the bookcase in front of him and pulled out *R.Kelly's* song *trade in my life*. He put the CD in the player which was the ritual when one of the brothers got married. Mike went to the front to grab a bottle of Moet. As R. Kelly began to sing on the disc, the laughing from the front room ceased and all the men in the house began to file into the back room. When they heard the first words to the song, they knew that the time had come. They also knew what the song meant to each of them. They listened as Jamie began to sing.

> *Sitting here wondering how things went wrong,*
> *Every night asking myself what happened to our happy home?*
> *Will I ever see you again?*
> *I need to know, my friend*
> *Chorus*
> *Now the past is gone away*
> *But tomorrow's gonna stay,*
> *And the sun is still goin down*
> *And I need you around, I'll trade…*

All the men in the room were married or had been married at one point or another. Jamie was the last one, the last of their pack to make the age old ritual. The men thought about their wives, those that were still married. Those that were divorced, all took time to remember the day that they asked their wives to marry them. It was a sobering song, but it was a good song also. As the chorus began, all the men in Jamie's home began singing in a circle around the nervous groom. Jamie sang the lead. It didn't matter whether or not you sounded like *R. Kelly* when you sang the song, or *Biz Markie*. This is what this circle of friends did before they walked what they called, "The last mile of the way." After the song ended, some men were laughing, others were crying and all were happy to be in one another's company. They had 20 minutes to drive to the House of Lynwood three miles south from Mike's home. The men straightened themselves out and walked to the fleet of black Cadillac trucks that were waiting for them outside. Jamie, Mike and the rest of the guys were all Ques. Mia made Jamie promise that he and the guys would not show up the wedding clad in their purple and gold. That did not mean that they couldn't show up and make their presence known. The brothers or the "bruhs" each synchronized their CD players and on the count of three, they all slid the purple CD's in their respective players.
Seconds later…Atomic Dog by George Clinton was playing over the Jensen speakers. The subwoofers were so loud and so full of base that windows on Jamie's block began to vibrate. Then at 20 miles per hour, they drove south on

Torrence Avenue, slowing traffic as they took their brother to the place where his bride awaited him.

MIA

Mia was nervous as hell. She wasn't nervous about being married. Hell, she figured it was about time that Jamie made her an honest woman. She was nervous about things going wrong on what was supposed to be her perfect day. She was at the Marriott a few miles south of the House of Lynwood. Her made of honor, Sonja, was at the actual hall making sure that everything was done according to her girl's instructions. Mia got dressed with the help of her longtime college friend Lisa. It was 20 minutes before the wedding was scheduled to begin and Lisa had just finished putting the finishing touches on Mia's makeup.

Lisa said, "You ready girl?"

Mia said, "Girl I was born ready."

"You think Jamie is ready?"

"Please, I think Jamie is at Mike's home right now flipping out, or on his way here right now flipping out. You know how men are when it comes to commitment and marriage."

"Amen" said Trina one of the bridesmaids.

"I just don't get it about men and marriage and why this day scares the hell out of them. I love Jamie and he loves me. We live together, so he knows what he is getting in a partner. I have been there with him when he was poor, been there with him when his Dad died and have been there with him through every triumph and failure that he has had in his adult life. So you would think that getting married would be a walk in the park. Just like any other man in America though, I bet all he can think about is losing his freedom."

Lisa said, "Yeah, well you can be hard on a man and that *is something for him to think about.*"

Mia said, "What? Come on girl, you don't even know us like that. I mean I may be a bitch to the rest of you all at times, but I treat Jamie like a king. He comes and goes as he pleases, I break him off a piece twice a week, and anytime he has come up with a new idea or goal I have been behind him one hundred percent. He could so a whole lot worse than marrying me."

"Yeah he could be marrying *me*" a voice interrupted.

That was the voice of Wanda, Mia's nosy ass friend that has hated Jamie since day one. It was obvious that the reason that Wanda hated Jamie was due to the fact that both always seemed to vie for Mia's attention. Wanda and Mia had been friends since the third grade. A friendship that has been strained since Jamie made his way into Mia's life. That friendship was also strained by the fact that two years ago after her divorce, Wanda came to the conclusion that she was a lesbian. Everyone else in the wedding party had a slight problem with this because they played for the other team. With the exception of Wanda, Mia's bridal part was strictly dickly.

Wanda said, "Girl are you sure that you want to do this?"

Mia said, "I am more sure of this than anything I have ever done in my life."

"Well, it's about time that he made this move, how long have you all been together? What has it been, ten years?"

Wanda's words stung.

Mia took in a deep sigh and decided to show restraint with her childhood friend.

"We have been together seven years Wanda, not ten."

Wanda said, "Girl all I'm saying is..."

"...Too much." Another voice interrupted.

It was Sonja. Sonja had finished making sure that all of Mia's expectations were met at the hall and had joined the ladies in the room to get dressed herself. She and Wanda did not get along. Sonja was a strong sister from the south side. She grew up in the projects, and was one of those sisters that you read about in magazines. She had beaten all the odds to get to the top of her field and was one of the city's most powerful attorneys. She had a thriving practice and was a well known civil rights leader and human service activist. She was the made of honor because aside from being the most organized woman that Mia knew, she didn't take any shit off anyone.

The two women eyeballed one another and in the far off distance if you listened hard enough you could hear the screech of a ghost cat as the two locked glares at one another. Sonja always tried to tolerate Wanda when she was around Mia, but she didn't like Wanda one bit. Sonja also felt that Wanda was crossing the line by bad mouthing Jamie on the day of their wedding.

"That's enough Wanda, it's their wedding day remember?"

"Hold up, Sonja just because you are the maid of honor does not mean that you are running shit."

Sonja responded, "You see now that is where you are wrong, maid of honor means *exactly that*. I am running shit."

"Well you ain't running shit in here."

"Here or Hurre? Since you are acting like a goddamned teenager, you might as well use the young people's language, god knows that you dress and act like a damned teen."

The two women started walking toward one another. Lisa dropped the makeup bag and went after Wanda and Trina went to grab Sonja. Mia shook her head and raised her voice as she spoke to both women.

"Wanda, Sonja, it' my wedding day remember? Can you two heifers put your differences aside for at least another four hours?"

The two women stopped their catting as they remembered why there were there. They exchanged further glares at one another and like two prize fighters, went back to their mutual spaces away from one another.

"Thank you." Mia said.

Lisa had a look of relief on her face as did Trina. Neither really wanted to be in the middle of that fight. It would have been like trying to separate Ali and Frazier back in the seventies.

"I'm sorry girl" Wanda said.

"I'm sorry too" replied Sonja.

"I just don't like that bitch." Wanda said.

"Sonja's eyes bugged out. She could not believe the audacity of Wanda.

"Bitch?" Sonja said.

"Bitch!" Wanda replied.

The room fell silent. It was in that minute that Mia knew that having both Sonja and Wanda in the same wedding party, let alone the same room was a mistake. Wanda was from the old neighborhood, but Sonja was from some place all together different. As *Steve Harvey* would say, Sonja was from the P-R-O-J-E-C-T-S.

Sonja's movements were cat like and fluid like some shit out of *The Matrix*. She was in a black *Donna Karen* dress that she wore to give directions to the caterers and photographer before the wedding. In one motion, she kicked off her pumps, slipped out of her dress and jumped on Wanda like white on rice. She began whipping Wanda's ass right there in her slip and she pounced on Wanda with such a force, that Lisa and Trina decided fuck it and simply got the hell out of the way.

Wanda was already in her bridesmaid's dress which was tight as hell. Wanda had a fat music video ass on her and was one of those sisters that considered herself to be thick, when the truth of the matter was she was about seven pounds away from being fat. Minutes earlier, Wanda had just finished putting on her makeup, makeup that was now all over Sonja's slip. Wanda looked like *Queen Latifah*. She was top heavy like the queen and had the complexion of *Sallie Richardson*. She was a strong woman and she could fight, but she was no match for

Sonja. Had she known how powerful Sonja was, she would have kept those last comments to herself just a few minutes ago.

Sonja was five feet three inches tall. She looked like *Jada Pinkett-Smith*. Although she was small in stature, she was one of those sisters that just didn't give a fuck. She could be a lady when she needed to be, but she could be a gangsta bitch when she needed to be also. Sonja grew up in the *Ida B. Wells* housing project on 39th street in Chicago. All her life she had been a fighter, and to go from her suburban lifestyle in Wilmette where she pulled in a high six figures, back to 39th street and in the "real hood" took all of three seconds. Sonja fought her brothers, fought injustice, fought for human rights and competed against whites, men, and backstabbing ass women all her life to get where she is today. She was a natural fighter in every sense of the word, and she whipped Wanda's confused and privileged ass for old and new. She began with a slap. She then countered with a right cross and followed that up with a knee to the midsection. After knocking the wind out of Wanda, she grabbed a fist full of hair and slapped her back and forth like an old school pimp from the movie *The Mack*. Wanda tried to get away but could not escape the flurry of blows that came from Sonja. Sonja was fast, strong, and all muscle. On top of that, Sonja was pissed. Everyone in the wedding party could see why men and women alike feared her. When Sonja became focused on *anything* she was a force to be reckoned with. Sonja began preaching to Wanda as she continued the beat-down.

"Bitch? I got your bitch! Your bitch is right here! [slap] You confused big-bootied bitch.

[slap] Who the fuck do you think you are? [punch] Bitch you don't know me, you…don't…fucking…know…me [punch] I'mma be respected up in here. You hear me? You won't ever dis-re-spect me ev-er a-gain up in this motherfucker. The next time you disrespect me up in here, Imma get straight up medieval on your ass."

It all happened in about 60 seconds, but that was all time Sonja needed to get her point across. It was a full minute later before she heard Mia's screams for her to let her friend go. By then Sonja had torn Wanda's dress completely off of her and worked up a sweat like she had just finished an aerobics class. Sonja looked at Mia and could see that her friend was crying. That was enough to get Sonja to stop. She let Wanda go and pushed her to the floor.

Sonja began fixing her hair and then she spoke.

"I'm going to the washroom. I hope that Wanda will have made an attitude adjustment upon my return. Mia I'm sorry. If you want me out of the wedding I understand."

Mia said, "No, that won't be necessary. I guess I just wanted the two of you to try and get along. I'm sorry I tried to make the two of you co-exist."

"It's not your fault. Two grown women *should be able to co-exist* especially on their girl's wedding day."

Sonja looked at Wanda with contempt before exiting the room. The room was silent for a long while. Mia was supposed to be getting married in 15 minutes. She looked at the clock. She then looked at her childhood friend who was bruised and broken as she lay on the floor. Wanda's pride was hurt more than she was physically. The four women were at a loss for words as time passed on what was supposed to be the best day of Mia's life.

"I am supposed to be getting married in less than fifteen minutes." Mia said to Wanda as if to infer that she started this whole mess.

"Black weddings never start on time" Wanda said.

"What are you going to wear?" Lisa asked.

Wanda looked down and her dress was completely ruined. Mia put her head in her hands and began crying. Her wedding day was not getting off to a good start.

LORETTA

Loretta arrived at the hall fifteen minutes before the wedding was due to start. She looked damned good for a thirty something year old woman that had just beat Cancer. She wore a green dress with matching shoes and pearls. She was a vision of beauty if she must say so herself. She used to have long free flowing hair, but since having chemotherapy, her hair was only just returning. She had a very small natural that she treated with an S-curl this morning to give it that short and cute wet look. Her dress looked elegant against her butter pecan colored skin. Because she won her bout with cancer, she had a new lease on life, which meant no stress, no financial worries and no more tears.

As she got out of her 2003 Maxima, she looked up at the hall and thought back to the day that she and Michael were married. That was just five years ago, but it seems like an eternity. Michael and Loretta met in school at NLU or National Louis University. She was studying Public Policy and he was studying Human Service Administration. Yet he became the politician and she became the social services administrator. It's funny how things sometimes work out like that. They both had classes together, and they both graduated at the top of their class. They fell in love while studying with one another in the wee hours of the night at the Harold Washington Library. They had what seemed like a fairy tale relationship. That is, until Michael was offered a Deputy Mayor position at the age of 26. From that point forward, their lives seemed to go in two totally different directions. Because she had political aspirations of her own, Michael assumed that she would be completely on board with his civic duties, and she was…until civic duty began placing a wedge between them.

Michael and Loretta never told anyone what really went wrong between the two of them. Although they were both thirty something now, they were from the old school when it came to their marriage. Both were firm believers that what goes on in their house, stays in their house. So when they both told family and friends that they were getting divorced, everyone was stunned. For a long time they had been that ray of hope and that model that other couples patterned themselves after. They saw no reason to shatter that image, which is why they are so very cordial with one another and seem like two age old friends that literally had irreconcilable differences.

Loretta put her keys in her purse and looked around at all the nicely dressed children and guests of Mia and Jamie. She allowed herself a half a smile as she flashed back to her life with her ex-husband.

To show the mayor how loyal he was and to better learn the ins and outs of the political game, Mike began keeping long hours. Loretta got a nine to five with a Catholic Charity and began working on opening her own community center. She kept herself busy with her grant writing and public speaking engagements, but the truth of the matter was she was already missing her man after just a year of marriage. Loretta and Mike dressed for various affairs and events that the city held. Many days they were afforded the time to dance with one another and hold one another close at these functions, but afterward they never got the chance to truly commune with one another as couples are supposed to. Whenever one of these events concluded, Michael would have to rush off with the Mayor or speak with some CEO with a palm that needed to be greased, or a citizen with a complaint or concern that the Mayor never seemed to have the time to address. Many days at these dances and events, Loretta held on to Michael for dear life. She knew as she held her man that it was just a matter of time before someone would be pulling him away from her. There were many nights that they were able to dance with one another, share a laugh or two and court one another. There were few times that they could cap one of these evening off with a night of making love.

Many nights Michael came in too late to consummate the evening. Other nights he seemed to be just too tired. When he did make the time for her, things were just as bad as if he had not been there at all. Some days their lovemaking was rushed. Other days he was not attentive and was simply going through the motions. Then there were the days that his body was with her, but it was painfully obvious that his mind was somewhere else.

Then there was the time that the Mayor fell sick with pneumonia.

That was when Loretta knew that she had lost her husband.

For three months the Mayor was on a medical leave of absence. For three months Michael was obsessed with running the city like a well oiled machine.

Michael was a damn good interim Mayor.

It was obvious that Michael was a damn good man in a crisis.

Michael then became drunk with the power.

He never abused his power as the interim Mayor. He never did any wrong as the interim Mayor. In fact, he did the job better than Mayor Howard Teague, and that was whispered throughout the political arena. Michael had found his place in the world. From the moment that sat in the big chair, new plans were set in motion. Mentally, Michael was working on his political campaign. From that moment forward, he and Loretta grew world's apart from one another.

When Mayor Teague returned, he congratulated Michael on the job that he had done. The problem that Michael was now facing was the fact that the Mayor showed signs of slowing down or relinquishing his seat. Michael often talked about putting in more hours and collecting dirt on the man that he had been loyal to for so long in the event that the two would one day be made to run against one another. That is when the arguing between Loretta and Michael began.

"I need more time with you" Loretta remembers telling her husband.

"Baby, I just don't have the time to give right now."

"If not now, then when?"

"I don't know. I'm working on a potential political campaign."

"And what about the campaign to save our marriage?"

"What? Are you saying that our marriage is in trouble?"

"I have been saying that our marriage is in trouble."

"Look, if you can't hang, tell me now. I need to know so we can get divorced now as opposed to when I am Mayor. I will not be able to deal with a distraction like this during the campaign and I really don't need it when I am in office."

Stunned, Loretta said, "Divorce? Who the fuck is talking about getting divorced? I was thinking about suggesting counseling. Where the fuck did divorce come from?"

Michael was somewhere else. He was completely obsessed with being mayor, so much so that he had no idea how insensitive he was being. Rather than saving his marriage, he was more concerned with the way that things looked to potential constituents.

Loretta sat back and leaned against the car as she began to tear and allowed her mind to flashback just a bit more.

When it finally dawned on Michael how stupid he sounded. He apologized to his wife. They never brought up divorce again while arguing or discussing politics. When it dawned on him that he might lose Loretta after all the two had been through, he got his head out of his ass and the chip off his shoulders and he began to court his wife again and made time for her. For three months they were a couple again. Then the Democratic convention hit nearby Chicago and Michael once again began to distance himself from his wife. Loretta was not willing to go through the possibility of losing her man again so this time around she went to appeal to a higher power. She went and had lunch with the Mayor's wife.

Loretta and Mrs. Teague had lunch at *Applebees* and talked about the difficulties that came with being a political wife. Mrs. Teague knew exactly what Loretta was going through as she lost her husband to the city years ago. It was a loss that she wished upon no woman that loved her man. Mrs. Teague told Loretta that she would tell her husband to tone it down. In the meanwhile she suggested that Loretta take more initiative with her husband if she was serious about saving their marriage.

"You know what dear? One day Mr. Teague was working hard on his campaign, day and night that it got to the point that we hadn't made love in three months. For me that was damned unacceptable. So I told Henry that if he didn't pay more attention to me that I was going to come to city hall butt naked and show the entire city my behind if he didn't give it the attention that it needed. Well I guess he didn't take me seriously until one day I went to his campaign headquarters and got on the intercom demanding that everyone get the hell out." Mrs. Teague said.

"What happened?" Loretta asked.

"I opened my coat with nothing on other than my birthday suit and we made love right there on his desk!"

"You didn't."

"I did, and it was worth it. Maybe you need to do the same thing. Just like the constituents, sometimes we have to demand to be heard."

I took the first ladies advice. I made myself available to my man at every opportunity, but the Democratic convention seemed to take priority over every thing else. One day Michael told me that he was working late at the office in City Hall and that he would order take out for dinner. I begged him to come home for dinner at the very least. He said that he was sorry and that he would make it up to me that following weekend.

I decided that the best thing to do was not to start another fight with him. I decided that fighting wasn't going to do anything except put distance between us and I wanted us to remain close. These last few weeks have been great and I was just beginning to enjoy having my partner again. I was not going to lose him to the politics game. I went to my closet and looked for some persuasive ammunition. Michael's favorite color was royal blue. I had a nice one piece lace bustier with black stockings, garter and heels. While he took the time to work late on his campaign, I was working on a campaign of my own. I did my hair, took the time to do my nails, showered and papered my body with scented lotion from the *Bath and Body Works* and sprayed just a hint of perfume in all the right places on my body.

It was too warm out to wear a trench coat, so I put a black skirt on over the garter and a white silk blouse over the top part of the bustier. I pinned my hair up just perfect, so with one pull, I could shake loose my free flowing hair and embrace my husband in one motion. When I looked in the mirror and finally approved of my wares, I decided that it was time for this girl to take action in holding on to her man! I jumped in my Honda Civic and headed to City Hall, it was now about 8:30.

When I got there the security guard, Ralph was sleep. Ralph was a senior citizen that the suburb put on the payroll so he would feel like he was of some use. Nothing ever happened at city hall, so there was no danger of him being hurt in trying to protect it. I took off my high heels so not to wake him, and tipped quietly by.

City Hall was a grand building that looked as if it could have been an old museum. I marveled at the paintings of all the past Mayors and all the framed news clippings of the many events that had taken place in history over the years in Calumet City. City hall was dark and quiet at night. I thought this was odd because it was as busy as a Metropolis during the day. There were no police officers present, and no additional guards other than Ralph. It seemed to be a place that was devoid of life. I walked up three flights of stairs to get to Michael's office. I walked past office after office where lights were off and people that perhaps should have been burning the midnight oil were at home with their families and loved ones. I resented that about Michael. The further and further I walked down the hall in my stocking feet, the more I realized that people in love went home at the end of the day and only put in the hours that Michael put in when they were hard up for the money that overtime brings…or being Deputy Mayor.

Michael's office was the largest on the floor next to the mayors. The Mayor's office was at the north end of the hall and Michael's was at the south end. I looked at the Mayor's office which was generally well lit, and it was pitch black. It was obvious that his honor was at home. I thought to myself, "The first lady must be putting it on him right now." I had a smile on my face at the prospect that the first lady won her man back from the politics game. I put a look of determination on my face as I was about to do the same thing.

As I got closer and closer to Michael's office I noticed that his office was just as dark as the mayors. "Now he said he would be here." I said to myself. Then I looked at my watch and discovered that it was 9:20. I thought that perhaps he went to get something to eat. "I've got something for him to eat." I thought to myself. I felt so dirty for thinking that, but the thought of Michael ravishing me once he saw me in this outfit, does make me kind of hot. I decided that I would wait for Michael at his desk in nothing but lingerie. This way when he came back from his lunch break, dessert would be sitting right there on his desk.

I pushed open his door which was not locked, and there was a stack of papers on his desk and no light on other than his desk lamp that I got him when we were in college. On his desk was a note to Ralph in the event that he decided to do rounds that said,

RALPH,

DO NOT LOCK MY OFFICE. I WILL BE RIGHT BACK. I JUST WENT TO GET SOMETHING TO EAT. IT'S 9:00 NOW.

—MICHAEL

I thought to myself, "I have great timing." I began unbuttoning my blouse in order to show off my cleavage. I then kicked my feet up on Michael's desk and let my hair down.

"Today, I am taking control of my marriage and love life." I said to myself.

A few minutes later I heard the rattle of keys and laughing. Then I heard a second voice in concert with Michael's. I began buttoning my blouse because it was obvious that Michael was not alone. It never dawned on me that he might be meeting with another politician or constituent. I went into a conference room that was adjoined to Michael's office to make myself look more professional rather than the slutty wife that had come to city hall to seduce her husband. The last thing that Michael and I needed was for me to ruin his image that he worked so hard for. If that happened, we would be arguing for the next four months.

I straightened myself out in the conference room. As I did that I heard laughing and joking and the second voice that I heard was one that I was not familiar with.

"Michael, if Loretta doesn't understand your drive and ambition, I think you should just leave her." The voice said.

I thought to myself, "Who the hell is that, and what the hell is she saying?"

Michael said, "It's not that easy, I love her, she has been by my side since grad school."

"That may be so, but it is obvious to me that she can't appreciate the man that you are and she may even be jealous of the man that you are trying to be. All I am saying is if she can't be the woman that she needs to be, and one day first lady of this city, then perhaps she should step aside and let someone else fill that slot."

I thought to myself, *who the hell is this bitch?* I was upset and hurt all in one instant. I began pinning my hair back up and pulling my earrings out. I don't know who the bitch is in the next room buzzing in my man's ear, but I am about to get straight up 43rd street on her ass!

Michael said, "Really, and just who did you have in mind to take her slot?"

The other voice said, "I think you know."

There was a silence that fell over the room. There was a silence that came over me as well.

I heard the woman's footfalls. It was obvious that she walked over to my husband. I waited on Michael to tell this woman to get the hell out of his office.

"Denise...I love my wife."

"I know you do."

"I'm not going to have an affair."

"No? Well your mouth may be saying no, but your body seems to be saying something else."

The lights went off. I was frozen with anger, fear and confusion. I could barely see into Michael's office, but I could see from where I was where this woman Denise had dropped to her knees in front of my husband.

Stop her! Do Something! Don't just stand there! These are the things that I told myself. Still, I made no motion. I thought to myself that if Michael showed some backbone and told her to get up and get out, I would help her out. I would kick her ass all over the office and possibly toss her out of the window. It did not dawn on me what course of action to take if Michael gave in to her advances.

From what I could see, this woman...Denise, was about 23 years old. She was obviously bi-racial and she looked like a younger version of me. From the back I could see that she was dressed in a pink *Phat Farm* form-fitting jogging suit. She had long brown hair, and she looked as if she should have been one of the girls in the *Chingy* video. She knelt before my husband and unzipped his pants. She then took his erect member in her hand and looked up at him as if seeking approval. She tossed her hair to the side so that he could watch her perform. She had thick lips like mine, and advantage that she could only have gotten from her African American side of her heritage. She licked her lips as she looked at his dick...my dick...with approval. She then took my man into her mouth. He offered *no resistance* and with that, he broke my heart.

Denise worked him like the slut she was. I stood there stunned as I watched her live performance with disgust. To make matters worse she took one of Michael's hands in hers and made him use the other hand to grab a fist full of her hair. Michael fell back against the wall. Denise leaned forward to balance herself and then the slurping sounds began. With each audible sound I grew weak, with each of Michaels' now audible moans, I became enraged. It's like *Darrin Lowery* said in his book *Handling the Truth*, "*Many an affair began with a blowjob.*" I came hear to please my man, instead I got my heart broken and lost my marriage.

I looked around the conference room to find something to fashion as a weapon. There was nothing of use in the large conference room. I decided at that point that it was time to go old school and "knuckle up." I rolled to the sleeves on my blouse and busted out of the conference room.

"Bitch!" I yelled as I jumped on the now *topless* Denise, and began whipping her ass for old and new. I don't know why I went after her instead of Michael, but I did.

"Lo-Loretta?" Michael asked, as if confused or hoping that he had been imagining things. After I slammed Denise to the floor, I kicked Michael in his dick which was now going limp. After kicking him, he doubled over and I slapped him and spit on him. Michael was down on one knee. Denise tried to gather her bearings and looked for a quick escape. There was none. I jumped back on top of her with all my weight and grabbed two fistfuls of hair. I then began banging her head into the floor as if we were women wrestlers in the *WWE*. Unlike in the WWE, I was trying to kill my opponent. Denise tried to fight back and she tried to use her youth to her advantage, but I used my experience and anger against her. I pretended that we were back on the schoolyard at Ryder grade school and I beat the hell out of her. She grabbed for my hair and pulled at it. With each pull she caught a right jab to the left side of her face. She tried to curl up into a fetal position to cover up from my assault. A minute ago she was a woman. Now she was nothing more than a young girl at the wrong place, at the wrong time, with the wrong woman's man.

I banged Denise's head into the floor until she was too dazed to resist. I then turned my attention toward a still stunned Michael.

"How could you? How could you fucking do this to me...to us?" I said to him.

"Loretta...baby, I'm so..."

"Sorry! Don't you say that! Don't you fucking say that to me! You can't be sorry that you did this. Otherwise you wouldn't have done it! If you are sorry, then you are sorry for getting caught and I don't want to hear that! Jesus Michael, what about me? What about us? Things were just beginning to get better between us again!"

"I know, baby I'm sorry, I love you."

"Love? Love? What the fuck do you know about love? Love brought me here with lingerie on underneath my clothes to try and hold on to our marriage. Love is my standing beside you in your every dream and accomplishment, Love is my unwavering support of your career. How do you reciprocate love in this relationship Michael? What are you bringing to the table lately other than *your wants and desires?*"

Denise began to stir, as she did I kicked her in the stomach.

"Go back to sleep bitch." Almost as if on que, Denise fell back onto the floor.

I turned back to Michael and said, "I loved you, and you betrayed me."

I looked at Denise on the floor and then looked back at Michael to speak. "How long has this been going on?"

"Loretta, this is the first time, I swear."

"When the fuck did you get an assistant?"

"Two months ago."

"Two months? Motha...Two months? Two goddamned months! When were you going to tell me."

Michael looked at me with guilt and said, "I was going to. Baby, I'm...I mean...I...I meant to tell you."

"And where does she get off telling you to leave me? What the hell have you been telling her about me, about us?"

Michael was at a loss for words.

I was through with tears.

I started to have the stereotypical argument with Michael. I started to scream more, and I started to beat the hell out of Denise some more. I surveyed the room however and came to a revelation about the type of women that I am.

I'm better than that.

I'm better than her.

I can do better than him.

I gathered myself together, fixed my hair and my clothing and I walked over to my husband and kissed him on the cheek. I whispered in his ear, "I loved you, and you broke my heart…never again, goodbye Michael.

I walked out of city hall and out of my husband's life. I went home, packed my things and went to live at my sister's home.

I never embarrassed him, never told anyone what really happened between us and I tried to keep the civil relationship that we have always had between us. We had a quiet divorce, a quiet breakup and we have spent the past few years re-building our friendship. I cannot see us ever getting things back as they once were. I can only hope.

He married Denise four months after I found them together in his office.

Four months after that, he was divorced from her as well.

Four months after that, I found out that I had Cancer.

I went through that ordeal by myself. Michael wanted to be there with me, but I refused his help. I already had one Cancer eating away at me. The loss of love combined with a failed marriage is like a Cancer all by itself. I pride myself on being a strong woman, but I could not handle both ordeals at once. I excluded Michael from that part of my life.

Here I am today, at his best friend's wedding, waiting and wondering.

As I sat there leaning on my car and looking at the hall, I wondered if Michael and I would ever be able to get back what we once had. I then asked myself if I even wanted that any longer. Perhaps it was time to move on.

Just then, a fleet of black Cadillac trucks pulled up playing Atomic Dog by George Clinton. Michael and all his fraternity brothers parked side by side in the front of the hall and began to step and stomp in unison right there in front of the hall and while dressed in their tuxedos. They looked sharp as hell, but the barking, flexing and shouting was upsetting the white people in the wedding across the hall from Jamie's. Michael saw me leaning on the car and smiled. He began to walk in my direction and the closer that he got the slower his pace became. He could see by the look on my face that I was not pleased with him.

"Hi." He said.

"Hello." I responded.

The hello was cold and flat. By the tone in my voice he confirmed that I was upset with him.

"Are you okay?" He asked.

"Yeah, I'm okay."

"Are *we* okay?"

"I guess so. I was just taking time here to remember our wedding."

"So they were good memories."

"Those memories were. After thinking about our marriage, I was all smiles. The problem came when I went fast-forward a bit."

"Oh." He said.

There was short silence between us.

"It's okay though." I said.

"Yeah?" He responded.

"Yeah, go be with your friends."

Michael leaned over to kiss me, and it felt good. He then went into the hall with his boys. I sat there reflecting in thought and wondering about the future. Just then, I saw Wanda, one of Mia's friends that I didn't particularly care for. She walked over to me and she looked a mess, like she had been in a car accident or something.

"Loretta, Mia needs you. She asked me to look in the hall and try to find you."

"What's wrong? And what happened to your face?"

"It's a long story, and one that I am kind of embarrassed about. The bottom line is she needs you to help save her wedding day."

"What can I do?"

"Just come with me."

MIA {COOL UNDER PRESSURE}

When Sonja got back from the bathroom, I cursed her and Wanda's asses out. I let them have both barrels. Today was my wedding day and both of these self righteous bitches messed it up like two high school prima donnas. I had to think of a way to save my wedding, otherwise Jamie and everyone in the hall was going to be disappointed. I sent Wanda to find Loretta, Michael's best friend's ex-wife. I don't know what it is about Loretta, but she is the woman that every woman in our circle aspires to be. She is poised, beautiful and mature beyond her years. I knew if anyone knew what to do, it would be her. Wanda led her in and I gave her a warm hug. She looked like Jeanne Sparrow from NBC. As always, she was beautiful. I explained to Loretta all that had happened that morning. She looked at Wanda and Sonja and scolded them both.

"You two couldn't set aside your differences for one day, one goddamned day? What does that say regarding love and respect for Mia? How do you both suppose she feels?"

Neither Wanda nor Sonja had the words.

Loretta thought long and hard about her next action. Then it came to her what she would do. She called an usher and asked *Sean Harrington* another of Jamie's friends to met her in the hall. Sean was a cop and a hell of a singer. She asked him to sing a song to the audience and explain that we were waiting on additional guests to arrive. Sean sang *For You* by *Kenny Lattimore*. Loretta then gave Wanda her Visa card and told her to buy a new outfit for herself in the boutique.

"I got it." Loretta said. "I will be the maid of honor, Sonja, you are now a bridesmaid, and Wanda, will have to wait in the audience."

Wanda said, "But I am in the wedding party, and your dress isn't even the same color as the rest of us."

"The maid of honors dress can traditionally be different. Besides, there is no way to save your dress. Now we need to make this work and today is not about you anyway. If you want to help Mia out, you will need to simply do as I say."

Wanda hated it, but she took the Visa card and bought herself a black walking suit.

And just like that, Loretta brought order to chaos.

THE WEDDING

Sean sang two songs after he finished For You by Kenny Lattimore. We were lucky that he sings as well as he does, otherwise people might have left. The minister asked the audience to be patient as the wedding would begin in just a few minutes. When Sean finished singing *Boys to Men by New Edition* he was given a prompt that the wedding was ready to begin. Jamie's friends began teasing him telling him that they thought he was getting off the hook. He smiled the smile of a nervous groom, but from what I hear he was actually looking for me and wondering what had gone wrong. Just then, the music began and the audience stood up as *Forever by R. Kelly* began to play.

One by one, my bridesmaids began walking down the aisle. Traditionally, the men would have accompanied the women down the isle with the groomsman. We decided that the men would be in place already (since they didn't care much for the ceremony anyway) and the women would be the ones coming down the isle by themselves. We were each strong, independent and doing our own things in the world of men. We made great strides in each of our fields and the significance of walking down the isle alone was to state to the world that we joined the men as *partners* and that with or without them, we could stand alone and strong. By joining with the men, the statement being made was that *united, we are stronger*. This was all outlined in the wedding program. Some people thought it was sexist on my part. Others thought that it was beautiful. At any rate, it was my day and what I said counted.

Each of the women walked down the isle and joined their respective partners. Lisa walked down and joined a groomsman, Trina joined with another, Sonja joined with yet another and there was a pause in the procession as Loretta walked in, right before me and walked slowly down the isle into the hands of her ex-husband. Michael had a look joy and surprise on his face as his eyes and Loretta's eyes met. Loretta teared a little as she walked down the isle to her former partner. If I didn't know any better, I would swear that Michael was ready to tear himself.

MICHAEL

Loretta looked like a vision of ebony loveliness as she walked down the isle. As she came closer and closer to me I was reminded of everything that was right in my life and everything that was wrong in my life. This woman, this remarkable woman, had been by my side through thick and thin. She had been to the wall with me, been there with me as I lost loved ones over the years, and she was a great part of helping me to become the man that I now am. She isn't my lady anymore, but I wish that she was. I want her back with all that is in me, but I have to wait for her to let me in. As she comes down the isle to be with me, I can't help but to think how so very lucky I am to have her in my life in any capacity.

I made the mistake of my life when I married Denise. After Loretta caught us in my office I felt as if I had nothing left in the world. I had my career and I had all these wonderful *things* in my life, but they meant nothing without her by my side. The thing with Denise was a one time affair. I did find her attractive from the first moment that I interviewed her. She was young, smart and sexy as hell. She looked like one of the women that you see in essence magazine or in a music video. I was taken with her from the moment I saw her. The fact that she did know as much as she did about politics only helped. I hired her for eye candy. I never meant to sample the goods.

I tried to resist her that night, but like Darrin Lowery once said, "Many an affair began with a blowjob." That is no excuse, but resisting her was not an easy choice for me. For a long time I blamed Loretta. If she was in the next room, *she should have stopped us before Denise dropped to her knees.* I hate to admit it, but I was powerless to stop her. This fine, young, firm woman wanted me. I found that so hard to believe, but she did. In that moment, a moment of weakness, I wanted her as well. I wish Loretta had stopped me that night. We might have fought and I might have been in the doghouse a long time, but my marriage would still be in tact. I still can't believe that she just left me like that.

When I got home the night of the affair, all of her things were gone. I tried calling her family members, but my every call was refused. With her gone, I realized that there was not only a void in my life, but a hole in my heart. I took for granted that she would always be there. To suddenly have her gone was a rush of reality that I was not ready for.

To fill that void I went back to Denise.

I fired Denise the moment that we got caught. After weeks of Loretta not answering my calls, I called Denise back. I should have kept pursuing Loretta, even if it meant pursuing her for the rest of my days. But instead I was even more selfish than I had been when I hired Denise. All I could think about was how bad *I was hurting*. All I could think about was how horrible I was doing without Loretta. I never gave one thought to what it was that she was going through, what I put her through. So to fill that void, Denise and I not only started working together again, we began dating…regularly.

"She is too old and out of style anyway, Loretta is lame, forget about her." She said.

Denise brought Loretta down verbally at every opportunity, and like a fool, I listened.

The next thing that I knew, we were married. After that, life for me changed drastically.

Denise wanted me to be the new mayor more than I wanted to be mayor. She wanted a lavish home, a lavish lifestyle, and she wanted everything that she thought I could provide for her. She never wanted me for me. In fact, the sex with her, which was mind blowing in the beginning, became almost non existent after marriage.

Denise didn't care that I worked the long hours. She never nagged me about spending more time with her. Initially, I thought this was a good thing, but it was becoming worse and worse as the weeks went by. I was working myself into the grave and she was spending every dime and every opportunity to advance her own goals. She contacted everyone from *Newsweek* to *Time* magazine to interview her as one of America's youngest first ladies. She took advantage of every social activity, every photo opportunity and every town meeting. I on the other hand, just seemed to be a stepping stone in her career path.

I can't believe how stupid I was in marrying her. I was taken with the sex and the fact that I was with this younger, and drop dead gorgeous woman. A few months into my new marriage and not only had Denise had an affair with the mayor, she was rumored to have gotten involved with the Governor. I caught her in lie after lie after lie, and still, I forgave her because I was so dependent upon having a woman in my life. Over the years, that I was with Loretta, I picked up some weight, loss a little hair and was so caught up in my career goals that I gave up on my own personal well being. My social skills began to suffer (other than politics and public relations) and I began to wonder if I could even get a woman as fine as Denise or as established as Loretta. My self esteem was suffering and Denise took full advantage.

At the Democratic convention, I was able to persuade the mayor to give me some extra time to devote to Denise. It was time that she was obviously not expecting me to get. I came home early to our condo, and found her in bed with a senator. I quietly divorced her as Loretta had quietly divorced me. The time alone was the worst part. That is when reality set in and I realized what it was that I had lost in Loretta. I loved my wife. In spite of all that had happened I loved her still. I had a few dates after Denise and I divorced. But being out there again was not all that I had imagined that it would be. I was this overweight, politician that did not have the time that was needed to devote to a relationship. Getting a woman to notice me was hard enough. Getting a woman to notice me and accept my schedule was even worse. I met a lot of women that wanted to meet, hook up, and satisfy each other's physical needs. This was fine in the beginning, but with each "booty call" the sex and the meaning behind the sex became more and more empty.

I missed the one on one thing. I missed telling someone that I cared about and that cared about me, all of the accomplishments and defeats that I had in life. I missed my partner, the one that I pledged my love to for life in front of God, my family and friends. After reality set in, then came the guilt. After the guilt came the full scope of the pain and hurt that I had put my woman through. When that set in, I wanted to find her, drop to my knees and beg her forgiveness.

I tried to get Loretta back immediately. This was hard because she knew of my marriage to Denise which made her hate me even more. To make matters worse, while I was married to Denise I tried a few times to see Loretta and each time she sent me away. After the last attempt I gave up trying. I now realize that in doing so this was the second time that I had given up on my marriage. I understood her hate for me. I now was beginning to hate myself.

I later found out on one of my subsequent visits that Loretta was diagnosed with Cancer. My world was shattered twice in hearing this. I was initially hurt because she actually had the big C. I was hurt a second time, because she elected to go through counseling and treatment alone. Her sister told me about the Cancer and she pulled no punches when she also told me what she thought of me. Her sister's name was Carolyn, and this was a sister that was the mother of all sister in laws. Carolyn was a fat and nasty woman that no man would ever want to deal with. She was a woman however that loved her sister. If you pictured the movie, *The taming of the shrew,* just imagine that *Elizabeth Taylor's* character was black and ugly to boot. That is what I had to endure in dealing with Carolyn. I remember the day that I went to her home to see Loretta to try and get her back. The memory is so strong that it was like it was yesterday.

"Hello Carolyn, is Loretta here?"

"No, Michael she isn't!"

"Why all the attitude?"

"Because you ain't shit."

"Excuse me?"

"There is no excuse for you. You ain't shit. You broke my sister's heart and it's killing her right now as we speak." She said defiantly.

"What are you talking about?"

"I heard that you got married again."

"Yeah, well I am divorced now."

"I heard that she was a hoe."

[sighing] "Yeah, well that may be true."

"How the fuck did you end up marrying the mistress. Don't you know that the man never leaves the wife? The minute you got caught, you should have had your ass over here every waking moment begging my sister to take your sorry ass back. You ain't shit! And now you are taking my sister, my heart from me."

Carolyn began tearing and if I didn't know any better, I would swear that she was ready to claw my eyes out. This was the second time that she referenced Loretta either dying or having some type of fatality.

"Carolyn, is there something that I need to know about Loretta? Where is she?"

"She is in the hospital you insensitive bastard! She is over at Mercy right now dying because of your stupid ass."

With that, she slammed the door in my face. She never offered an explanation. Because she would not open the door, I raced over to the hospital to see Loretta. On the way over there, all I could wonder about was whether or not Loretta had committed suicide or made an attempt on her life. When I got to the hospital, there was no evidence of her being in the emergency room. I told the triage nurse that I was Loretta's husband and begged her to check the system for her name. The triage nurse said that she did not have a Loretta Downing in the E.R. but she did have a Loretta Downing in the Cancer ward.

I remember thinking to myself, "Cancer?" then it dawned on me that although it was far fetched that I was the cause, it somehow was feasible to me that I was in fact responsible. I thought back to my psychology studies in under-grad and thought about my studies of diseases. I thought about the word disease and broke it down into dis-ease. Then I thought about all the dis-ease that I had brought into Loretta's life. I felt like shit. Psychologically, I felt as if I was in fact the culprit of my wife's agony.

I made my way up to the Cancer ward and told everyone that I encountered that I was Loretta's husband. When I finally got the opportunity to see her, I was broken hearted with how she looked.

The first time that I saw her, she was asleep. She had lost a ton of weight and lost all of her hair as well from the treatment. She looked decimated. She looked like she was half the woman that I had come to know over the years. I had come to know her as a pillar of strength and this powerful being. This disease, this hor-rible disease was eating away at her like nothing I had ever known. I sat beside her as she slept, and I held her hand. I cried like a little baby when I saw what this disease had done to her, what I had done to her. Hours later, she awoke. When she recognized that it was me holding her hand, she used the last of her strength to take her hand from mine. That broke my heart.

She then spoke in a voice that was a little above a whisper.

"I don't want you here."

"I want to be here for you." I said.

"Go be with your wife."

"I'm not with her anymore."

"That changes nothing."

"Baby…I'm sorry."

"Michael…I can't do this. I can't fight Cancer and deal with what you put me through. Do you understand? You are killing me. I can only handle…one thing…at a time."

I said, "Loretta, I love you, I need you."

She summoned up the last of her strength and said, "It's not about you. If you love me, if you ever loved me…you will go away and never come back."

"I need to be here for you." I said

"You needed to be here for me before this. Our situation might have precipitated this. Go away Michael…Go away."

"Will I ever see you again?" I asked.

She took a long pause and a single tear streamed down her face.

"We'll see. No promises."

Her words cut me like a double edged sword. They cut swift and deep. Loretta drifted off into unconsciousness. I kissed her hand and watched her for awhile after she dozed off. I hated myself for all that I had put her through. I went home and curled up in a ball in my bed and cried as if I were three years old.

Loretta beat the cancer. In my heart of hearts, I knew that she would. She was a warrior and she was not giving in to the disease. Not only did she beat it, she beat it into submission or remission. My biggest hurt was that she endured the whole ordeal alone. After the treatment, she and I became friends again. It took a long time, but she agreed to meet me once a week at IHOP for breakfast. Breakfast was always my treat and the conversation always went in the direction that she wanted to take it. The problem that I am running into now, is the fact that she sometimes goes out on dates with other men. I see other women from time to time, but I know that nothing will ever develop from those relationships. My greatest fear, is that she will replace me with one of the men that she goes out with now. I freely admit that I am jealous as hell, and scared to death of losing her. I also realize that I am the one that put myself in this position to begin with.

Here she was coming down the isle. As she walked down the isle toward me, I imagined that we were getting married all over again. I imagined that all was well in our world and that she and I were young and in love again. I teared as she walked toward me. She teared as well. As she took my hand, it took a world of restraint not to kiss her deep on the mouth.
"You look stunning." I told her
"You look rather dapper yourself." She said smiling.
I looked deep into her eyes and said, "I love you. I plan to tell you everyday of your life that I love you and you mean the world to me."
Loretta smiled a deep smile and whispered to me, "Let's go for a walk when all this is over and talk."
"I'd love that. It's a date."

LET NO MAN PUT ASUNDER
JAMIE

The wedding was beautiful. I always thought that the wedding day was nothing more than a big elaborate production for the woman. I have to admit, it was the single greatest day of my life. As Mia walked down the isle toward me, I felt like a king that was on top of the world. My beautiful black princess was coming to me and I to her, humble and proud that of all the people in the world, we found something so special with one another, that there was no need to search further. Being married was a *powerful thing*. I never realized how powerful it was until my wedding day. My woman and I were married and I was moved to emotion.

When the minister stated, "This thing that the lord has ordained this day, let no man put asunder." I cried before, during and after I saluted my bride.

FAST FORWARD ONE YEAR
JAMIE

Time passes as time does, and things between Mia and I were great for the first nine months that we were married. She was doing her thing as a feature editor for *Black Woman Chicago* a new magazine that she helped to get off the ground. I was also doing pretty well as a Public Relations rep for a number of clients that I had nationwide. I left town at least twice per month on business, but each trip never lasted more than two or three days. Since my clients paid my way every-where that I went, Mia and I had a lot of mini vacations together. We had regular trips to New York, California, Colorado, Phoenix and Las Vegas.

As Black Woman Chicago began to grow, Mia had less time that she was able to spend with me. The more the fledgling magazine grew, the less time Mia and I began to spend together. I hated it at first but Mia insisted that the time apart would help us to appreciate the time that we did get. She also explained that as a young couple, we were just securing our futures. There were many days when she would say to me, "Baby, it gets greater, later." As time went on, that was a phrase that I was beginning to hate. There were many days where I would wake up with that 5:30 AM hard on, and I would wake her up with it. You know how we do. I would give her that "Hey, are you sleep" poke with my penis. Some days Mia would oblige me. Many more days, my probing was just an alarm clock for her to get up and start her day. There were many days that she would promise me the sex of my life that evening. These were of course promises that were not kept. Some days she would work late and I would be in the bed in my silk boxers and with *Floetry* sitting in the CD player cued up to play the song, *say yes*. Mia usually got home at 6:00 in the evenings. Those days were becoming few and far between that she would get home on time. Many nights I would be there alone with my hard-on and some romantic CD. By eight or nine o clock I would just fall asleep or do some work myself when it was obvious that she was not going to make it home.

The weekends were worse, because for me, that is when a great deal of my cli-ents got into trouble with the law or the media. As their public relations rep, I was the one that had to talk to the press about the drama that my client's often caused. Sometimes it would be pro-football players in hotel rooms with drugs and under aged women, or it would be the friend of one of my clients that dragged my client into a troublesome situation. Naturally, the press would not hound the person that committed the crime. They would instead hound my clients. Many nights on the weekends, I would have to catch emergency flights out to different cities to explain the very juvenile behaviors of grown ass men. Not only was my job having an affect on my marriage, but my lady's job was doing the same thing.

I hated what was happening to us. I tried to talk to Mia about this regularly, but no matter how civil we would be when the discussion started, it always ended up with screaming and yelling before it was all over with. At one point I just told Mia that she needed to leave the magazine all together and be home where I needed her. I remember that argument all too well.

"Be home? Jamie are you out of your mind?" Mia said.

"Our relationship is in trouble, I think that is what is best for the both of us." I responded.

"Do you think that is what's best for *us* or what is best for *you?*"

"What is that supposed to mean?"

"I mean, how in the hell does my quitting my job, help *us*? It sounds to me like you just want me at home to be there at your convenience."

I gave out a long sigh as I knew that we were on the verge of having the mother of all arguments. I needed to convey to my woman that I simply wanted her home more so we could spend some quality time together.

"I do want you to be home, and I do admittedly want you to be there for me when I need you. It might be selfish but there are a lot of men that don't give a damn where there mate is or how much they work. Besides, I make more than enough money to support us both."

Mia said, "Money is not the issue. I didn't go to school and take out all these loans just to sit my black ass at home. I am a strong independent woman and you need to get over yourself and your insecurities!"

Mia's words cut deep. The reality of my own selfishness was more obvious to me. I loved the fact that Mia was a strong independent woman. That is the type of woman that I always wanted as a partner. She is the type of woman that I want raising my kids one day. I need her to continue to be the strong woman that she is, in the event that I ever need support. She was right in her desire to keep her independence. I was wrong to even allow myself to speak about taking that away from her in any capacity. But that did not change the fact that we still had a problem.

"Mia, I love you. It's that simple. I also miss you. I miss us, that is all that I am trying to say."

Mia gave me a small smile. "Then say that Jamie, tell me how you feel, but don't ever make demands of me."

"No demands at all?" I said with a wry smile.

"What did you have in mind?" She said smiling back.

"A little makeup sex."

"That wasn't really a fight that we just had so much as it was a disagreement."

I interrupted with, "Bitch."

Mia said, "What?"

I said, "Bitch. Now, since I used the B word, I guess that constitutes a fight…right?"

Mia began laughing, "No, that constitutes me cutting your ass."

"I'm sorry baby, Maybe you should spank me."

Mia said, "Boy, you nasty"

Jamie said, "You know it. Now come here."

Mia looked just like Nia Long in the movie *Love Jones*. She had long black hair, perfect c-cup breasts and dark brown piercing eyes. She had that same mahogany complexion and her makeup was in earth tones which accentuate her African American features. She almost looks as if she could have a quarter of Asian in her. She also has a smile that could stop time.

I walked over to my five foot two inch princess and grabbed her baby making hips. The thing that I think I loved most about Mia was her smile and her ass. She had a butt that was so big that you could see it from the front via her hips. All my boys envied me when they first saw Mia. I mean she was the cats meow for me when we first met and everyday that we see each other now. Man, I love her hips. When she is walking toward you, all you can see is hips. Her hips are so wide and so curvy, that most men love looking at her from the front and can't wait to see the back. From the first moment that I saw her, I was hooked.

I kissed Mia deeply on the mouth and cuffed her firm round ass. I ran my other hand up the small of her back and ran my fingers through her hair. I kissed her as if it were for the first time, as if it were our first date, and as if we just began courting all over again. I then turned her back to my front and kissed the nape of her neck. I then cupped both of her ample breasts and she turned her head to meet mine and kiss. I ran my hand down her front and reached for the V between her legs. I unbuttoned her pants with my years of skill and was happy to discover that my kissing alone had already begun to make my bride moist. My heart was racing, her heart was racing and for a brief moment we were like teenagers again, hot, excited and innocent.

As my fingers found the slippery rosebud at the peak of my wife's lips, She let out a gracious moan. Her breasts began to heave up and down and she began to grind her perfect ass against my penis. The more I gyrated my finger, the faster that she began grinding against me. She let out a primitive moan, as did I. I then bent her over, while still playing with her clit, and used the other hand to slap her ample behind.

While she was bent over, I stopped my love play with her kitten long enough to take her top off. I then removed her pants and exposed a navy blue two piece laced bra and panty set. I then began grinding my penis against her ass. I also leaned over to kiss the small of her back and ran my tongue up her spine and kissed the back of her neck. I planted slow wet kisses all over her back and shoulders. I cupped the sides of her breasts as bathed her backside in kisses. Mia tried to get away from me, but I pulled her to me and kissed her deeply again and asked her, "Where do you think you are going?"

I picked her up and cradled her in my arms, kissing her the entire way to the bedroom. I laid my bride down on her back and told her to be still. I looked at the vision of loveliness that she was and smiled to myself with pride.

"I am a lucky man." I said aloud.

"Yes you are." Mia responded.

I kissed my woman from head to toe. I began at her feet which were manicured and painted red with polish. I kissed the tops of her feet and the back of her calf. I held her foot and calf with both hands as I bathed her leg in kisses. I then began to kiss her inner thigh and slowly make my way back to her love box. I could feel her trembling with anticipation as I kissed her everywhere…but there and occasionally liked the protruding rose bud, over the panties, but forcefully with the tip of my tongue. After teasing her for minutes on end, Mia let out a gracious moan as I tongued her lower lips. Soon the room was filled with the aroma of her sweet scent and her soft whimpers. She let out soft cries of, "shit" and "right there" and the occasional, "Yes, Jamie…just like that." I took my time with my woman. Tonight I planned on giving her something to remember me by.

Mia's breasts began heaving up and down. The more her mounds of flesh rose and fell, the more I devoured her. I loved watching her whimper. I loved making her move like this. I loved making her feel like this. Her nipples became more and more obvious as they stood erect and north stretching the delicate material that was holding them in. Mia cupped her breasts and played with her nipples as I ate her. She knew that I loved it when she did that. She knew that shit turned me on. I ate her and ate her and devoured her life she was my last meal. Her juices ran down the crack of her ample ass and my face and I treasured every drop. She began trembling with great force after some time, and tried to get away from me. I knew that she was about to come with quake after quake of pleasure and orgasm. As she moved to get away, I locked down hard on her with my fore-arms and devoured her precious little kitten at an even faster rate. She began bucking and her screams became louder and louder as she began saying my name. "Jamie, oh shit, Jamie…oh damn, damn Jamie damn! Oh shiiit!"

She pushed away at my forehead with the palm of her hand as if the weight of the world was on her and she was trying to get it off. She pushed my head just out of the reach of her vagina as she tried to get her composure. I then used my tongue and stuck it out as far as I could and continued to lick the very tip of her clit with the very tip of my tongue. The two delicate pieces of flesh barely touched, but the slightest touch from these two organs had a powerful response. Mia pushed my head back so far that I thought she might snap my neck.

"No more baby, No more." Mia kissed me deeply on the mouth and then reached for my package.

"Your turn."

CHAPTER 2

▼

ALL WORK AND NO PLAY

JAMIE

Mia and I never made love like that again. We didn't have the time. I began taking on new clients and she turned what was once a fledgling idea, into a powerful magazine. *Black Woman Chicago* was turning into a powerhouse the likes of *Ebony, Jet and Essence*. Mia's phone, email, and pager stayed busy. Even when she and I would go to dinner, she would receive messages. I was no better. My phone stayed full with messages and my former agent from my days of playing pro ball was constantly sending new client's my way.

To make matters worse, Mia began picking up weight. That slamming body that she once had, was beginning to slip away. With her busy work schedule, she had less time for everything including me, working out was one of the farthest things from her mind. She tried the at home gym thing, that didn't work because whenever she was at home she was working. You would think that she could do all that she was doing from the treadmill, but sometimes whoever was on the other end of that phone would get her so pissed off that she could not concentrate on walking.

We still made love from time to time, but it was more out of routine than it was genuine lust. I hated that. I hated fucking as opposed to taking time to make love to my woman. Every Thursday night around 10:00, we ended up in bed and grinding against one another like teenagers. The problem was that our once all night sessions of sucking, fucking, playing and sweating, changed into this quick nut that we both needed to help us get through the reminder of the week, that required little effort. Our all night sessions were reduced to fifteen minutes. This included foreplay.

When Mia could tell that I was starting to pull away she would give me the most fantastic blowjobs. She would pin up her hair, lay me down and go to work on me like a fat kid in the Mississippi sun, in the middle of August, with a popsicle. She would slurp, tease and jack me off with a fever that made me want to propose all over again. I swear, there were days that she gave me head so good, that I would have trouble sleeping at night because she sucked the dreams right out of my head. She would work me like spandex on a fat woman and I would come so hard that my head would hurt. Seriously, there were some days that I thought I had burst a blood vessel in my head, Not only that, but she would swallow and suck me past the point of climax and for 15 or 20 minutes I would be her bitch. Here I was a former pro football player, and this little woman would have me screaming like Chris Tucker in *The fifth element*.
That was in the beginning, now? Forget it.

Those blow jobs that she used to give me were the bomb. They began to drop off as well. Here I was, married only a short time, and I was getting little sex, little head, and little time from the woman that I pledged to spend the rest of my life with. When Mia took the time these days to give me some "special attention" she would hand me a kiss-o-mint condom. She said it was so I didn't cum in her hair and it also was to help with taste. I didn't mind so much but she didn't even present it to me in a romantic way. It was more like "here, put this on." Then, rather than place my member in her mouth and tease me or let me feel the warmth of her mouth, she went right into jacking me off and sucking. I guess I should be lucky, because many of my boys get no head at all. The routine and flat tone that Mia took with me sometimes, made me feel like I was a baby that she was trying to rock to sleep so that she could get back to her work. I remember thinking to myself the last time, "If you don't suck this motherfucker right, I will find someone that will." That was the first time that I had ever thought about cheating on Mia. It was not the last time.

TROUBLE IN PARADISE

Mia began traveling that following June. The magazine was sending her out to meet with potential funders. I began seeing less and less of her and seriously began giving thought to cheating on her. I called Michael to ask him what should I do.
"Don't do it." Michael said.

"Dawg, Mia has picked up all types of weight, she isn't taking any time out for a brother and everything has changed, even the quality of the blowjobs."

Michael began laughing. "What, are you talking about Jay?"

"Dude, the blowjobs even suck, no pun intended."

"How can a blowjob suck? No pun back at ya."

"She gives me a kiss o mint condom, that's new. She goes right into jacking me off, and gets frustrated if it takes me longer than ten minutes to bust."

"So how long do you take?"

"Man, that's not the issue. I mean she is gives head like she is doing me a favor."

"She is doing you a favor."

"You know what I mean. She gives head like it is inconvenient."

"How convenient do you think it is."

"That's part of her duty."

"Duty?"

"Yeah, you know, duty as in what a man and woman share with one another."

"Jamie, the vows say to love, honor and cherish, not love honor and suck dick."

"Yeah, okay. You know what I mean."

"I know what you mean dawg, what I am saying is, these are things that can be worked on, things that can be discussed. Cheating is not the answer. Besides, once you open that door, sometimes you can't close it. Remember what happened to my cousin Michael and that crazy woman Karen that he was dealing with.

"Yeah, well I think that was the exception to the rule."

"Maybe, but you never know."

"I hear you Mike, and I appreciate the advice, but I think I am going to have to make some rough decisions in upcoming weeks."

"There is no decision to make. You promised to love, honor and cherish that woman in front of your friends, family and God. To honor her means that you will not cheat on her. To cherish her, means that you hold dear all the reasons that you married her to begin with, and to love her means just that, to love her and only her. To fuck around on her is breaking your word as a man, husband and a partner."

"You sound like you have been down this path before." Jamie said.

There was a long pause on the phone that seemed to confirm what Jamie was thinking. After a minute Michael finally spoke again to Jamie after he gained his train of thought.

"Jamie, all I am saying is that you can't un-ring the bell. Think about this before you do it. Think about what it will do to her to find out. Think about how you would feel if she fucked around on you."

"I know that I would hate it if she fucked around on me. I know this. But that does not change the fact that I want someone new in my life." Jamie said.

"So is it that you want someone new, or that you and Mia's problems are so bad that you feel you need to cheat?"

"What difference does it make?"

"The difference is, if you just want someone new, say that. Don't put the blame on Mia. The other thing is, if your problems are just that bad, then maybe there is no need for counseling. In either case, there is a third option that you haven't brought up yet."

"What's that?"

"Leave."

"What?"

"Leave. Jamie, if you just want someone new so bad, then that means that you were never ready to get married to begin with and I should have let your ass walk away from Mia on the wedding day as you were originally thinking. On the other hand if you all have problems that are so bad, then maybe counseling isn't the way to go, maybe you just need to break up."

"What kind of fucking sense does that make? I'm not leaving Mia, I am just talking about getting a little something extra on the side to supplement what she isn't doing at home."

Mike said, "If you aren't leaving her, then that tells me that you still care. If you are going to fuck around, that means that you aren't man enough for her."

Mike's words were beginning to piss Jamie off. Jamie called and knew that he was in store for a lecture; he knew that he would get an earful. He did not plan on his best friend being straight up mean to him.

"What do you mean not man enough? Men have been doing this type of thing for years."

"Weak ass men." Mike interrupted.

"What?" Jamie asked.

"Weak ass men, look dawg, I love you as a brother, but I need to keep it real with you. Niggas have been cheating on women for years, it's true. But we cheat for all the wrong reasons, the chief being that we are selfish as hell. I could see cheating if your wife was incapacitated, maybe. I could see if you were in a bad situation that you needed to get out of. I could even see if your woman was no good and a burden. But you have a beautiful, strong black woman that not only contributes, she has your back. Dawg, you really need to think about this before you do it. If you love that woman then you need to respect that woman. Talk the issue out, don't take on a mistress."

Michael's words made sense but I was fed up with Mia and what was going on with her job taking precedence over me. Michael had more experience at this type of thing, so I decided to give him and my relationship the benefit of the doubt and talk to my woman. I do love Mia, so I guess my relationship with her is worth saving.

"Okay Mike, I guess you are right. I will talk to Mia this evening."

THAT EVENING

I knew that Mia would be in really late this evening. I didn't want that to be an excuse to argue or to let this issue go. That being the case, I decided to be diplomatic in my approach to discussing her either leaving her job or making more time for me. I made my world famous lasagna, garlic bread and put a bottle of champagne on ice. I also lit some candles, prepared a salad and played a little *Najee* over my system at a volume low enough for us to speak, yet loud enough where we could enjoy his saxophone.

Mia made it in at about 11:30 that night. She came in beat and worn out. She was surprised to see that I was still up waiting for her. I had her bath drawn and the candles lit on the table. I told her to get into the tub while I placed the lasagna and bread into the oven. I poured her a class of champagne and sat on the edge of the tub as she got undressed.

"Mia, I wanted to talk more about trying to make time for one another in spite of our respective careers."

"Jamie, not tonight."

I took in a deep sigh. I knew this was not going to be easy. The ambiance and everything was to cushion the blow of the things that I wanted to say next. I was not going to ask for a divorce, cheat or anything like that, but whether Mia likes it or not *we are going to discuss this shit this evening.*

"Mia, we have to talk, our marriage is in trouble."

"Is our marriage in trouble or is it that you are not getting enough attention?"

I could hear the defense in her voice and tensed up for an argument. I then remembered the purpose of the food, champagne and music. The smell of the lasagna and the ricotta cheese, spices, sauce and Italian sausage, three other cheeses and ground beef, seduced my senses.

"I don't want to argue. I want to talk. I want us to talk over dinner, over candlelight, and act like two professional adults that are in love with one another."

"Mia was about to say something sharp. I could tell because although we have only been married three years, we have been together ten. I know when the wheels are turning in her head and when she is going to say something hurtful and sarcastic. After ten years of being with someone, you tend to know their tendencies. She would say something really evil, but she would say it in one of those tones that suggested that she means no malice behind it. Ten years has taught me that the tone is camouflage. When Mia says something mean and hurtful, she means to be hurtful. I guess the lasagna was playing the same tricks on her senses that it was playing on mine. She decided to get undressed and enjoy a warm bath.

Being a former pro athlete afforded me many nice things in life. Our Jacuzzi in the Master bathroom was a corner unit that was six by six feet. It had coils underneath the marble setting to keep the water warm and at any desired temperature for hours. Ten years of being together gave me the inside track on the perfect temperature for Mia's body, eighty three degrees. The water was warm with scented oils in it and a little bubble bath that I got from *Bath and Body Works.* I used my remote right there in the bathroom and although the speaker system was four rooms away, the remote signal found the stereo and adjusted the volume. Najee was breaking his way through Mia's defense system. I thought to myself that not only might I get her to cut back some of the hours that she had been working, I might even get laid in the process. Then the unspeakable happened.

Mia and I had not had sex since the last time that we discussed her job and making more time for me. That was only a few months ago. In between, I have been getting the occasional oral love from my wife, but no "nookie." I knew that Mia was gaining weight, but I had no idea how much weight she gained in the last few months. I thought it was just a cute seven to ten pounds that I was worried about turning into twenty, when in fact it was twenty pounds that looked like it was changing into thirty. At first I thought I was imagining things. My suspicions were confirmed when Mia, my wife, was somewhat apprehensive to undress in front of me. She looked at me and gave a half smile that almost suggested that I leave the room.

"I'm not going anywhere." I thought to myself.

When it was obvious that I was not leaving, she gave another half smile and got undressed.

Today she had on black slacks, a belt, and a red cashmere short-sleeved sweater. She had on a pair of designer shoes and stockings. I had seen the outfit a million times before, but somehow, today it looked different. As Mia got undressed, I noticed a few things.

Her belt was tight as hell around her waist, so much so that she had been cutting off the circulation to veins on the side. I could tell because she now had stretch marks on the side *only where her belt would have been.* She also had that imprint around her waist that said that her belt was on way too tight. As she bent over to take off her stockings, the slight pouch that she had for a stomach was twice the size that it was since I last saw her. Mia actually had a small potbelly on her. Her ass which I always thought was perfect, was even bigger. I didn't mind this so much, but it seemed like the spread that I expected Mia to have at age 40, she has now while in her thirties.

I smiled as if none of this bothered me. I then thought about the fact that she had not been going to the gym like she used to, not going to see her girlfriends and family like she used to and virtually every night she has brought in fast food for dinner and left me to fend for myself. I have been cooking for two, but she seldom comes in on time. I have been hitting the gym alone, whereas she used to always go with me when she could. I used to go for long walks with her on the weekends in downtown Chicago. Now all we seem to do is walk past one another as we prepare for another day in the rat race. I didn't let on that her weight was an issue. Right now, it wasn't. Right now, I wanted her to make more time for me and now, more time for her health. As she finally got undressed and slipped in the Jacuzzi, I took her clothes from the floor and told her, "I will hang these up for you. Tell me about your day."

Mia began telling me about her day, and I walked into the Master Bedroom which was adjacent to the Master Bath. We had a hottub in the bedroom as well, but it was not as nice as the master bath. Mia's clothes are hung up according to color in a walk in closet that we have that is bigger than some people's bedrooms. I hung up her outfit where I knew it belonged, and then I made yet another discovery. I had seen this outfit a thousand times before, or at least I thought I had. When I went to the space in the closet where I was going to hang it up, I saw the exact same outfit hanging in the closet, only the one hanging, was in a smaller size. As I examined her closet, I noticed that a great deal of her regular outfits were doubles. One size two to three sizes bigger that the other. Mia was buying clothes that fit, in the same styles that she previously had. Because I kept seeing the same thing over and over again, I didn't notice exactly how much weight she had picked up.

"Maybe I shouldn't be feeding her lasagna." I thought to myself.

Mia went on and on about her day and I listened attentively as I looked for an opening to segway the conversation into our marriage and her need to get in someone's health club. As she continued to tell me about her day, I prepared the plates and gave her a very small helping of lasagna on her plate and a small slice of bread. I poured her more champagne and set the food out to begin cooling again. I then walked into the bathroom where she was getting out of the tub and helped her to dry off.

"You know, I can dry myself off."

"I remember when my drying you off was not a problem."

"Well, I feel a little self conscious. I have gained some weight."

"I think the weight gain has come from the extra hours that you are working."

"Here we go."

"Yeah, here we go. Please, come sit down and let's have dinner."

The weight gain was out there. The reason for the meal was out there. The fact that I did not plan to let this rest in spite of the fact that we both have to get up early in the morning was out there. I prepared to be as diplomatic as possible and she tensed up her whole body and prepared to do battle with me by way of tooth and nail if need be. We both prepared for what was turning into a verbal war that we seemed to be engaged in at least once per month.

"I am not quitting my fucking job." Mia said.

"I'm not asking you to. I am asking that you work no more than 35 to 40 hours and that you make more time for me and this marriage."

"Why does everything have to be about you?"

It's not about me. I supported your going back to school and I supported your wanting to run this magazine, but I will not take a back seat to it."

Mia interrupted with, "I supported your playing pro football."

"Pro football is the reason that we have all the nice things that we have. You may have supported my playing pro ball, but pro ball is what supported us, remember?"

There was a silence between us.

"Are you minimizing my contribution in this relationship?"

"No baby, I'm not. God knows that I would not have made it this far without you. You were there when I blew out my knee. You were there when I rehabbed it. You were there when I was drafted, and you were there when I got cut. You even helped to research ways for me to invest my money so when my career was over, we could live comfortably. Neither of us expected my career to end so early, and if it were not for your planning I would probably be working in McDonalds right now. We are partners in this. What I am saying is I do not feel like your partner lately."

We went back and forth as we ate our food. What I was expecting to be a straight up battle, was more civil than I thought. We had the occasional smart ass remark toward one another, but for the most part we didn't argue like either of us expected. I guess we were both just sick and tired of discussing this.

"You could quit *your job*" Mia said.

I almost choked on my damned food.

"My Job?" I said.

"Yes, your job. I think you could quit your job and I could take care of the two of us."

"My job is what got us here."

"No, playing football got us here when that was your job. Being a public relations representative for present athletes does not carry us."

"It does help with the day to day operations of our household."

"It does, but so would my job with the magazine."

"I was thinking about being a sports agent."

"So you have other career goals, is that what you are saying Jamie?"

"Of course, why wouldn't I?"

"My point exactly."

I was stumped. We had been going back and forth since midnight and it was now 2:30 in the morning. We both have to be up in three and a half hours and we have accomplished nothing. I hate it when that happens. We agreed to disagree, and we made love before going to sleep. Making love was not like it had been in the past. In fact, it seemed like we had just been going through the motions. Tonight we reached an impasse in our relationship. As we said goodnight it was obvious in our eyes that neither of us knew what was next for our marriage.

Mia said, "I love you."

I said, "I love you too."

Both of us were probably thinking about the other, "You don't act like it."

END OF THE ROAD

I threw myself into my work. I stopped being a PR rep and went on to join the players union and became a sports agent. I got the occasional TV time and sports spot on cable to discuss pending deals for my client's. The magazine that Mia was working for was steamrolling and becoming a powerhouse among periodicals. We made time for one another at least once a month, but I wanted more. It made no sense that I was a former professional athlete with a great body, money and looks, but could not get laid on a regular basis. I felt like *D.L. Hughly* in the movie *The Brothers*. This was becoming a bigger problem now that I was a sports agent. Many of my client's were first round draft picks in basketball or football which meant that they had millions. Millions of dollars meant huge parties in my client's huge homes.

There were many days that my clients wanted me at their homes for their parties. This was great for me, because I got to make more contacts with up and coming athletes. They would see how good my client was doing and think that I could get the same thing for them. What many of them need to realize is that my client's talent sells itself most days. I do play a part in the negotiations, but it's not like Hollywood would have you to believe. I am no *Jerry Maguire*.

One of my clients, a running back named JJ Johnson or 3J as he was known in the press, invited me to a party at his home to celebrate his rushing for over a thousand yards in his first season. 3J lived here in Chicago and played for my old team, the bandits. He had a beautiful house up in Evanston. I was bored at home as well as lonely, so I went. I got in my three year old BMW and drove from my lake shore condo to his beautiful north suburban home. As I pulled up, there was valet parking, women everywhere, and all of 3J's no good ass friends that were nothing but hangers on.

"Hey, your agent is here!" I heard one of them yell.

Upon saying that, women looked at me as if I was Jesus returning to claim his saints. They gravitated toward me and began introducing themselves.

"So how much to do you make?" One woman asked me brazenly.

"Where do you live?" Another asked.

"So what's your name?" Another asked me.

All three women were drop dead fine. It was obvious that they were all about one thing…the benjamins. I looked each one up and down and smiled at them. I walked up the long walkway to the house where my superstar athlete was waiting to dap me and give me a hug.

"What's up Jay Dawg!" That was my client's nickname for me.

"What's up 3J? How are you feeling brother?"

3J looked at the ladies and decided to build me up some. He said to them, "Ladies, don't let this brother's conservative style fool you. This man right here got me the six year fifty six million dollar deal that I signed.

I felt each hand that the ladies had on me get tighter. They were each fine, but they were obviously uneducated about contact deals. Yeah, 3J got fifty six million, but my fee was only about a half million dollars. After taxes that is actually about a quarter million. More than half of that goes into my retirement account. The rest equates to mortgage, insurance, and bills. In downtown Chicago, that's nothing. I mean. I live nice, but no where near as nice as 3J. When I got injured, I had to sell the monster of a house that I had. When I look back on that moment, I almost expected Mia to trip when I told her we would have to down-size everything. I expected her to snap to be honest. I knew that she had become used to the large house that took her almost three years to furnish. I knew that she would hate giving up her kitchen that was almost 600 square feet. She also had to give up her garden, horticulture and indoor pool. I remember being nervous about telling her that I had been cut from the team. Instead of tripping, she apologized for my losing my job, kissed me deeply, and told me that we would be okay. I remember telling her, "With no contract renewal, you will have to give all of this up."

She said, "As long as we are together, I will be fine."

I smiled when I thought about that moment. Mia has always been supportive. She has always been there for me. When I thought about that day, when I was at my worst, my woman was at her best. We made the most memorable love that night. Somehow, I had forgotten how wonderful she can be at times.

I took my arms from underneath the ladies and told them to enjoy themselves for the remainder of the night. I then walked into the party to try and secure some more clients. As I walked into the grand foyer, I saw plenty of my old team-mates and some of the new players that were 3J's teammates. There was cocaine and heroine everywhere, call girls, video girls and a few rappers and their entourage. The music was blasting and Special K, a brother named Kelly that looked like *Suge Knight* was spinning all the latest cuts from Chingy, R. Kelly and that new joint from Outcast.

3J hollered out for me to enjoy the party and feel free to tour the home that I helped him to buy. Each time that he gave me a plug, women approached me in droves. I still looked like a player, but these days I was nothing more than a spectator. I didn't see anyone worth approaching about a new contract, so I decided to tour the home. I walked up the grand stairs and looked at how the place was decked out.

3J lived in a white mansion that looked every bit just like the White House. 3J called it the Black House. All throughout his home was photos of famous black people from Mahalia Jackson, to Malcolm X. The photos looked nice, but for what he paid for an interior decorator, he could have done better. I walked up the stairs that had to total seventy, and checked out each of the rooms on the second floor. I opened one room and it was 3J's trophy room. There were no trophies in it other than the Heisman. I remember 3J telling me that he planned on having many more to add to the case. When I opened the door to the trophy room, there were three of 3J's teammates triple teaming a white call girl with implants. They saw me and gave me the universal head-nod.

"Yo dawg, you want some of this?"

I looked at them and said, "I'm straight."

I closed the door and walked further up the hall. Each room had a different surprise. Each room had someone either doing drugs or having sex in the room. One room even had a Chicago celebrity tied up while girls that looked younger, were giving him a golden shower. The girls were dressed in plaid skirts and made up to look like high-school girls in pumps and bobby socks. I looked in that room and gave a look that said, "What the fuck?" The Celebrity screamed at me to get the hell out.

"No problem." I said.

I walked into 3J's library and was even more surprised at what I saw.

There was no one in here.

I thought to myself, "Niggas. It figures that the one place that they don't go is where there are books." I was doubly surprised that 3J even had a damned library. Hell, I wasn't even sure that the boy could read. At 22 years of age, he looked like a young Tony Dorsett. He partied like a young rock star in the seventies.

I surveyed the wall and there were law books, philosophy books, books on war and strategy as well as scholarly books on African-American History.

"This boy paid someone to select these books for his ass." I said out loud.

"He sure did." A voice said behind me.

I turned around and there in the doorway was a fine young sister that looked like she was back and Asian mixed. She stood maybe five feet tall, she was high yellow, and she had long brown hair. She had on a plain mock turtleneck that was short sleeved and black. She also had on black slacks and designer glasses that looked as if they were from Europe. Beneath the slacks she wore black designer boots. She looked militant yet professional, model like but also an intellectual. She was just as pretty as any of the music video women that were downstairs and had an ass that was proportioned just right on her small frame.

"Hi, my name is Jamie." I said.

"I know. My name is Yvonne."

"So how do you know 3J Yvonne?"

"I'm his sister."

She had 34 C breasts. I thought they were a bit small, but on her frame she would topple if they were any bigger. If I didn't know any better, I would have thought that the perfect woman was standing right in from of me. She reminded me of a black *Leeanne Tweeden from the Victoria's Secret catalog.*

"You are related to 3J?"

She smiled and said, "We have different fathers, but yes, he is my brother."

"How did I not meet you? I mean…I thought I knew everyone in 3J's family."

"I keep a low profile." She said.

"Why?"

"To protect my brother's interest."

There were tables in the library as well as a mini bar and stereo. These were things that obviously did not belong in the library and were direct contradictions to the various items in the room, but they were items that 3J insisted upon. Yvonne asked me what did I normally drink and I told her Bacardi and Coke would be fine. She mixed me an excellent drink and without thinking I sat and began talking with her. I was taken in by her beauty and about to be equally taken in by her intelligence. Yvonne told me how she helped to furnish 3J's home and how the library was her personal favorite, minus the minibar and stereo. I sat up and listened to her tell me how she and 3J grew up and how they had nothing. She was a few years older than he was at 26, and she insisted that he not only play sports, but that he remain in good academic standing. Once 3J decided that he was going to quit school and run with a gang in their home state of Louisiana. Yvonne found out that 3J dropped out of school and not only did she drop his ass back in, she whipped his ass and fought with the would-be gang members for his freedom. This girl was not only fine, she was courageous.

We talked and talked and talked for hours in the library. We talked so much that we forgot that there was a party going on beneath us on the first floor of the house. We laughed, we told jokes and as much as we tried to fight it, three hours into the conversation we discovered that we had chemistry.

"So why are you sitting here with me chatting instead of hemmed up in one of these rooms getting your dick sucked?"

I was surprised by how frank she was. Yvonne was so fine that you didn't expect anything foul to come from her mouth. In the same token, this was the same woman that used to discipline and beat up my star running back downstairs. To respond to her question, I began fingering my three carat wedding band.

"This is why."

"There are plenty of men downstairs with one of those, what makes you any different?"

"I love my wife."

"Do you?"

"Why do you ask?"

"Well, it's 2:00 in the morning. Why are you here with me instead of home doing what married couples do?"

I responded, "Married couples do very little after a decade."

There was a long silence in the room.

"You make it sound so depressing." She finally said.

"Sometimes…it is."

"Do you want to talk about it?"

There was another long silence.

"Yeah, I think I do."

I bared my soul to a perfect stranger, a stranger that didn't seem like a stranger, a woman that I wanted to get to know better.

BACK HOME THAT NIGHT

Nothing happened. That is, with Yvonne and I. I got home at 5:30 in the morning. Mia was sleep and didn't seem to mind that I was gone. I turned on ESPN and watched clips of my client from last weeks game. I saw my client, but all I could think about was Yvonne. I reclined in my lazy boy recliner and turned on the massaging unit. I undressed to my boxers and tried to lose myself in the electronic fingers that massaged my entire body. A few minutes into it, I began touching myself. This is what I was reduced to after ten years of marriage.

I envisioned Yvonne was in my home and standing in the doorway dressed as she was earlier. I envisioned that I walked over to her and placed one hand in the small of her back and the other on the back of her head as I ran my fingers through her long silky hair.

I then slowly pecked her, kissed her, sucked gently on her bottom lip and then on her earlobe. As I began kissing the nape of neck and planting soft wet kisses all on her neck and collarbone, I occasionally tongued her passionately. I imagined that the room was filled with the sound of our soft wet kisses and passionate moans. I touched myself as I got off on how hot the kissing was alone.

I thought about my hand making its way to Yvonne's soft round butt. I imagined that it was creamy to the touch and giving to my primitive grabs. I then imagined that as I kissed her she ran her hands through my locks and kissed me back as if she wanted me just as much as I wanted her. I then pictured raising her shirt just enough to expose her bra, which I imagined to be laced and white. I envision my kissing the tops of her breasts as I take each one in my hands. I then begin to kiss her ribs, her sides, and all over the front of her body. I hear her let out a moan as I kneel before her and begin to unzip her pants.

"Jamie what are you doing?" A voice interrupted. "Where have you been?"

It was Mia. She got up to pee and noticed that I was lost in touching myself in the easy chair. I don't think I have ever been more embarrassed. Not wanting to spoil the opportunity I said, "I was just thinking about you, you wanna help me out with this?"

Mia looked down at me and said, "I don't think so." She then began to walk off to the bathroom.

I was mad.

If she didn't mean to help, then perhaps she could have left me the fuck alone to finish. The fantasy was just about to get good. The wheels were turning in my head now. I knew that I was about to say something that I didn't need to say. I knew like all men knew, that there was something inside me fighting to get out, something that was fighting to be said, yet I also knew it was something that I shouldn't say. I remember Michael's words saying, "You can't un-ring the bell." Still, I didn't care.

"You know if you don't help me with this, someone else might."

Mia stopped where she was. She didn't even turn around.

"Has it come to that?"

There was a short silence.

"No. It hasn't come that. It will never come to that."

There was a long silence in our home. But we were on the same page with one another.

"Don't ever let that walk out of your mouth again."

Mia went to our bedroom without even turning around. I went to the linen closet and grabbed a blanket. There was no sense in going back in our bedroom.

I thought to myself, "I shouldn't have said that shit. There is no way that I should have said that shit. Damn."

It's true that you can't un-ring the bell.

CHAPTER 3

▼

LOVE DON'T LIVE
HERE NO MORE

I went on with my new job as agent and made a killing financially. The more successful I became, the more opportunities there were to cheat. I kept my composure and I did everything that I could to hold on to my marriage. Mia and I had sex once a month and that is all there was to it. In the last year I have com to notice a drastic change in my wife, a change that was not for the better.

Mia picked up thirty or forty pounds all together. She stabilized somewhere around 165. She went from being what I thought was a fine ass "thick" black woman to a cute "heavy set" woman. She was still pretty, but I didn't sign on for just pretty. I wanted the woman that I married, you know, that fine motherfucka that walked down the isle and made me say, "Damn." I wanted the woman that used to wear her hair down for me. I wanted the woman who stayed shopping in *Fredrick's* and *Victoria's Secret*. I wanted the woman that would break me off twice per week instead of once a month.

I think back to a time where she and I were both in love and hungry for knowledge. I remember once in college when I had to take on a job as a security guard when financial aid screwed up my loan information. Mia stayed by my side throughout that ordeal and even fed a brother when funds were short. I remember being in her dorm room one day tired as hell. Mia surprised me by getting dressed up in my uniform top, fish net stockings, my Barney Fife hat, and high heels.

"Freeze Nigga, your ass is under arrest."

[playing along] "I'm sorry officer, what did I do?"

"I don't know yet! But I am betting your ass did something. Get yo ass up against this wall!"

"Aren't you gonna read me rights?"

"You don't have any rights right now, in fact, shut the fuck up."

Mia tossed me up against the wall (while in heels) like she knew what the fuck she had been doing, or as if she had been arrested before. She then began searching me like she was really looking for some shit. She reached for my package from behind and grabbed it with a vise like grip.

"Unh hunh, I got something here, what's this?"

I started laughing.

"What the hell are you laughing at? What the hell is this? Just like I thought, you are under arrest for concealing a weapon."

"But officer that's not a weapon."

"She turned me around and grabbed my package again. I was harder than Chinese Arithmetic.

"Feels like a weapon to me. It's long, it's hard and I think it's dangerous. I think I am gonna have to confiscate this here."

"You can't confiscate it" I said.

"What?"

"You can't confiscate it."

"The hell I can't, give up the dick nigga, strip!"

I stripped, took some more verbal abuse, and was thrown to the bed and made passionate love to by my woman. Those heels, stockings and the way she looked in that uniform had my heart racing like a school boy about to get his first piece. Damn she looked good that day. Her hair was down, nails were done, make up was perfect and she rode my ass like a jockey at the races. I hated the fact that I was a security guard for some time. She made me look at that uniform in a whole different light.

That was when I was at my worst.

The next year is when I began playing football. She was there for that as well. The more I think about it, Mia was with me before I had even thought about playing organized sports. She and I did not have to have this lavish lifestyle. We could have ended up in a small suburb somewhere and I could have still been a security guard and I think we would have been okay.

Where did I go wrong?

These days we made love…or rather had sex, out of routine more than any other reason. She was accommodating, but that is all that she was. We still had great conversation from time to time and we still made time for one another's social events, but we were slowly drifting apart. Initially it was just my mind that was wandering, now it is more my heart.

MIA

I love Jamie. I love him with all that is in me. I need to focus right now, and he needs to understand that. I have been with Jamie for a time that seems like forever. I was with him *before* he became the pro football player. I was with him *before* he signed his first contract. I have been with him through thick and thin. Now it is my time. Most women lose their men when they play college and pro sports, especially when the men don't marry then before they ink their first deal. A lot of women would have trapped Jamie and gotten pregnant. That is not my style and I hate the bitches that do that sort of thing. They give us real women a bad name. I always knew that I would marry Jamie. I always knew that we would not only marry me, he would marry me on my terms. I was more than the fine ass round the way girl that Jamie fell in love with. I was his best friend.

Back in the day I gave him some lovin two to three times a week. No matter what his dream or his inspiration, I stood by him. Hell, if that nigga told me that he wanted to begin catching frogs for a living, I wouldn't trip. I would say something like, "Okay baby, what is the plan for catching these damn frogs?" If he didn't have a plan I would create a marketing plan for him. That is the type of woman that I am. I have my man's back no matter what. It's time now that my man began showing me that same type of loyalty. I wanted to call my best friend, but Wanda has been so busy lately appearing in music videos and modeling. The last time I talked to her on the phone, she was trying to trap some rapper into a pregnancy scam. It was then that I saw exactly how trifling Wanda's ass was. I wondered why I ever wanted her in my wedding in the first place. I needed someone to talk to so I gave Loretta a call. I explained to her all that Jamie and I had been going through and asked her how did she and Michael get through the problems that they had.

Loretta said, "Girl, I hear you in wanting to be your own woman and wanting Jamie to stand by you, but did you let him know what your plan was?"

"No I didn't quite tell him what my plan was, but I think no matter what my plan is, he should be supportive."

"How can he be supportive of a plan that he knows nothing about?"

"I don't know. I just want him to be there for me regardless of what plans I have. I mean I know that he wants more time and attention, but this magazine is important to me. When I was standing by in support of his dreams, I did so without question."

"And you want him to support you without question, is that what I hear you saying?"

"Exactly." I said.

"Mia, have you been on top of your womanly duties while you are putting in all these long hours at the magazine?"

"Womanly duties?" I said "Girl you are sounding like my momma now with that old school verbage."

Loretta laughed. "Yeah well, you may have a ton of duties while you are with the magazine, but every woman has duties that they have to perform as well *no matter how tired they are.*"

I asked, "Do you keep up with your duties all the time?"

"When I have a man I do. Remember what the comic Monique said, "What you won't do, another bitch will.""

"Jamie actually said something to that affect the other day."

"Then that is a sign that he is already thinking about it and you need to get back on your square."

I asked, "What about his responsibilities and the part that he plays in all of this? It's not fair that I have to bend over backward to please him. I mean damn, I plan on our spending more time with him after I make this dream of running this magazine a reality. I mean I am doing great things at Chicago Black Woman Magazine. I have brought in seven million in funding, written additional grants and have signed all types of celebrities to help jump start the magazine's first year anniversary and celebration."

"Mia do you hear yourself?" Loretta interrupted.

"What?" I asked.

"I hear that you love what you do, but I am also hearing where you are obsessed with your job."

"Is there something wrong with being driven?"

"Driven, no. I admire your passion for your work and I have no doubt that you will be successful, but sweetheart what about Jamie?"

"What about Jamie?"

"The passion that you have for your work, Jamie has to now share. I am sure that all this passion that you speak with was all exclusively given to him before you took this job. Girl, sometimes a man needs to feel needed. Also, men are like babies, that want all of your attention, all of your love, and all that you have to give just about all of the time."

I said, "You know Loretta, I hear you, but lately I just do not feel that Jamie has been as supportive as he could have been."

"Hasn't he? I mean I know that you have been there for him, but didn't he pay your tuition to graduate school? Didn't he take your mother in when he signed his first contract? When you first began raising money for the magazine, didn't he cut the first check?"

"Yeah, but that was when he thought it was just a passing fancy."

"Fancy or not, he was there for you. He is still there for you, and based on the little bit that I have heard, it sounds to me like you are now pushing him to the side."

'Loretta it's not just him that I have placed to the side, It's everything in my life. I mean I have picked up weight, I have lost sleep, I am putting all that I have into my career."

Loretta interrupted with, "If you don't put more into your marriage, you will lose Jamie."

Mia said, "Jamie might run his mouth and say he would step out on me, but he ain't going nowhere."

There was a short silence over the phone.

"Never say never, Mia, those words have a way of coming back and biting you in the butt."

Loretta's words sounded so convincing that I almost wondered if Michael had cheated on her and if that was the reason that they quietly divorced. Everyone in our circle of friends knew that they were no longer an item, but no one, not even Jamie knew why. I thought that Michael must have cheated years ago. A year after their divorce, Michael was married to a younger woman. Me and all my girls figured that she had to be in the picture way before Loretta and Michael got divorced. Jamie said that wasn't the case. Jamie said that Michael was tired of being alone and opted to begin going out with younger women. Jamie stated that the woman Michael married, I forget her name, just happened to be the one that he settled down with. I have to admit that she was pretty. I also have to admit that she was smart. It still made no sense to me that a year after his marriage was over to Loretta, that Michael would marry another woman. They are such a good couple together, that you would assume that a year later they would be working on getting back together. Even at my wedding they looked damned good together. Still, if Loretta is cautioning me against my behaviors with Jamie *maybe I ought to check myself.*

54   Down Low, Double Life

"Okay Loretta, I will give some thought to all that you have said."
"All I am saying Mia, is talk to your man and let him know what is on your mind."
"Sounds like a plan, thanks Loretta."
"Anytime girl."
"Loretta, can I ask you what happened between you and Michael?"
There was a long pause over the phone.
"Mia I am really not ready to talk about it."
"After all this time?"
"After all this time."
There was another short pause.
"Okay girl, I understand."
"Let's meet for lunch Friday at Applebees." Loretta said.
"It's a date, I'll talk with ya."
I hung up the phone and thought long and hard about whether or not Jamie would cheat on me. I thought about how long we have been together and the fact that he hadn't. I then thought about all the sex he could have had while playing pro ball. Not once did he cheat on me or bring any outside babies to our situation. Not once did he go to an event without having me on his arm sharing the spotlight with him. If he didn't cheat then as a pro player, it made less sense for him to cheat now. The fiscal year ends in thirty days. I will finish up my work and then arrange for he and I to go to the Bahamas and kick it for a second honeymoon. He will only have to wait four more weeks. In the meanwhile, I think I need to get my ass in the Gym. I think I will head out to Bally's in River Oaks.

LORETTA

It was hard as hell not to pour my heart out to Mia. I started to tell her to do whatever she can to hold onto her man because there are some trifling ass women out here that are probably chomping at the bit to get their claws into someone like Jamie.
Damn, I miss my man. But he put the wedge between us. I have been punishing him for some time now. I need to get myself together. I think that is why I started going to therapy. I am seeing a Master's level therapist named David Allen, that seems to bring peace into my life each week that we meet for session. The problem is, I have become very attracted to him as of late, and I do not know how to control my emotions. David had made me think more and more about my marriage. He has also convinced me to explore my fantasies about my husband. David looks like Shemar Moore, that alone makes me weak in the knees some

days while in session. The more I let myself go and the more that I think about a better life with Michael, the more fantasies about David sneak in there.

That is not my only problem. Another brother at the agency that I work for named Keith Bryant has been sweating me hard to go out with him. Keith is also a therapist, but he works with teens and children. This brother looks like Moris Chestnut and also has his winning smile. Keith has a thriving private practice, he dresses like something out of a magazine, and everyday without fail he compliments me and tells me how wonderful I am. Every now and then I get flowers on my desk that have been sent anonymously by 1-800-FLOWERS. Each time that I receive them I smile. Each time it is a dozen roses. Each time the roses are a different color with a card attached that says what the color represents.

All this borderlines sexual harassment, but I would not trade this attention in for nothing in the world. I once got flowers from Michael. I could tell that they were not from Keith because the flowers that Michael sent were the ones that were part of the special that they always advertise on the Internet. They were pretty, but there was little thought behind the offer. Keith walked by and saw the bouquet that Michael sent, although he did not know who they were from, and chuckled.

Keith and I have only been working together for a short time. I think he has been with the agency for a year and a half. He doesn't know that I was once married and he doesn't even know that I had my bought with Cancer. I'd like to keep it that way simply because one, it's not his business and two, I don't want him treating me any differently than he does now. Every morning I come in and I hear him say, "Hey pretty lady" in that soft, deep, radio voice of his and I just tingle all over. I have wondered on more than one occasion what he would be like in bed. I know that all I need do is say that word and I could find out. But I still needed closure with Michael, or I needed to begin reconciling my marriage. The problem was, I didn't know which I wanted to do. I discussed this in therapy with David.

"I just don't know what to do, I want my marriage back, but I almost feel as if I am missing out on something by not giving other suitors a chance."

"Why do you think that you are missing out on something?" David asked.

"I just feel like these other men that are interested seem so nice, so warm, and as if they would never hurt me. They are attentive, caring, and they compliment me often."

"Don't all men do that in the beginning? Didn't Michael do that? What makes these men that you are mentioning any different than your ex-husband other than the fact that they are new in your life?"

David's questions got me thinking, hard. His questions were such that he helped me to stay focused and helped my objectivity. His line of questioning was the main thing at this point keeping me out of bed with Keith. The more I thought about things, the more I realized that Keith could be a dog as well as a player. God knows I didn't want to trade one bad situation for another. At least with Michael I know what I have. There was still the matter of his cheating on me.

"What about his cheating on me?" I asked David.

"What about it?"

"He betrayed my trust."

"Years ago."

"That doesn't take away the pain."

"No it doesn't, but let me ask you this, why do you meet with him once a week for breakfast and twice a week for dinner?"

There was a short pause as I processed my response.

"Because I still love him."

David asked, "You all go out, have a nice time, you go to dinner, dancing and the movies, what is the difference between what you have now and what you had when you were married?"

"Well for one, we are no longer married. Two, there is no sex, and three, we are not living together."

David asked, "Beyond that, what is the difference?"

I thought long and hard during the silence. There was no difference. I was dating my husband and had been for some time. We went on dates that were great. We went to many concerts and events like we did when we were younger. There was no difference between what we were doing now and what we used to do other than the fact that we are not under the same roof and we are not having sex. David made an excellent point.

"What is to say that he won't place his job over me again?" I asked.

"There are no guarantees, but he is making time for you now isn't he?"

"I don't want to be hurt again."

"I think he knows this, don't you?"

"That other woman had my husband's dick in her mouth!" I snapped.

"You had every opportunity to stop that."

That hurt. *I mean that really, really hurt.* My attraction to my therapist for the most part was gone when he let that walk out of his mouth.

"Are you saying that this is my fault?"

"No I am not saying that at all. Let me ask you though, what do you think would have happened if you had stopped the woman from giving head to your husband?

You were right in the next room. From my understanding of your account of the story, the other woman took the initiative, your husband even tried to resist…"
I interrupted with, "It was a weak as attempt at resisting."
"It was an attempt nonetheless. Now I am sure that you have asked yourself this question a million times. Now I am asking you, what would have happened had you stopped them?"
"I'm not clairvoyant, how am I supposed to know?"
"That's bullshit."
"What?"
"That's bullshit, answer my question to the best of your ability."
David had never taken this stance with me in therapy before. I was hurt by it, but also glad that he challenged me on it. I don't know what I was feeling. I was confused, hurt and angry all at once. Then the unspeakable happened. I felt something that I hadn't felt in all this time regarding my husband's affair. I felt responsible. This was <u>not my fault by any stretch of the imagination</u> but I did play a small part in all this. I should have stopped the two of them when I had the chance. Who knows where we would be now.
"I guess had I stopped them, Michael would have been embarrassed, she would have been fired, and he and I would have fought for months, but we might still be together. We might have even gone to marriage counseling."
"How else could you have handled this differently?"
"I might have gotten separated instead of divorced."
"Is there anything else that you might have done differently?"
"I think that I would not have persecuted him as much as I have. I guess I have been mean to him, but I was hurting. I think that I was not only punishing Michael, I think that I might have been subconsciously punishing myself."
For the first time in therapy, I began crying. Not that weeping we do when we realize that we have been hurt, but that sho nuff crying that we do to cleanse past pain. I put my man through the ringer as I should have, but I also overdid it. I have pushed my man so far to the left, that I almost could never see right. Michael hurt me, but he was a good man. A good man that I punished for years on end because of what *almost happened.* Rather than stopping it when I had the chance, I might as well have pushed the two of them in bed. I cried when I realized my part in it, cried when I realized his part in it, and cried for women everywhere that lost their man to a whore.
"I think we just made a breakthrough" my therapist said.
"Now what?" I asked.

"Now, you are free to make the decisions that you need to make and make them objectfully. Should you decide to see other men, at least you can see them for what they are rather than what you hope for them to be. Perhaps if you begin dating again, you will be able to appreciate a date for just that, a good time with no strings necessarily attached. Who knows? Seeing other men that are out there that only want to take you to bed, may actually help you to appreciate your husband."

"Do you think I should see other people?"

"What do you think you should do?"

"I think that it couldn't hurt."

"Then I fully endorse it."

SEEING THINGS FOR WHAT THEY ARE

I went back to work with new lenses to view the world. When I got back to the office the next day there was Keith with his winning smile and his dashing good looks. He looked like a piece of fine chocolate to me, and I have to admit, I really wanted a taste. There is nothing like a man that is clean cut, smelling good, and has muscles that show even when he has on a dress shirt. Keith was fine, but now that I had a new lease on how I viewed things, I knew that more than wanting to get to know me, he wanted me on all fours talking trash and hitting it from the back. I wanted that too, maybe…but if it ever came to that, he would have to work for it. Prior to therapy, I was ready to give him the cookie on a silver platter.

Initially I thought that Michael's flowers were cheap in comparison to Keith's. That is not the case. The flowers that Michael sent are beautiful. Those flowers that he sent said, "I am thinking of you." The roses that Keith sent, said, "I want to take you to bed." The more I thought about things, the more I began to see them for what they really were. Sure Keith was smooth in a Keith Washington, Barry White sort of way, but he also had an ulterior motive. Still, I was glad for the attention and I loved the games that we played.

"Hello pretty lady." Keith said as I arrived to the office.

"Well hello right back at you Mr. Man."

I had on a pair of black slacks and an electric blue silk dress shirt. I walked past Keith smelling of body lotion from the bath and body works and a hint of Eternity Perfume. My hair had that short and cute wet look and today I was feeling every bit of being Jada-Pinkett Smith's twin sister. My look was simple yet elegant, professional but alluring. My slacks were very tight around my ass and bell-bottomed at the ankle. I had my earth tone make up on with the exception of ruby red lipstick that accented my Maybelline-like lips. I smiled at Keith as I walked to my office and lightly licked my lips to get them moist as I said, "Talk to ya later Mr. Man."

Admittedly my walk had a little more bounce and my ass had a little more shake, but I see no harm in a girl feeling proud of her wares. I then sat at my desk and dialed Michael to ask him out for dinner. Michael picked up the phone on the first ring.

"Hello, this is the Deputy Mayor."

"Hey Baby, how are you?"

"Fine now that I am talking to you, what's up?"

"I was hoping that I could see you, ya know, talk."

"Just name the time and the place."

"Your place at about 10:00 PM. See you then."

"Oh…kay…I guess I will see you at ten."

With that I hung up. I decided that I had punished Michael enough and it was time that we both shared a little more than an intimate embrace if we were going to get things back on track. Michael might not be the only one that I see however. I think it's time that I made use of this freedom and "Check my options" to see what else was available to me.

Just then, I noticed that Keith was standing in the doorway—Smiling.

"Was that my competition on the phone?"

"Competition? Why Keith whatever do you mean?" I said in a sly and sexy voice.

"Well, I guess that is your man on the phone or at the very least an interested suitor. I am kind of wondering where he stands in relation to where I stand with you."

"What makes you think that you are even in the running?" I responded.

"The way that you smile when I compliment you; The way that you move when you walk away from me, and the smile that you sometimes have for me for no reason at all."

Damn. Was I that transparent? I thought to myself.

"Keith, I do enjoy your compliments. I do enjoy your company and your singular wit. But I do not date co workers."

Keith smiled a smile that said, "not yet."

"Okay miss lady. I hear you. Does that mean that I should stop?"

"No, do what you feel."

"Really? What I feel?"

Keith walked further into my office and closed the door behind him. I was seated in my leather office chair with my legs crossed. He walked over to me wheeled me around in a position to get a better look into my eyes, and smiled one of those winning Morris Chestnut smiles. He then separated my legs with one hand and slowly caressed my inner thigh as my legs opened for him as if they had a mind of their own. His hand slid all the way up my thigh almost to my kitten. I inhaled with anticipation expecting that he would touch me there. Rather than touch me where no man but my ex-husband had touched me in years, I felt the light touch of the back of his index and ring finger as they ran tiny circles around my left nipple. He caressed my breast for a brief second before giving it a light squeeze. He then took the same hand and grabbed my chin ever so lightly. He gave me a single wet kiss and then began nuzzling on my neck. The room fell silent with nothing but the sounds of his kissing my lips and neck. I let out a soft sigh that you could barely hear as he sucked my earlobe and tongued my inner ear. He then kissed me passionately on the mouth, eyes closed and with a fire I had not known since my early college years. He pulled me to him with one arm and I felt safe in his muscular grip. He stood me up with one arm as if I were a little girl and then skillfully grasped my ass with the other hand, palming it's roundness and exploring it as if he had never felt something so soft and so curvy. I felt him get hard between my legs and became light headed as I began to kiss him back. He then ran his fingers through my short wavy hair, touching me just right at the base of the back of me head. He looked me deep into my eyes and then spoke.

"No more office games. I want you. I think that you are a beautiful, intelligent, strong black woman. You are the type of woman that I need in my corner and the type of woman that I need in my life. I know I don't really know you. But I want that opportunity to get to know you. I want to know your likes and dislikes. I want to know your fantasies. I want to know your dreams. Most of all, I want you in my life in whatever capacity that I can have you. Loretta, I am asking you for that chance. Go on your date with whomever was on the phone, but when you are ready, I'm here."

He kissed me once more on the lips and then he turned to leave. I almost started to ask him to stay, but then I thought about the words that he spoke. I forgot about that whomever person that was on the phone. Just like that, I had forgotten about Michael.

Damn. This was going to be harder that I thought. I picked up the phone and began dialing. A voice answered.

"David Allen's office can I help you?"

"Yes, I'd like to schedule an appointment to see David again, this is Loretta."

"Is it urgent Loretta? You are not scheduled to be back for two weeks."

"I'd like to see him again as soon as possible."

MICHAEL

I do not know what has gotten into Loretta but I am glad that she is finally beginning to come around. The mayor has let me know that he does not intend to run
another term and that he and his wife plan to retire and enjoy their lives and
rekindle their marriage. On the outside looking in, it didn't appear that there was
anything wrong with their marriage. I could see where if I was not careful, things
would turn out the same way for Loretta and I. We are on the verge of getting
back together, I can feel it. I'm glad too, because I was at the point where I was
beginning to say the hell with it and stop pursuing her all together.

We have dated for a while now with no sex. My boys all think that I am crazy
for still pursuing her, especially my boy Don. Don is a friend of mine and Jamie's
that just doesn't know when to let things go. Just the other day, he and all of our
frat brothers were over at my crib playing spades, bid-whist and poker, when after
a few drinks it looked like my entire chapter might end up coming to blows. It
started when Don started suggesting that we hit Mississippi Valley State College's
homecoming this year and have an old fashioned road trip.

I told Don, "Bruh, we are really too old for that sort of thing."

Don said, "You mean you are too old. Besides your ass couldn't go anyway with
your precious political career"

"Well, it wouldn't look right with me in a hotel room somewhere with some
young girl."

"Young girl my ass, nigga you know even if you went you wouldn't do anything.
Your scary ass is probably still pining away for your ex-wife. How pathetic is that
dawg? I mean damn, are you ever gonna get back on your square?"

"Hey yo, lay off that. Don't start hatin on me because I have a real job with a real
career and a real woman by my side."

"Real Job? Hold on son, who the fuck are you talking to? What the fuck is wrong
with my job at the Railroad? Nigga I make $23.00 an hour."

"Yeah and you don't have a damn thing to show for it."

"Nigga what?" Don said.

"You don't have anything to show for it. You have what—two babies by two different mothers that are bleeding your ass for child support, both of them were
welfare bitches to boot, and you still live in your mother' house. I mean come on
dawg, we are cool but don't start hatin on me cause I'm doing what I want to do
while you are living paycheck to paycheck off a hookup that you got from
another brother."

Neither of us should have been talking in the tone that we were talking but that Hypnotic and Hennessey kept the conversation going. Jamie tried to slow us down but to no avail.

"Hold up guys, be cool. Both of you niggas is drunk." Jamie said.

Don finished his hand and continued to talk shit. "That's a Boston nigga, ya'll asses is out! Hold on…Now Mike—what the hell do you mean disrepectin me up in here?"

The tension in the room mounted. There is nothing worse than an angry, drunk Que.

"Up in here? Nigga up in here is my house. You hear me? This is my spot. If anyone is being disrespected up in here it's me. You don't come up in my house talking about my job, my ways and my woman."

"What woman? You ain't got no woman remember? She divorced your ass. And why is it that your divorce was so fuckin hush hush? Don't nobody in here even know why yall got divorced, not even Jamie who is supposed to be your boy. What's up with that shit?"

I interrupted with, "No one knows because it ain't no one else's business but mine."

"I bet you couldn't get it up. We got some bruhs that are doctors you know? Maybe one of them could get you some Viagra or something. I hear that political mother fuckers like you got stress and can't satisfy your woman."

"That's retarded, you know Don, You are a simple mother fucker."

"I bet that's it. That's why you don't wanna go on no road trip. Either that or you are so pussy whipped by that pretty bald bitch of yours that you can't go on with life without begging her to take your simple ass back. Fuck that bitch Mike. Let's go to the homecoming and fuck some of them young girls, ya know, get that Que oil up in em and tear that ass off."

"Nigga Naw." I said.

Don said, "See, your punk ass is soft. I bet you got a soft dick too."

"Don, why do you keep referring to my dick and my lovelife? What the fuck, I mean are you trying to come out the closet on us?"

That sobered Don up some. It also pissed him off.

"Nigga, your bitch likes it." Don said while grabbing his crotch.

"Yeah, right nigga you're drunk. One of you guys take Don's ass home."

"The bitch *used to like it.*" Don said.

Generally, I would have given Don no attention because he was drunk. Hell, we were both drunk. I was going to let the whole thing go until I saw the looks on some of my frat brothers faces as they tried to usher Don out the door and to their cars. Many of them started gathering their things like the entire chapter was in on a secret that I was not privy to.

That sobered me up.

"Hold up, Don…what the fuck are you saying Bro?"

They were pulling Don out onto the lawn to drive him home and he got louder and louder.

"I'm saying that the bitch used to like it. Before you was with her, I was all up in her. Back in the day, she was my bitch. Before you transferred to the school, I was tappin that ass on the regular. Then she met your square ass and I was only hitting it about once a month when you all first started dating and then it was every now and then when yall got serious, but you can bet your ass it was ALL THE TIME WHILE YOU WERE PLEDGING!"

I graduated college years ago.

Loretta and I have been together as long as I can remember as far as meaningful relationships go.

Let Don tell it, they fucked well into the first two years that Loretta and I were dating.

I looked at Jamie's face for confirmation, but I brought Jamie in and he met Loretta later, so there was nothing to confirm. The looks on the other brothers faces were all damning.

I charged Don.

I hit him over and over and over again. I pummeled him even though he was drunk. I pummeled him even though he was my frat. I tried to kill his ass with a fury of blows. Fortunately for us both, I was drunk too and my punches barely connected. The brothers separated us, and our boy Justus, took Don home.

That was a week ago.

Don and I have not spoken since then and tonight Loretta was coming over.

I know that I have no reason to question Loretta and chances are that Don is lying. If I truly want to reconcile, I will let it go. Being a man, that is next to impossible. Don's timing could not have been worse. Loretta and I have been doing fine. She finally seems like she is ready to come around. We finally appear to be back on the road to reconciling our relationship and perhaps our marriage. Now I have this shit in my head fucking with me. Damn.

I wanted the house to be perfect for Loretta's arrival. I cleaned and cooked and even paid a maid service to come in and clean behind me for $50.00. I always thought that was funny about me. I have used a cleaning service on more than one occasion, but whenever I used them, I cleaned up before they got there. I think it's crazy to clean before the cleaners get there. It kind of defeats the purpose. But I wanted the house to be picture perfect. I wanted Loretta to almost imagine what it would be like to live where I am living. She has her apartment I know, but I would love to have her here with me in my new house—our new house, where we could start fresh.

The maid service arrived an hour later. I played a little Keith Sweat to clean to and poured myself a glass of lemonade. I then booted my computer up so that I could feign as if I were working while the fine ass Hispanic women came in and did their thing.

I was elated like a schoolboy at the prospect of Loretta coming over. If she was coming over at 10:00 then that could only mean one thing…the wait was over and she was ready to be physical with me again. If that was the case then everything had to be perfect. I broke out the crystal, scented candles, and my best wine. I placed satin sheets on the bed and laid out my silk pajamas. I went to my computer and made a short grocery list with cheesecake, flowers, ice cream and all of Loretta's favorite things. I put bubblebath on the list as well so she would have no reason to leave and I could pamper her in the morning. When I thought about all the preparation and how excited I became at the prospect of getting my wife back I thought, "Maybe Don is right, maybe I am pussywhipped."

On que as if the mere mention of Don was enough to spark karma, my screen said, "YOU HAVE MAIL!"

I expected it was Don making the first move to apologize for our drunken behaviors.

I was wrong.

The email had no written content…just attachments.

I opened the email.

I think my heart stopped.

There were at least 20 photos of a young Loretta and my Frat Brother. Some were before me, some were during me, and others were after I gave Loretta my heart. I know because in the beginning pictures I hardly recognized her. In the second set, she had on my ring on a chain around her neck. In yet another photo, she was in her cap and gown and nothing else.

I was at her graduation—we were two years in love at her graduation.

Loretta broke my heart…long before I ever broke hers.

I never went out for the groceries. I stared at the photos over and over and over again until the doorbell rang at 9:45. I opened it and there was my ex wife looking as if she was ready to take me back. The problem we now faced…was whether I wanted her trifling ass back in my life.

She said, "Hey Baby, what's wrong?"

CHAPTER 4

▼

CHEATERS NEVER PROSPER

JAMIE

I can't believe that Don used to mess around with Loretta. What's worse is the way that he clowned my boy in his own home. Don has always been jealous of Michael and all that Michael has accomplished. I guess that includes not only the ability to bed Loretta, but the ability to hold on to her as well. Mike and Loretta built a lot with each other. Mike could have easily played pro ball as I did but that is not where his heart was. He was in love with Loretta from the first time that he saw her. They are the ideal couple in my eyes, no matter what anyone else has to say.

I started to go to Don's house and kick his ass for the way that he played Mike, but I needed Don's advice on some things so I decided to give him a pass. Each day that went by, I thought more and more about Yvonne. I went to a lot of 3J's events including another house party where we celebrated his getting an ESPY award from ESPN. 3J also did a lot of charity work on the team's behalf and at the behest of his sister. I went to a great deal of these events to sign small talent as well as get a look at Yvonne and the stylish way that she had about her. Our conversations became more and more intimate as the weeks went by, and the more in-depth the conversation, the more I wanted Yvonne all to myself.

Mia and I might as well have been living in separate living quarters for all I care. We had the occasional sex, but that was just her way to appease me. She insisted that she had a plan and that things were going to get better between us really soon. Well, really soon never came. The minute that she finished on project for the magazine, the more responsibility she took on. I didn't give a damn anymore. When I made love to Mia, these days, I imagined that it was Yvonne. I must have one hell of an imagination too, because the feel of Mia lately felt just as if she had a frame identical to that of Yvonne. Had she lost weight and I not noticed?—nah, couldn't be,

At any rate, I called Don and told him that I was en route to see him. I know that he thought I was there to kick his ass because the first thing out of his mouth was an apology.

"Hey Jamie, listen I don't want any drama over this shit with Mike."

"I'm not here about that Yo. I think what you did is fucked up and a sign of insecurity, but that is between you and that man."

Don seemed surprised about my response almost as if he slept with Loretta *last night* or something. When he saw that I truly wasn't there about his altercation with Mike, he opened up and welcomed my visit as if we were age old friends.

"Okay bruh, so what's up?"

"I met this honey and I want to have an affair with her, but I don't want to get caught."

Don looked surprised. "You are about to step out on fine ass Mia? The world must be coming to an end."

I responded with "Yeah well, Fine ass Mia is too busy for a nigga these days and I think it's time to call in some backup."

"I feel you. Mia is your Michael, this other honey is your Scottie. Tell me about her."

I went in, closed the door, and told Don everything that there was to know about Yvonne.

I told him how fine she is, how sophisticated she is, and how I wanted her in my life to fill a void and who knows? She may actually end up replacing Mia.

"Replacing Mia? Dawg, you are damn near as bad as Mike."

"What is that supposed to mean?"

"It sounds to me like this broad Yvonne has you pussy whipped *before you even got the pussy.* Plus you are breaking one of the cardinal rules of cheating when you have a *good woman* at home."

I interrupted with, "Yeah, what's that?"

"When you cheat, you never have another actual *relationship* with the other woman. You should simply use her for sex and nothing more. Talking about how fine she is, is one thing. Talking about how intellectual and simulating and getting to know the bitch as an actual person is something all together different."

I was thinking to myself that Mike was right, *Don is a simple and stupid mother-fucker.* But he has more experience at this shit than I do so I decided that I would let him help me to the best of his ability.

Don said, "I will need fifteen grand."

I said, "For what?"

"Just trust me dawg, if you want to do this…cut me the check. I'm not gonna spend one dime on me."

"I'm not giving your ass fifteen grand. What I will do is go with you and you can show me what the fifteen grand is for.

THE BLACK MAN'S GUIDE TO CHEATING

Don took me out to Park Forest where we purchased a co-op for eight grand. I had no idea that you could buy a place that cheap anywhere. But low and behold, there we were at the Park Forest Co-Ops signing a lease. I was about to sign a lease for the co-op in my name, when Don reminded me that it would be all too easy to trace the place back to me if Mia were to catch me up in a lie. So we put the new place in Don's name and mine. Don wanted me to place it in just his name, but I don't want to have to kick his ass later over some bullshit. I figured if push came to shove and Mia found out, I would simply tell her that I co signed a crib for my frat.

Next we got a phone in Don's name at my new place and went to Harlem Furniture and bought a leather couch, love seat, and brand new furnishings. We also went to Walgreens where we bought a $12.00 answering machine with my voice on it. We stocked the fridge with liquor, bought a mini bar for living room, and a full size bar for the basement. In just under three hours, I had a second place, phone line and new life. Don called over some women that he knew and gave them each a thousand dollars of my money to go out and buy nice things to furnish the remainder of the co-op. This included paintings, vertical blinds, an entertainment center, and an aquarium. Don called in a favor from some street thugs that he knew worked the docks at a local electronics store. For another thousand in cash, I was able to get a plasma screen TV. The one I have at my house cost $12,000.00. I was thinking to myself, "The next time that Mia wants to go shopping, fuck the store, she needs to see Don."

I thought about Mia. I am not supposed to be thinking about her at all. When I thought about all that I had done today and the lengths that I have gone through to keep my marriage in tact yet pursue another woman, I felt like shit.

"Stop it. Stop it right now. Stop fucking thinking about Mia" Don said.

"I wasn't, I was just…"

"Just thinking about your wife. Nigga you ain't slick Jay, every brother that I know has been through this and you are no different."

"The other brothers have done this too?"

Don said, "Too? Dude, Jeff, Keith, Crip and Chuck have a crib right out here in this same complex. They each have a co-op just like yours except theirs have two bedrooms instead of three."

"All those brothers are happily married." I said in a confused voice.

"Yeah, just like you are happily married. Now dawg, come on, we have work to do."

We then went to the cell phone store to get me a separate phone, relay for the phone with advanced call waiting, text messaging, encryption code, and an answering service. Then Don gave me strict instructions.

"This phone is for everyone except Mia. When you are with Mia, shut it off and put it away. If another bitch calls you, she gets the service or the standard answering message. No matter how much a woman complains about having access to you, tell her to deal with the arrangement that you have or to step. If Mia ever asks you for the code to your phone because she thinks that you are hiding some shit, that is where the relay comes in. It's an extra fifteen dollars a month, but it will save your ass. Tell her the code is 8631 and it will allow her to get all your standard messages from your family. When family calls, to leave a message, they will have to key in 8631. This places them in a separate mailbox from the women you fuck around with. Their code is 5304 which spells hoes upside down on a calculator and in a numeric pager. When the phone is on, people putting in that code will ring different from family and friends. When you hear DMX's song, *What these bitches want from a nigga,* you know that it is one of your hoes calling.

My head was reeling. I could not believe that Don had this shit down to such a science. "The text messaging system is your back up when you need someone to call you, cover for you or get you out of a jam. Those messages will only come from another one of the fellas. Finally, if Mia ever cuts your phone on or picks it up, it will not unlock without a key code. Give her the 8631, and it will cut on to standard numbers of friends and family. When you want to access your outside women, cut the phone on with the 5304, got it?"

"I think"

"Don't think Jamie. Get this shit down to a science dawg, otherwise you are going to get caught up nasty. Now the next set of rules is simple. When you meet a broad, just as a backup, give her a guys name. For example, if you meet a woman named Donna, put her in the phone as Don. Phyliss is Phil, Michelle is Mike and so on. Your phone system should never be exposed to Mia, but just in case, it covers your ass if there are all male numbers in the que. Now I need to go over the Kobe sheets with you."

"The what?"

"Kobe sheets. Since you used to play pro ball along with some of the other brothers, I had them get a lawyer to create a sheet of paper stating that these women you meet give written consent to sex with you."

"Don, you are bullshitting me, are you serious?"

"As Cancer baby. Check this shit out."

Don showed me a yellow sheet of paper that stated by signing your name on this sheet of paper, you are entering into a contract which explains that you are about to engage willingly in consensual sex that may or may not include the following acts...oral, anal, S & M, and role playing.

I asked Don, "Do women really sign this sort of thing?"

Don said, "Yeah they do, especially for pro-athletes, former pro athletes, celebrities and people of influence. That is not to say that all of them will sign it. There are plenty of women that will tell you to go to hell. There are others that are going to give you every reason why they should not sign the card. Most of the women that refuse to sign the card are running game. No matter what excuse a woman gives you, if she doesn't sign that card, don't mess with her."

I asked him, "What woman with any self respect is going to sign a card like this before having sex?"

"The type of woman that chases after men with money."

"What if I come across a woman that is into me for me and not the money?"

"Then you leave her alone until you are divorced from Mia."

"What?"

I was confused by Don's response. Of all of us in our clique, Don was the biggest dog and biggest player of us all. Here he was telling me to leave Mia rather than cheat on her or get involved with someone else.

"Don, not you too. Why is everyone telling me how to deal with Mia?"

Don said, "I'm not trying to be all up in your business brother, but there are rules to this shit if you are going to mess around. For starters, you have a good woman at home, a damn good woman, don't cheat on her if it can be helped. If it can't be helped, then you do any and everything you can to protect her from hurt. That means, no babies, bringing your own condoms when you do fool around, and bringing home no STD's. You also do not need to get into another full fledged relationship. Women can forgive you fucking around at least once. They have more trouble understanding when their man not only cheats but has another *full or part time relationship with another woman.* I mean, think about this for a minute. How would you feel if Mia fucked another man? You would be mad as hell. Now imagine *how much more upset you would be* if you found out she was having romantic dinners with someone else, joking and laughing with someone else and enjoying all the special nuances of your relationship. Fucking another man will send you into a rage, having a relationship and sharing her heart with another man, will linger with you for life. If you have someone else that you are interested in dog, just leave. Mia will respect you more. If you love her, you will do right by her."

I could not believe that this walked out of the mouth of Don, the master player of our chapter. If he was saying this, then maybe I needed to think long and hard about my next step.

"Don, when did you get on this holier than thou trip? I mean, no offense, but you are the biggest dog that I know."

Don thought long and hard about his response. It seems that the older that we get, the more thinking that we do. It seems that the more thinking that we do, the more we seem to grow as individuals. There are many days after all this thought and soul searching, that each of us is finding out that we are looking in the mirror, and not liking what we see.

"Jamie, I'm going to tell you something. I ain't shit and I know that I ain't shit. I am the way that I am because of the relationship that I had with my own mother. Back in the day my old man used to slap my moms around. Back in the day he was controlling as hell to the point that she had a half hour each night to get home from work otherwise he was accusing her of cheating. When she was late, he would beat her ass. I would try to stop him, and I in turn would be beaten."

I was surprised at Don's response. I had never known this about my frat, and apparently I was about to learn a lot more about him.

...."My mom eventually left my father. Rather than take me with her, she left me with him. From what I hear, she went from relationship to relationship after my dad, each one was with a man that was abusive. One day, they found my mother in her apartment with her head caved in. The man that did it, her then boyfriend, was never found. I never got over her death. I never had anyone to talk to about it either. My father did not allow me to speak of my mother in his house. When I did, he simply referred to her as that no good tramp bitch. I saw my dad date woman after woman after woman. He encouraged my behavior and I gladly obliged him. My father and I were never like father and son when I was coming up. We were more like buddies or roommates.

I dogged women all through high school and college. I can't tell you how many babies I have out here. I can't tell you how many times I have been to the clinic for treatment of STD's. I dogged women all of my adult life. That is, until I fell in love. I met a woman once named Kenya. She was special to me. She had a body out of this world, and a smile that was so warm, that it could melt a glacier. We met at First Chicago Bank downtown. I was hooked on her from the moment that I saw her. She waited on me while I was making a deposit, and I fell in love with this sister from the word hello.

At any rate, after turning me down request after request after request...I finally got her to go out with me. We dated and discovered a chemistry that I have never known between a man and a woman. She was...my everything. Kenya had two kids, a boy and a girl. I treated her children as if they were my own. I supported her when she wanted to return to school and I supported her every ambition. Eventually, we moved in together. Maybe a year after that, her mother moved in with us as well. I had no idea, but her mother had a cocaine habit. Her mother began stealing from us and pawning our belongings. One day I put my foot down and checked her mother into treatment. This proved to be a bad move because when the mother left the treatment center, she went home to Ohio. As it turns out, Kenya was from Ohio, but told me that she grew up here in the Chi on the south side.

One day I came home and in my living room was Kenya and another gentleman that looked like Prince. Kenya had a black eye and a bruised chin. She then introduced me to her husband that I never knew existed. Her husband was from Ohio. She had been running from him for three years. He was abusive and a stalker. He learned of where she was from Kenya's mother who traded information with him for a hit of coke. Me and this dude naturally came to blows and I whipped his ass. Kenya then told me everything that she had been withholding from me all these years we had been together.

We moved. I leased another apartment in Indiana and took Kenya to another state entirely. I also asked her to marry me. She said yes. I went on working and received promotion after promotion at the office. This is when I was working at Lowery Enterprises. I was about to make regional manager when one day I came home to an empty apartment. Kenya was gone, the kids were gone and all my belongings were gone. Kenya left me a note explaining that she was going to give her ex another chance. She remarked that after all, he was the father of her children. She left me, and she left me brokenhearted.

A year later...he killed her.

I was devastated.

I moved back home with my step-mother, lost my job, and it took me a long time to bounce back from that shit. From that point forward, I decided that I would never fall in love again and from that point forward, I would only fuck women. I decided that I would never trust them again with my heart."

"And you never have?" I asked.

"I didn't love again for a long time. When I did love again it was after I returned to school."

"What happened with her?"

"I loved her for a long time. We had something equally special...then one day after I had been drinking, I beat and raped the woman that I loved."

"Beat and Raped?" I asked.

"Yeah."

"Why aren't you in jail or something?"

"Because that is not the type of woman that Loretta is."

"Loretta?"

"Loretta."

Don told me that he used to date Loretta well before Mike got into the picture. The two were apparently very much in love and like Loretta and Michael, they seemed like the ideal couple. Everyone in our chapter was happy about this because apparently Don was very devastated by the death of Kenya. Don was even in therapy for a time after her death to help him cope with his loss. I had no idea that he was carrying all this emotional and psychological baggage with him.

He explained to me that Loretta is a damn good woman and that he misses her terribly. He explained to me that he never stopped loving her and probably never will. He was hurt by the fact that she took up with Michael so soon after their breakup. He also explained that their breakup was precipitated by a rape. He came home one day drunk out of his mind and decided that he would come to Loretta's dorm room to sleep it off. When he got to her room there was another man in her dorm room. Without asking, Don grabbed the young man and began smacking him around. Loretta was no where in the room to be found. That didn't matter, Don was mad and had become a drunken raging fury.

The young man was Loretta's roommate's new boyfriend. Loretta and her roommate had gone to the 7–11 to get munchies. The young man fled the room for his life. Don was not only our frat brother, but he was the fullback on our football team years earlier during undergrad. He stands 6, 3 and weighed about 240. When he was upset, he was a force to be reckoned with. Loretta saw her roommates boyfriend leaving the building with blood running from his mouth and bruises all over his body. She charged into her dorm room to yell at Don. Don locked the door and slapped Loretta around like an abusive father. After he beat her, he sodomized her. All this time, people were banging on the door trying to get in. Loretta's roommate was with her boyfriend so no one else had a key. The R.A. on the floor was not in the building. The onslaught went on for minutes on end. Finally, the police got there and pulled Don off of Loretta.

The boyfriend pressed charges and Don was charged with assault and battery. He plead that down to simple assault and did community service. Loretta never pressed charges. She never repeated what happened to her to anyone. All my frat brothers knew. Don left the campus and took a year off from school. He spent that year in therapy. He confessed that Loretta even joined him in one session so that he could apologize to her. That was years ago. He never got over losing Loretta nor did he ever get over what he did to her.

"Damn that's deep. Does Mike know all of this?" I asked.

"Mike began dating her while I was away in therapy. I imagine that she never told him. The rest of us in the chapter keep it to ourselves."

"So I am confused. Why talk shit about you and Loretta to Mike after what you did to her?"

"Jamie, I was drunk. What I did was inexcusable. To answer your question, I did it because I still love Loretta. I did it because I am jealous of Michael. I also did it to hurt Michael—and I guess, to hurt Loretta also."

"Why would you want to hurt Loretta?"

"I don't know, I guess because she gave Michael another chance but didn't give me one."

"Don, can you blame her?"

"I guess not—I mean, no, of course not. I don't know what I mean anymore."

"You owe them both an apology and an explanation."

"That will probably never happen."

"Why not?"

"That night…after we had the confrontation, I sent Mike an email."

"What was in the email?"

"Pictures."

"Don, you didn't."

"Jamie, I wish that I hadn't."

LORETTA

Michael has lost his damned mind. He had every chance to get on the road to reconciling with me and he blew it. I came over with every intention of being intimate with him and then he went off on me. As soon as I walked in the door I was getting the third damned degree about my dealings with Don, a matter that I tried to mentally block out myself.

"Come in, we need to talk." He said in stern voice. Never mind that I was dressed sexy as hell in a Black Donna Karen evening gown that was form fitting and loving my hips and ass. Never mind the fact that I had on black suede pumps and stockings to match with a sexy garter underneath (that he didn't get a chance to see), and Never mind the fact that I came over with the intention of giving him the most mind blowing sex of his life.

"What's wrong Michael?"

"This is what the fuck is wrong!" He slammed prints down on the table that he got off his printer. They were pictures of Don and I that I had forgotten existed. They were from a time when I was younger, had *the perfect body,* and a time that was not long before Mike and I got involved, but as far as I was concerned, it was eons before my falling in love with Michael.

"What the fuck is this!" He demanded.

"Where did they come from?"

"What? What fucking difference does it make where they cane from? That's you in the photos isn't it?"

My head was reeling with pain and confusion. I picked up the photos as if looking for confirmation, knowing damn well it was me. I was a lot freakier then too.

"Yes, Michael, that's me."

"Why didn't you tell me that you went out with Don?"

"It was before you and none of your business."

"None of my...what the fuck are you saying? Are you saying that you fucking my frat is not important?"

"No, I don't see where it was important."

"Well, it is. I already kind of hate Don's ass already, the only reason I tolerate him now is because he is frat. Otherwise I would have probably kicked his smug ass years ago. Now to find out that he used to fuck my girl—My wife? And this mother fucka has proof?"

I interrupted with, "Those pictures were taken years ago, Mike..."

He interrupted with, "I don't give a damn if they were yesterday or yesteryear. A nigga that I hang with and loathe, has been fucking my woman. How long were you together?"

"A few years."

"You love him?"

"I did."

"You suck his dick?"

"Stop! You stop right there, right now. I will not be interrogated and berated for my involvement with Don. It was before you and again not your business."

"The hell it isn't. We were married, remember? What if we had still been married. How long was I supposed to go on not knowing that another nigga has photos of my woman, had his dick in her…what the fuck am I supposed to do? How am I supposed to look at you now? It's not like we don't have enough fucking problems between us already. We are supposed to be trying to get back together and work on our fucking relationship!"

"That was why I came over."

There was a long silence between us. Michael was mad, very mad. He was also wrong in his line of questioning me. I am not proud of having ever been involved with Don. I hate him for what he did to me. When Michael and I got together, he came to me at a time in my life when I needed something good. I believe in my heart of hearts that the Lord himself sent Michael to me. I have never loved a man the way that I loved Michael. Today it seems that instead of making up with him after pushing him away for so long, that I have unknowingly placed a permanent wedge between the two of us. Where the fuck did he get the photos from anyway? *Was Don mailing photos of me to other people? Didn't he and I make a video too? Damn.*

Michael looked me up and down with Fire in his eyes. If looks could kill, I'd be one dead sista. On one hand I can't blame him. On the other, he has no idea what his *frat* put me through. Michael's eyes softened a little when he saw how good I looked. I almost expected him to compliment me. Instead, more foolishness came out of his mouth.

"You fuck anyone else I need to know about?"

"Excuse me?"

"You heard me. Are there any other frat brothers, friends, church folks or constituents that I should know about?"

"Michael that is not fair."

"Isn't it?"

Still, another long silence.

I told him, "I came over here to try and work things out with you."

"I don't know if we can get past this."

I was stunned that he would say such a thing. Is my relationship with him truly over just when I was looking to make things right between us? Jesus, what have we come to? I thought long and hard about what to say next. I thought about my therapist and what he might say to me under these circumstances. I definitely had some shit to talk about in therapy this week.

"Michael…Let's Talk."

There were tears beginning to well up in Michael's eyes. Every muscle in his body was tense and each muscle was rippling with definition and cause, demanding to be seen. Michael controlled his breathing as he spoke.

"Loretta, I think you should leave."

I could not believe that he was putting me out and not willing to at least talk about this situation. I was hurt—then I became angry. I grabbed my coat and walked to the door. I stopped just short of the door.

"He raped me."

Stunned, Michael said, "What?"

"Don—raped me. That is why we broke up. I think I am your chapter's biggest secret. Everyone knew, but you. It happened before you transferred to NLU. I was a sophomore and he was a grad student. I never pressed charges because I once loved him. That is why we broke up. The photos are from freshman year. I was young and impressionable and he was a Grad student. I was almost young enough to get him caught up on statutory rape."

Michael was at a loss for words. I didn't wait for him to find the words. I walked out of his place and perhaps walked out of his life.

MICHAEL

Raped? I was stunned for minutes after Loretta walked out of my front door. I was still hurt by the fact that he and she were an item, but he had to be feeling just as weird then as I feel now knowing that he used to be with her and I was with her for so long and later married her. Don was one of the older brothers in the chapter, but he was one of the most loved also. I never really cared for him too much, but because everyone else revered him, I dealt with him and was more than cordial to him. I can't believe that he raped her. I mean damn, how could someone with that in their history be liked or be one of my fraternity brothers?

Don was at my wedding. He was at our home whenever we had a celebration. How could she even tolerate being in the same room as him if he raped her? How could he be around me knowing that he raped my woman? She was his woman first, but we were *married* we had a home together. Was this something that wasn't my business? How could everyone be in on a secret like that and keep me in the dark? How could everyone treat me like this including my wife?

I asked myself a lot of questions as it began to rain outside. I did this as I loaded a clip into my nine millimeter handgun. There was a bottle of jack sitting on the shelf. I took a long hard swig of it and tried to decide on my next move. I was mad and I think I had a right to be. My woman betrayed me, if not by sleeping with us both, then by keeping their involvement from me as long as they had.

I took another swig of Jack. Had Don been pining for Loretta all this time? Did he want her back? Had he been fantasizing about *my woman* under *my nose* in *my house?* Oh hell naw! I took another swig of Jack and began sifting through the photos.

Loretta was right, she was younger when these were taken. There is more youth and innocence in her face. She is a lot thinner in the photos also and less curvy. In one shot she has on a short teddy and silk panties. In another she is wearing a thong. In yet another she is in a bathing suit. There were other couple photos that Don emailed me as well. They were photos of what looked like a young couple in love. Only she was probably the only one in love. If Don was in Grad school, that means he is at least 25 or 26 in the photo and Loretta is just 18 or 19 years old. *This motherfucker was a rapist long before actually raping her.* Don was at my wedding, so was Loretta's parents. Did they know too? Did the whole fucking world know what happened between my woman and a nigga that was supposed to have been my boy? I took another swig of Jack and placed my gun in my jacket. The rain began to beat down on the roof with a melancholy rhythm. The thunder and lightning soon followed. I had a nice little buzz going on about now. I thought about going to see Loretta and apologizing. That Jack began speaking to me and said, "Fuck her!" Then the Jack Daniels said, "Let's go see Don." I said, "Okay."

MIA

I have been hitting the gym like crazy lately. I guess it is true that you can easily put the weight on, but it is hard as hell to take the weight off. I was trying to get my figure back to the way it used to be if not better. I went from looking like Nia Long to looking like that girl from *The Parkers* or maybe not that bad. The magazine is doing well. I have gotten a second satellite office up and running that is closer to our home and with the money that Jamie has given me and 80% of my own salary I will soon be the sole owner of the magazine. It took some doing, but I convinced Sonja to be the general manager of the magazine. I am training her now to take over, so I can give Jamie the time that he needs. He is such a big fucking baby, but he is my baby, I guess. He has been busy as hell lately, which I do not particularly care for. I thought that he was trying to make himself as busy as I am, but it seems that he is trying to make his latest dreams come true. Either that, or he is trying to distance himself from me.

Jamie has been traveling from city to city and has been seen on TV in the background with many of today's high profile athletes. He tried to get me involved in his new career by introducing me to all of his latest prospects, but I wanted nothing to do with meeting them or anything associated with football. Don't get me wrong, I love Jamie and I actually have a genuine love for the game, or at least I used to. Football is the reason that we have all the nice things that we have. Football is the reason why Jamie was able to send me back to school for my Masters. But it was football that also kept me away from my man all these years.

When Jamie decided to go out for the team in college, I thought it was a pipe dream. Most of the guys on the team were great high school prospects that had been playing regulation ball all their lives. Jamie wasn't like that. He played ball on his block, but he had never played organized sports in his life. When he initially told me that he was going out for the team I expected him to fail. I never told him that, but I'm not supposed to. I was his woman. Whether he made the team or not, I planned on supporting him. I was genuinely surprised when he made the team. The coach stated that he was a natural talent. That was the beginning of his career, and the first step that put distance between us.

Jamie had to study, and practice, and hit the gym. Although he was a natural talent, he needed some work body wise. I liked Jamie's body the way that it was. All of a sudden, he was getting bigger and bigger and eating more and more food than I had ever seen him eat before. When he wasn't studying, he was training, when he wasn't training he was practicing, when he wasn't practicing, he was on the road. Games were usually on Saturday, but that meant that he was practicing Monday–Wednesday, and leaving me on Wednesday nights. There were many weeks that I had no contact with him and had to be satisfied with just a phone call. There were other weeks when he was home, that he would be too sore to perform. The off-season was just as bad because there was summer camp, mini-camp and pre-season camp. Still, I stayed by my man and remained faithful to him. I gave him quality time during the little time that he was able to give me. All I want from Jamie is the same loyalty that I gave him. I know it's not easy. I have been there! Just like I was patient, I want him to be patient just a little bit longer.

When we were younger, I turned down a lot of quality beef myself. He was a pro football prospect, but I had just as much opportunity with men that are pro basketball players, politicians, and brothers that now head fortune 500 companies. If it was just about finance, I could have been with any other man or made my own money. I stayed because I love Jay. He needs to understand that I also love my Independence.

His wait is almost over. Sonja understands the ins and outs of the magazine and as an attorney, she is going to bring a strong work ethic and a host of other skills to the magazine. I plan to one day make her partner. In the meanwhile, I hooked my girl up with a nice six figure salary. I threw so many zeros at her, she had to leave her firm to come and work with me. She is also going to have to learn to play well with others also. Wanda is my fashion editor. With her taste in clothes, men and her connections to the Hip-Hop community, we will always be up on the current styles and new designs by *Ecko, FUBU, Phat Farm, Baby Phat,* and any other styles that are banging in the hood. From *Rockawear* to *Sean John,* Black Woman Chicago will be ahead of the game.

Now all I have to do is get my ass back in shape. Damn, getting back to my old self is going to be hard. I have been training with Barry out at Bally's Health Club in River Oaks. I am also on a high protein-low carb diet. According to every magazine that I have been reading on women's fitness, this is the way to go. This is how Wanda gets in shape to get in music videos, commercials and magazine layouts. I have already lost about 14 of the 40 pounds that I have gained. Losing the first 10 pounds was easy, these last pounds are going to be the stubborn ones.

My body is supposed to be my temple. Well, I have been treating my temple like shit. I was eating all throughout the day and when I did eat, I ate wrong as hell. McDonalds, Wendy's and KFC became my best friends. Between my poor diet, lack of exercise and stress at the magazine, it only took me a few months to blow up like a balloon. I was discussing this with my loan officer Connie Stevens, when she said something that helped me to see how fat I was becoming.

"All career women have trouble with their weight. Believe it or not, weight gain is a sign of success. Independent women like us, don't need teenage bodies to state that we have made it, we have our financial portfolios. Besides, there are men out there that love heavier sisters like us."

"Heavier sisters like us?" I was thinking to myself, "Bitch Please." Then I sat there and thought to myself, "What does she mean like us?" Connie was fat. She was cute, but she was fat. Me? Brothers have told me that I was "Thick" all my life. Shit, I kickbox (or at least I used to) Run (or at least I used to) and I have a figure that will make brothers drool from Chi-Town to Memphis. Only a dog wants a bone, I'm thick like a milkshake baby!

Connie's words stayed with me when I went home that night. I was just about to jump in the shower when I walked past the full length mirror in the hall of our home.

"Who the fuck is that?" That is what I thought to myself as I saw my own nude body in the mirror. I had stretch marks that were never there before in my youth, quite a little belly on me, and my ass, my bee stinger as Jamie called it, was big as hell. I used to be an apple-bottomed girl, it seems that someone added a little cottage cheese to my precious dessert.

Shit.

No wonder Jamie has stopped looking at me the way that he used to, I wouldn't want to make love to me either. First thing tomorrow, I am on a diet. That was an eye awakening evening for me. I have been hitting the gym since, walking up stairs instead of taking the elevator, and parking my car far away from the entrance to the magazine. Next week I plan to go back to kickboxing, begin aerobics, and jump some rope. I want my body back!

JAMIE

I raced over to Don's house after getting an eerie phone call from Mike. He sounded like a desperate man. This scared me because Mike was the one that was always in control and the one that kept the rest of us in line. He not only kept our clique in order, he helped to run an entire city! If he was off balanced, something was wrong.

"Jay, meet me over at Don's house. I need you here. Dawg, if you don't come and help me, I don't know what I am gonna do."

I raced back over to Don's house. Scared of what it is that I might find. I knew that Don and Loretta used to deal with one another. Don told me about the photos that he sent to Mike. Now I am just hoping to God that Mike hasn't bust a cap in Don's ass and wants me to help him dump the body. I will…I think—or I would like to believe that I will, I mean, that's my guy—but murder? Damn. He couldn't have…could he?

I was doing 70 miles per hour on the Dan Ryan expressway trying to get to my friend in hopes that he hadn't committed a homicide and in hopes that I was not about to eyewitness one. I got off the expressway at 55th, headed east to Stoney Island and over into Hyde Park to Don's place. The tires on my BMW screeched like something out of an old *Starskey and Hutch or Barretta* episode. I got out of the car like I was a superhero and raced up Don's stairs.

When I got to Don's front door, the door was open and wet, muddy footprints led in from outside. It had been raining all evening and now it was the early hours of the morning. I could smell the faint scent of liquor and what smelled like something awful burning in the interior of the house. As I walked in I called out to see if anyone was there.

"Don? Hey Don are you in here?"

No answer.

"Mike? Don? Anybody? Is anyone here?"

No answer.

The house was still and quiet, like something out of a Hitchcock flick. The burning smell was that of weed that I imagine Mike had been smoking earlier and a lamp that was knocked over and just beginning to start a fire on the floor. I put the small fire out and replaced the lamp on the table that it looked like it fell from.

"Damn." I thought to myself.

"Now my goddamned fingerprints are on the lamp."

I walked cautiously into the grey stone praying that I was not going to find the worst possible scenario. My heart was pounding inside my chest and I was giving a lot of thought to phoning the police. Then it dawned on me that Don lived at home with his step-mother. Where was she? My head began spinning with all the millions of possible scenarios that went through my head—none of them good.

"Mike? Don? Anyone?"

I waited a full thirty seconds in the home and stood still as I listened and prayed desperately for a response. I swear I could hear my heart beating audibly as I walked toward the stairway and began to look upward. I then heard a voice that was more than a whisper, but less than a yell.

"Up here Jay...We are up here."

It was Mike's voice. But that is all that it was. I began my ascent up the stairs.

As I began walking up the stairs, I noticed more and more things that had been knocked over. There was a fight here. A fight between two huge men. Don played football years ago before Mike or I transferred to the school. Mike was no slouch either and could be a force to reckon with as well. When I think about the two of them clashing my faced winced as if in pain. That is one fight I would hate to try and break up. Breaking up Don and Mike would be like trying to separate *Ali and Frazier*, *Tyson* and *Holyfield* or the Jealous man that fought with Bad Leroy Brown in the *Jim Croce* song.

I thought to myself, "They tore some shit up."

I continued to walk up the stairs and I noticed drops of blood on the stairs.

"Oh shit. Please God don't let me be walking through evidence."

I continued up the beige carpeted stairs where the drops of blood became more and more pronounced. It got to the point that I had to walk through the blood just to continue to ascend the stairs. There was no turning back now. This must be how O.J. felt.

I walked to the top of the stairs and spoke out loud. "Mike? Don? Where are you?" Once more I heard my long time friend's voice from behind me. I walked into the bathroom where there was Don, covered in his own blood, Mike who was bruised and also bloody. Mike had a gun in his hand and a bottle of E & J in the other hand. Don was in the tub bloody and broken, but breathing. I walked in the small room where Mike was sitting on the toilet weeping. He looked up at me as did Don, and the three of us fell silent while we thought about what we were each going to do next.

I spoke first. "Mike—you okay?"

"Yeah, I'm okay Jay."

I looked to Don and spoke, "Don—you okay?"

Don spat out blood and was breathing heavy as hell and struggled to speak. He said, "Yeah, just peachy."

Another long silence fell over the room. Again, I had to break the silence. I had to. I think I was the only one present with any logic left in him.

"Mike…where is Don's step-mother?"

He thought long about his response as if to remember that Don did not live alone. He wiped tears from his eyes and said, "I don't know Jay, she wasn't here when I arrived."

I looked to Don next and asked him, "Don…where is your moms?"

Again Don struggled to speak as his breathing was labored. "She is at her boy-friends, undoubtedly…spending the night."

That was funny, but not really. Don's Mom was not really his mom, but his step mother. We all used to joke about how pathetic this was because not only did Don still practically live at home he lived with a woman that was not even his mother. He lived with a woman that used to fuck his father. A woman that was in her late fifties, and at her man's house getting her freak on and undoubtedly wishing that her stepson would grow the fuck up.

For the third time, I had to break the silence.

"So what now Mike? You obviously won the fight. What are you going to do now?"

"I plan to kill him."

That sent a chill through me to my spine. Don was too hurt to fight back and he looked just as stunned as I was when Mike confessed to his plans. Because Don was a proud man (though he had little to be proud of) he didn't beg for his life or begin to bitch up. He looked as if he resigned himself to the fact that he might not live to see tomorrow.

"No." I said.

"No what?" Mike responded.

"No, you aren't going to do this. I can't let you throw your life away."

"My life is already forfeit behind this. I am the Deputy Mayor, remember?"

I let out a heavy sigh. I saw where Mike was going with this. All that he is and ever was stemmed from his political career. Here he was waist deep in controversy, so he figured that he had nothing else to lose.

"What about Loretta? What about your marriage? Aren't the two of you going to work this out?"

Mike took a swig of the E & J before he spoke. "That's over."

"What do you mean that's over?"

"Loretta came over to my crib earlier, and I kicked her out. I told the love of my life to basically go to hell. I did all that because of this nigga here. I mean to kill his ass Jay."

My heart was heavy with anguish. I thought long and hard about all that Mike and I had been through, how hard that we both worked in our respective careers to be at the top. I thought about the fact that if I didn't do something and fast, we were both going to end ass up on the wrong end of a scandal.

"Mike...we worked too hard to get where we are today for you to throw it all away over some bullshit. So what are you going to do after you shoot Don? What are you going to do, shoot me next?"

"Of course not Jay, I didn't mean to get you involved..."

I interrupted with, "You got me involved. You got me square in the middle of this shit. I believe in my heart of hearts, that you called me here because you wanted me to stop you."

I walked over to the tub and placed myself between Mike and Don. I then looked into the drunken pupils of Mike and all I could see was pain. This man was hurting on a number of different levels. He was trying to self medicate with alcohol to take that pain away. I reached out to my longtime friend and took the bottle of spirits out of his hand and poured the alcohol down the bathroom sink. I then placed both hands on the gun and held Mike's hand firmly. Initially, he wouldn't let go of the gun. I took my hands and brought the gun to my chest. With tears in his eyes, Mike let the gun go.

"My car is downstairs, I will drive you home."

Mike got up in a drunken stupor, and dragged himself out of the 3 x 5 bathroom. He looked back at Don with disgust and then made his way downstairs. Minutes later, we heard Mike go out the front door. Don and I sat in silence for a long time.

"Are you pressing charges?" I asked Don.

Don tried to sit up but couldn't. It was weird seeing a guy that could easily be mistaken for a pro football player, being folded up in a regular size bath tub.

"I think I have done enough." Don said.

"What happened here tonight?" I asked.

EARLIER...

Don explained to me that he saw Mike's car out of his front window in the rain, and opened the door for Mike to come in. Mike sat in his car for some time obviously debating about what he was going to do. Don thought that he might be able to talk Mike down and he was hoping that he and Mike could talk civilized. When Mike finally got out of his car, Don met him half way up the driveway. He didn't smell the liquor on Mike's breath until the last minute.
Don said, "Look man, I'm sorry. I guess I was just jealous..."

POW!

Mike hit Don in the mouth before he could finish his sentence. Mike was not concerned with Don's apology or his jealousy. He had come here to do battle. He kicked Don in the stomach, punched him with a downward right cross, and gave him a knee to the face with his left leg. Mike then hit Don over the head with the empty Jack Daniels bottle that he brought with him and began punching him with a fury that said that he wanted to kill Don.

Don's head was reeling with confusion. He had taken blows to the head and could not think. He had just finished smoking a joint that had been laced with some ingredient that he had not paid for and that ingredient was just now starting to kick in. Don was both high and in pain and he was giving his all to sober up. He was in the fight of his life, but could not shake the intoxication. Each punch that Mike threw looked as if it was coming in slow motion. In spite of that, Don could not escape any of the blows that came at him. Initially he thought that he was hallucinating, but the pain that followed the blows was all to real to him. The pain was killing the high, but it was not giving him back his reflexes in order to react.

Don heard the word rape among the swears that were coming out of Mike's mouth. He put two and two together and did the best he could to shield himself from Mike's rage. Then at one point he did actually begin to sober up. He thought to himself that if Mike killed him right now it would be no more than what he deserved for his transgressions in life. Don fought back as best he could but he was no match for the rage of a jealous husband who loved his wife more than he loved himself. Mike whipped Don's ass for old and new out in the rain. Don's block was quiet except for the thunder and no one saw the two combatants outside. After several minutes, Mike took the fight to Don in the house. Don was on his hands and knees at that point crawling into his step mother's home trying to seek sanctuary.

Don crawled in the house and up the stairs trying to get away from Mike. "Man—Mike, bruh…I'm sorry."

"Sorry? Yeah you are sorry. You are one sorry excuse for a human being!"

Mike gave chase up the steps. Don had just made it to his feet when Mike tackled him from behind. They fell forward into the bathroom and fell head over heels into the tub. Mike heard a snap, and Don fell into unconsciousness. Mike thought that he killed Don. Don wished that he had.

Reality set in for Michael. He thought to himself that he had killed his frat brother in a crime of passion. That was when he called me and told me to come to Don's. After getting off the phone with me, he must have seen the bottle of E & J on Don's dresser, and decided that he would drink his pain away until either I showed up or the cops. As far was Mike knew Don was dead. For that, he had no regrets. He hated himself for having no regrets or remorse. He sat there on the toilet weeping about his situation with Loretta and the crime that he had committed.

20 minutes later Don awoke, much to the surprise of the now wasted Michael. Don tried to get up but couldn't. We still haven't surveyed how bad the damage is. When Mike saw that he hadn't succeeded in killing Don, he pulled out his gun and aimed it at Don's head. Mike would most likely miss if he shot at Don. The problem was that even if Mike missed with the first round in the chamber, he still had a full clip in which to bust a cap in Don's ass.

"You raped my woman."

"That was years ago."

"The timeline changes nothing—you raped my woman."

"I was drunk when I did it. I was just about as drunk then as you are now."

"I'm drunk…and guess what? I ain't thinking about raping nobody."

"When I was drunk, I didn't think about raping her either. I thought I caught her with another man. I beat him, beat her and then I…I…"

"Say it!" Mike interrupted.

"That's when I raped her." There was a long silence as Don began weeping.

Mike said, "I loved her!"

Don said, "I loved her too."

Mike said, "I love her still."

"I never got over her." Don said. "I just could never get over her. She meant the world to me at one point and in a single instant, I fucked all that up. Then somewhere along the way you came along and made everything in her life right. You and she had what she and I had and I hated her, me and you for allowing that to happen. I never thought that I could find happiness again after Kenya. I was fortunate enough in my life to have found love twice...and twice I lost. For a long time I hated Loretta. For an even longer time I hated you. You not only were able to make her happy, you made her your bride, your partner, your soulmate. You love her...well...I never stopped loving her."

"You have a million bitches that call you everyday and a million of these hoes that you sleep with, how the fuck can you still have feelings for my woman?"

"Those other hoes that I fuck with don't mean anything to me. They are just there to help me fill a void in my life. If nothing else, I have learned that in therapy. I know that I need help. I'm thinking about giving my life to God."

Mike responded with, "I'm thinking about giving your life to God *for you.*"

For a long time the two talked. The whole time both thought long and hard about two things, Death and Loretta.

BACK IN THE HERE AND NOW

That is some heavy shit. Wow, that is some heavy shit. This shit could have gone south quick. I almost walked in on a murder. Instead, I am hoping that I had a hand in saving a few lives. Just then my cell phone rang.

"Hello?"

"Jamie, hi, it's Yvonne."

"Hey Love how are you? Look, I am kind of in the middle of something right now, can I call you back?"

"Um, sure. I was just hoping that we could maybe get together soon—I mean, have some coffee or something."

"That sounds like a plan, but I need to let you go okay?"

"Okay."

With that, I hung up. I was in the middle of a goddamned soap opera. I didn't need to be in mack mode or trying to arrange a booty call. My best friend's life had just been turned upside down and I needed to try and help him to get it right side up.

"So you are not pressing charges?" I stated it as a question, but I was hoping to actually get some type of confirmation from Don that he was not going to pursue this matter any further. That would at the very least save Mike's political career.

"I won't press charges on one condition."

"Name it."

"One, you take me to the hospital. Also, promise me that you are not going to cheat on Mia with whomever that is that just called you."

"What makes you think that was a booty call?"

"It's three in the morning. Women that are not your girlfriend or wife only call you for two things in the middle of the night or early in the morning, bad news or a booty call."

I thought to myself, *Damn, did these two niggas just cost me getting some ass from Yvonne?*

"Do we have a deal Jamie?"

"We have a deal Don, let's get you to the hospital."

"Great. Help me up."

"One question though, how is it that you live with your stepmother after she divorced your father and you are 37 years old?"

"Why do you think she left my father?"

I looked at Don eye to eye with disgust.

"Gross. You know you are a nasty motherfucker."

"I know."

"You also need Jesus"

"Yeah, I know. I have an appointment to see him Sunday at his house."

"You almost met him this evening."

"Mike wasn't going to shoot me."

"How do you know?"

"Mike's a good man. I have always known that about him. Besides, if he did he wouldn't see Loretta again. The two of them are destined to be together."

I took Don to Mercy Hospital on 35th street. He had three broken ribs, a cracked jaw, and a concussion. Mike must have really put in work on his ass. I called Mia and told her where I was. She drove to the hospital to meet me although I told her it was not necessary. I tried to call Loretta, but got no answer at her place. It was 4:00 by then and Michael was in my car sleeping off the liquor.

CHAPTER 5

▼

BEDSIDE BUDDIES

JAMIE

The next day, I called Yvonne back and explained to her all the events that took place last night. I told her how I was almost a witness to a murder and how all my boys these days seem to be locked up in drama. She thought the whole thing was funny and told me that me and my guys sounded like we were the toys are us kids. She went on and on about how we obviously never wanted to grow up. She then asked me how were things going between me and Mia.

"Things are fine I guess."

"You guess? So are you going to reconcile your differences?"

I was not going to allow her to control the conversation or distract me from the fact that she might have given me some ass last night, so I deflected her question by acting as if I hadn't heard her at all.

"So when you called last night what did you need?"

"What?" she said.

"last night, or rather this morning when you called, what was up?"

"Oh, well I called because 3J called me frantically stating that the quarterback from Oregon called him to welcome him to their team. Are we moving to Oregon?"

I was thinking to myself, "Oregon?" Yvonne actually called me on business. I talked with the general manager of the Oregon team about a possible trade next season, but that was *next season,* and illegal on my part to even discuss it.

I told Yvonne, "I did have some preliminary discussion with the GM of the Oregon team, but nothing definitive."

"How could you make such a decision without talking to 3J first?"

"Like I said, it was just a discussion."

"You had no right!"

Yvonne was upset. Quiet as kept so was I. I had every right to discuss a possible trade. Oregon needed a good running back for there west coast offense. 3J would not be used as much as he is here in Chicago, but that means a longer career, and more importantly, more money. With 3J on their team, Oregon became an instant playoff contender. Ii had to make Yvonne see that.

"Look Yvonne, 3J will be in Chicago at least another year. I do plan on talking with the Oregon team at the end of the year and I had planned on talking with both you and 3J about the possibilities."

"Well, 3J is on ten at the thought of moving to Oregon. His season ends in three weeks and already it seems like Chicago is ready to ship him off as if to blame him for the sorry season that they have had this year."

I explained to her, "It's actually quite the contrary. Chicago would only ship 3J if it looked to be worth their while. Oregon has more salary cap room and when I last spoke with them, they were willing to give Chicago two draft picks."

I hated explaining my rationale to Yvonne. Managing 3J was my job, my responsibility and I knew exactly what it was that I was doing. Signing with Oregon meant at least 8 million more dollars. That meant a cool 1.5 million for me. After taxes, that meant another 800k.

"Look Yvonne, why don't you and 3J meet me downtown at the Hilton. We will have a meal and a drink in Kitty O'Sheas. I will tell you how talks went when I last spoke to the Oregon team at the beginning of this season."

"What time do you want to meet?"

"Let's make it for 7:00 tonight."

"Done."

I was supposed to have dinner with Mia tonight, but if she can put me off for work as often as she does, she shouldn't trip if I do the same. I pulled up in front of the house and there was a note on the fridge from Mia.

JAMIE

I WENT TO THE GYM. I HAVE TO GO TO THE OFFICE AFTERWARD, SO WE ARE GOING TO HAVE TO TAKE A RAINCHECK ON DINNER. I WILL MAKE IT UP TO YOU TONIGHT I PROMISE.

I LOVE YOU,

MIA

Figures. This is what my marriage was reduced to. Leaving notes for one another rather than arguing or talking. That is the only reason that Mia left a note, she didn't want to talk to me or face me after canceling on me again. Fuck her. I am glad that I have plans. She could have hit me on the cell at any point today, instead, she opted to write me a note. How did my marriage get into such disarray?

I changed into a Navy Hugo Boss suit with a gold silk tie. I then put on a pair of Bruno Vittali shoes and broke out my platinum Movado watch. I then threw on some Hugo Boss cologne and called Mike.

"Hello?"

"What up Mike, how you feelin today man?"

"Like a car ran over my head."

"Yeah, well you were pretty wasted last night."

"I'm going to jail, it's just a matter of time before Don calls the police."

"Don's not calling the police, I took care of all that."

"What did you do, put a bullet in his ass?"

"No, I did what you should have done and I talked to him. He feels that he is just as much to blame for last night as you are. He knows the role that he played in all this. Enough about him though, have you spoken to Loretta?"

"Nah, I have called her all day today and left a number of messages on her machine. She is not at work today either."

"Well, keep trying, don't give up the faith."

"I'm not giving up, but I think I do need to give her some time."

"You know her better than anyone else dude. While you are giving her space though, you should be sending flowers with I'm sorry cards for the next three days."

"Now that's a thought. Listen, I have been in the house and in the bed most of the day. Do you wanna run and get something to eat?"

"Wish I could dawg, but I have a 7:00 meeting downtown."

"New Prospect?"

"Naw, I have to convince an old prospect, 3J to consider moving to Oregon for a trade."

"We just got a good running back, why the fuck would he leave here? Mike asked.

"Actually, I have been behind the scenes working on this move for a few months."

"Jamie I don't believe you. This city has been starving for a great running back since *Walter Payton* played for the Bears, and you go and snatch the only bright side in the Chicago Bandits offense? Why can't he stay here in the Chi?"

I told him, "Because one, it's cold as hell in the Chi in the wintertime. Two, it means more money for us all if he leaves, and three Chicago will get two high draft picks for 3J which means they can get another running back and finally a real quarterback."

Mike thought about my plans and said, "Jamie, you are a genius. Do you think you can pull it off?"

I told him, "I am on my way to seal the deal right now."

THAT NIGHT AT DINNER

3J and Yvonne arrived at the Hilton at 6:45. I was already seated and just finishing my second Rum and Coke. I didn't think that Yvonne could be more beautiful than the last time that I saw her. I was wrong. Today she looked down right delicious. She already looked like a supermodel with a body out of this world. Today she was dressed like she was the last temptation for black men. She had on Black Donna Karen boots, and a micromini dress that looked as if it was made out of the finest silk. The dress stopped *just an inch or two below her crotch.* Her hips were hugged by the material and it touched her body in ways that I could only dream of. She didn't have on a bra and her nipples were erect through the material. The top of the dress had spaghetti straps. The dress itself was navy blue. Although you could see that her nipples were erect, you could only imagine what her breasts looked like because the color and the material was not at all revealing. The dress was like the ultimate tease. She had such lovely breasts. They looked perky as if she had on a push up bra. What was even more enticing was that fact that she didn't. Her breasts were just—perfect.

I stood up as my fantasy girl and client approached my table. Yvonne was looking good as hell, but I had to hide the fact that I noticed from my client. I am sure that he would not appreciate my looking at his older sister with lust in my eyes.

"Hello 3J, Yvonne, how are you guys?"

"Not too good Jay, what is this shit about my going to Oregon?"

3J sounded pissed. The only reason that he came and hadn't fired me was because Yvonne convinced him to give me the benefit of the doubt. I explained to 3J that if he did agree to go to Oregon at the end of the season, it would mean a win/win situation for everyone and that it meant possibly another 12 million to his contract. I had secured him a six million dollar bonus this year with a five million dollar base and incentives this year also. To switch teams meant that he was getting almost 13 million dollars absolutely free. I also explained to him that by playing in Oregon, he had a better chance of going to the championship and earning a ring. 3J liked that prospect a lot.

"But I don't know shit about Oregon." 3J said.

You don't need to. You can keep your crib here in Chicago, along with your charity, and just get a condo or summer home in Oregon. Your life does not have to change drastically. There are a lot of pro athletes with six and seven homes. You would only have to maintain two homes. With a house in Oregon, you can live in Chicago all of the summer and spring and spend the cold months in the warm comfort of the west coast."

3J thought long and hard about the prospect and eventually warmed up to the idea.

"I'll do it. I will finish these last few weeks here, and I will do it. Jamie, you are my man."

After an hour of negotiating, 3J and I came to an understanding. Then he said something that messed my head up.

"Jamie I need a favor."

"Anything 3J, what can I do for you."

"You and my sister fly down to Oregon and get me a house down there with all the works. My sister likes to shop and she knows what is best for me. You can begin negotiating the deal for me as early as tomorrow."

I almost spit out my drink at the suggestion of Yvonne and I spending time together finding 3J a house. I wanted very much to take advantage of the opportunity, but I had to play things cool, kind of like R. Kelly in the extended version of down low with Mr. Biggs.

"You know, 3J, I am not your private assistant. You can hire someone to spend money for you."

"I don't mean any disrespect Jay. I just remember seeing the crib that you had when I was in high school. I saw you on MTV cribs and I think that you have good taste. I was hoping that you could just pick out the house, and my sister would stay up there for a few weeks furnishing it, like she did with my crib here."

"Oh, okay. I guess I can do that for you." I said.

"I would appreciate it."

Yvonne was looking at me with a wry smile as if she could read what was going on inside my head in spite of my trying to be cool. She also gave me a look that said she wasn't going to give me any. As far as I was concerned, she was beginning the age old game of cat and mouse. I was thinking to myself, "Let the games begin." I said my goodbyes and began to head home.

I wanted to get a moment alone with Yvonne to say something witty and charming, but I decided against it. There would be plenty of time for that later. Besides the best way for a man to get in a woman's pants is to act as if he really isn't interested anyway. Granted both parties know that the man is always interested, but some women see it as a challenge to make the man give up this façade and chase after her like the primitive beast of passion that he is. Yvonne was no different. She was a gorgeous young diva, and I was a former player. So I didn't mind the cat and mouse, the flirting or the challenge. I had all the time in the world now that my wife was working like a Hebrew slave.

I went home that night and the house was dark. I thought this was odd because it was hardly 9:00 and I know Ms. Work-a-holic wasn't in bed yet. I walked into the house where there was candles lit, music by Frankie J on the CD system and the smell of strawberries in the air.

"Mia?" I called out.

"Be right there." I heard from the upstairs.

That's right. Her note said that she was supposed to make up missing dinner tonight. She must be upstairs trying to slip in some lingerie or something. I resented her trying to distract me with sex to make up for the fact that she had cancelled on me again. If she thinks that I am giving her some lovin, she is crazy as hell.

Our large home was dim and warm. The music was enticing, but I was in no mood for one of Mia's quick sex episodes. We made love so fast these days when we did get around to having sex, that too often it seemed like a goddamned race. I sat on the couch and thought about Yvonne and what making love to her would be like. She was young, she had a tight body, and she was new. I bet given the chance she would make *slow, passionate love to me.* THAT was the type of loving that I wanted. That was the type of loving that a man needed. It was that type of lovemaking that I enjoyed most from my wife. For almost two years, we had been doing nothing but going through the motions.

I have to admit, this Hispanic brother Frankie J was tight. I thought he was black when I first heard this CD, but after checking out the cover, it was obvious that the brother was Latin. I got up from the couch to admire the Cd and then went to the bar to pour myself some Bacardi and Coke. I sipped the drink that I had been drinking since I was eleven, and looked at the CD cover. Frankie was just beginning to sing his song. "Don't wanna try" where he tells his girl that there is no use in them even pretending anymore, their relationship is in so many words—over. I thought this was the most appropriate song to hear this evening as I gave my first thoughts to asking Mia for a divorce. Then my mind changed like day to night. I saw Mia at the top of our stairs.

Mia and I had made love off and one during this job thing of hers, but I hadn't actually *seen her* in a couple of months. You know it is when you are both rushing to bust a nut, neither of you really gets to see what it is that you are getting or gets to explore one another's body. Well, today I might just have to do some exploring. Mia walked slowly down the stairs and was looking fine as a motherfucka. She had on red pumps, sheer black stockings, and a bright red teddy. Her breasts were swollen and ready to pop out of the delicate material that held them in, and her stomach somehow appeared flatter. As she came down the stairs ever so slowly, her baby making hips swayed east to west as if to imply that she was back to being the thick dream girl of every mans dreams. Her hair was down and had light brown highlights in it. Her makeup was back in earthtones and she looked like she was about to do a commercial for both Revlon and Penthouse. When she got to the bottom of the stairs she stopped in all of her glory to show me what I was getting. She looked so fucking good that I dropped the CD cover and I think I literally had drool drop from the crack of my mouth.
"You like what you see?" She asked.
"Yeah, hell yeah…fuck yeah—girl come here!"
I couldn't tell if I was hallucinating or not, but Mia looked better right now than she ever had when we got married. She reached in her top and pulled out a joint. She lit it, took a hit and walked over to me and placed the joint in my mouth. I took a long hard hit and inhaled the Jamaican stash. It had been years since I had a hit of weed, going all these years without made my first hit in years just as powerful as my first hit as a teen.

Frankie J was now singing, "I'm digging your style." Mia backed away and began to dance for me. Back and forth she moved and her ass and breasts bounced up and down. She then turned around and began bouncing up and down like s skilled stripper from one of the high end exotic clubs downtown. Her ass pulsated underneath the material, popping like something from a music video. The teddy was short, so it gave me a teasing glimpse at my wife's lower butt cheeks. I wanted to see more though, so I reached out to her. Mia danced away from me as if she wasn't ready for me to see her hidden treasure. I wanted so much to grab that ass. After all, that was my ass, I earned the right to that ass. She wasn't having it. She stuck her finger in her mouth like a young girl that had been naughty. She then walked seductively to me and wiggled back and forth like a harem girl. She stuck her beautiful swollen breasts in my face and held each one in her hands. She then grabbed my head and placed them in between her breasts as she juggled them back and forth. Her breasts smelled like strawberries. I grabbed them both and began to knead and massage them. Just as I was ready to unharness them, she kissed me deep and danced away from me again. This was beginning to frustrate me some, because my dick was so hard that it hurt. I thought I was going to explode. She danced toward me again and I let out a gracious sigh. She kicked her right leg up and I saw a black laced garter with crotchless panties that were sheer. Through the panties I could see that Mia had cut her pubic hair in one of those designs that you see the supermodels cut theirs into. Mia rocked her pelvis back and forth, making her lower body do the snake or the worm. Her delectable sex smelled like fresh strawberries as well. I leaned my head forward and savored the fruity smell. I then placed my tongue in that familiar place and was equally surprised to taste strawberries on my wife's private parts.

I began to savor the snack that was now my wife. Frankie J was singing. As he sang, I created my own remix which was a mix of Frankie J's music and my wife's seductive moans.
"Oh...Jamie....Yes, yes baby, right there...oh damn baby...Jamie....Jay—me...yes."
I ate my wife out as if it was our first time making love. I took my time and devoured her as if she was my last meal. I felt her leg trembling minutes later. She grabbed a fist full of my dreads and began to grind her pelvis against my face, her juices running down her thigh. Grabbing my locks hurt, but her moans sent me so far in ecstasy myself, that I was soon oblivious to the pain. Had she fallen, I would be bald as hell on the back of my head, that is how hard she held on. Mia began to tremble and shake which told me that she was about thirty seconds from climaxing. I grabbed her ass to balance her and was even more to my surprise was

the feel and shape of my wife's perfect ass. Either I was dreaming or she went somewhere and went and got her ass back from the pawnshop. I grabbed her J Lo ass and helped her hips rock back and forth as she came. She tried to pull away from me and I almost snapped my own neck as I forced my tongue even deeper inside her. Mia screamed a scream of passion as she came. She then straddled me and kissed me for what seemed like an eternity. She could not move—I know. She was trying to keep our passion rolling as she tried to compose herself.

She took another hit from the joint, as did I. She then stood up and turned her back to me. She then rocked side to side and occasionally up and down. She made her ass bounce so that the material bounced high enough to give me a glimpse of her ass. This dance that she was doing was spectacular. Not only was it great, it had to be rehearsed. I pictured my wife practicing dancing just for me. I smiled an all tooth Stevie Wonder type smile at the prospect of my wife going through all these lengths just to please me for one night. Mia loved me. Only love can make a woman go through all that preparation for one night of making love.

Back and for the she moved, rocking her hips and bending over teasing me. Finally she grabbed both sides of the teddy and slowly lifted it up as if raising a skirt. Slowly upward she peeled the delicate material until finally there it was. Her ass was even more perfect now than it had ever been any time that we were together. Mia made her butt cheeks clap as if to applaud herself for getting back into peak shape. I sunk back in the couch and let out a sigh that said to her, "Perfect."

When Mia finally turned around to face me, I was butt naked on the couch stroking my member. I thought I might burst right there after viewing her perfect ass. There is nothing in the world like a fat ass on a black woman. I would take a perfect ass like Mia's over money, food and water on most days. Mia approached me and kissed me deeply on the mouth tasting her own juices (which always turns me on) and the taste of fresh fruit that was once coating her special place. I ran my fingers through my wife's long hair and ran then up and down her back. Frankie J was now singing *Ya No Es Igual*. My wife handed me my drink of Bacardi and Coke and offered me a sip. She then had a drink herself and we both had another hit of the now finished joint. As Frankie J continued to croon, I reached for the remote and set the CD player to repeat. I never knew what the fuck it was Frankie was saying when he sang *Ya No Es Igual*, but I loved the hell out of that song. Mia knew it too which is why she chose this out of all my CD's. She kissed me deep once more and then lowered herself to the floor. She then took my member in one hand, Moved her head and hair to the other side and slowly took me in her mouth.

Her warmth and passion took me somewhere I hadn't been in years. She made love to me slowly with her mouth, slowly she took in my flavor. She was patient with the special attention that she gave me, and I was most appreciative for it. I sunk further in the chair and became weak as my wife worked me like a rig drilling for oil. I ran my fingers through her long free flowing hair with one hand and braced myself with the other. I closed my eyes high on weed, Bacardi and passion. I lost myself in my wife's warmth. Not wanting to cum, I brought her to her feet and had her straddle me right there on the couch. Again I kissed my wife this time tasting my own juices and salt. I slowly penetrated my wife and slowly guided her down on my now throbbing member. She and I both let out a gasp in unison.

I then took both hands and slapped firmly my wife's firm round ass. I then helped her to rock back and forth taking my member all the way in, back to the tip, and all the way back in again. Mia and I both wept as we made love. It had been so long since lovemaking had been on this level, this passionate and this giving of one another. It had been too long since we shared a passionate embrace and felt *this good.* We made love for hours as we told one another how much we each loved the other. After a marathon of positions, caresses, sweet whispers and I love yous, I came in my wife. For the first time in a long time, my wife and I made love to one another. We had that good love, that gangsta love, that primitive, lusting yet powerful lovemaking that you only see in the movies. Her lovin was so good that shit, she could keep her job. Just make love to me *like that* twice a year and shit—I'm good. The love we made tonight will last a while.

I cut on the fireplace and we laid right there on the floor, naked on top of a fur rug that I picked up years ago. Mia stared off in the fire and I kissed her shoulder, the nape of her neck and her cheek. I rubbed her back and sides as I treasured every square inch of her body.

"So how is work?"

"Work is fine, Jamie. How is your gig?"

"Fine. I have to fly to Oregon tomorrow."

Mia took my hand and brought it to her breast. She then covered my hand with hers and began spooning me. I thought she was going to possibly drift off to sleep.

"I have a surprise for you." She said.

"Another One?"

"Yep. I made Sonja my chief executive at the magazine. I will only be working 20 hours a week, more if I am needed."

"Really? You did that for me?"

"I did it for us. I love you Jamie. I love us also and the life that we have with one another. I was working as hard as I was to prove my independence to both you and the world. It seems that in working so hard, I was placing other aspects of my life on the back-burner. I can still keep my identity while working 20 hours a week."

"Is there anything that I can do to help?" I asked.

"Just respect my decisions no matter which way they go. And never stop loving me."

"I may not always agree with your decisions, but I have always respected them. And I could never stop loving you."

I kissed my wife deeply on the mouth and we made love again and again and again that night. Things in my world were back as they should be. I have a damn good woman in my arms. I can never…ever let her go.

LORETTA

I cannot believe the gall of Michael. He practically called me a hoe to my face the last time that I saw him. I heard that he and Don got into a fight. That is just like men to resort to violence when something doesn't go their way. That is why I had to get away. Coming here to this time share in Beaverton Oregon was a great idea. I could never afford a place like this. People with homes like this remind me of the type of person I always wanted to be as a little girl on Chicago's south side.

My new beau is upstairs sleep. I wonder whether or not it is too soon for me to be seeing another man. I have been divorced for a few years now, but I always denied myself and left the door open to the possibility of Michael and I getting back together. I am not closing the door entirely to that idea, but I am shutting the door some. All this time I kept denying myself a relationship with another man. Sleeping with another man last night other than Michael was not only thrilling, it was liberating. God knows that I have carried around a lot of baggage these past few years. Who would have thought that a massage and some good lovin would relieve some of the pressure. That is not to say that I am problem free just because I got some dick recently. That is to say that good dick can take a woman's mind off of her problems—even if it's just for a little while.

I think I will let him sleep while I go into town and do some shopping. First I will get some clothes, then I will go look at homes that I can actually afford down here, and then I think that I will get some groceries and do some cooking tonight. I might even stop by Lovers Lane and pick up a teddy or two. I never met a man that would willingly give me his credit card and an expense account and tell me to spend his money like it was my own. I could get used to this shit. I miss Michael already, but I think before I go back to the who is sleeping with whom and the whole father figure routine, I will test the waters a little and see what other options are available to me.

JAMIE

I met Yvonne on the plane at Midway airport, I was so glad that she opted to leave out of Midway rather than O'hare. I hated driving to O'hare airport. It was like a city all by itself, it was so big. When I got on the plane in first class, I saw Yvonne seated and holding a seat for me. Today she was looking plain and dressed conservatively in jeans, a Tommy Hilfiger t-shirt and a Tommy girl hat with her hair pulled out the back into a ponytail. The good thing for me was that she wasn't looking as good today as she was yesterday. The bad news is that even on her worst day, Yvonne was still fine as hell.

After the lovemaking session that Mia put on my ass last night, though fine, Yvonne isn't as tempting as she once was. I don't know if that is because I am no longer mad at Mia or because I am spent and couldn't get my dick hard right now if I wanted to. After last night I think that I could remain pussy free for the next three or four months. I get chills just thinking about last night.

"Hello Mr. Kennedy."

"Hello Yvonne, how are you?"

"I'm fine, how did you sleep last night?"

"Oh, Great!"

I didn't mean to sound so enthusiastic, but after last nights session I slept the sleep of the dead. Mia kept me up most of the night with our lovemaking *but when I did sleep I slept the best sleep I have had in years. Yall hear me? My shortie put it on a nigga last night!*

I broke out my lap top and the flight attendant told me that I had to put it away until we were in mid flight. This meant that I had to talk to Yvonne which at this point I really just didn't want to do.

"So what were you going to do on the laptop?"

"A friend of mine that plays for Oregon said that the ideal place to love is a town called Beaverton. I was going to show you some photos of files that I downloaded with virtual tours of certain homes."

"Really, I didn't think that you would be so prepared."

"Well, although I hate the idea of acting as someone's personal assistant, I do love spending other people's money. Besides, I have a few connections with Realtors nationwide. I plan on getting a kickback from somewhere no matter what home your brother buys."

"Always trying to make a buck, huh?"

"I have to. I don't make the millions that I used to. I live nice, but my lifestyle now pales in comparison to when I played. Whether it's announcing, coaching, acting as an agent or just a guest appearance on a TV spot, I have to get paid. In order to keep the lifestyle that I have created for myself, I have to work—hard."

"I know the feeling."

"Do you?"

She laughed. "Hell Yeah. 3J pays me a salary of $50,000 to act as his assistant. The truth of the matter is that I am his financial manager. Because he let's me live in the same mansion that he is in rent free, he feels that $50,000 is an adequate amount of money."

"Well, I think that is a lot of money to get paid along with free rent don't you?"

"Not when I am paying all the bills, budgeting his money, scheduling his appearances on TV and running his charity. Running the charity should have a separate salary all on it's own. I still have to be his sister, mother and confidant *and* make sure that he doesn't get hooked up on drugs, make sure he doesn't get one of these groupie hoes pregnant, and make sure that everyone from you to the team owner doesn't fuck him over."

"Me? What makes you think that I would take advantage of 3J."

"I didn't think that *until* you made this Oregon deal. Just talking to the other owner is a violation of league policy. 3J started to pick out his own home down here, But I told him that would just create more problems in the press. He kept going on about how "fly" your home was on MTV cribs, so that is why I suggested that he ask you to come down here and get things ready.

"So it was your idea?"

"Yeah, it was."

Yvonne looked at me and smiled. I thought that she was trying to seduce me with her smile, so I was glad when the flight attendant began with the pre-flight procedures. That took my attention away from Yvonne and kept me focused on the task at hand which was to purchase a crib in Oregon and get back home to Chicago. I told Mia I wouldn't be gone any longer than a week in Oregon. Only I told Mia that I would be in Portland at the Hilton. When I checked the Internet earlier today, it seemed that Beaverton was the place that a pro athlete should live.

We went through our pre-flight instructions and then shortly after began to take off. Once we leveled off I was worried that Yvonne might ask me about Mia, to which case I would tell her that everything was now okay between me and my wife. Just when I thought that Yvonne was about to begin interrogating me, one of the white flight attendants walked over and asked to see our tickets.

"Why?" Yvonne asked.

"I'm sorry Ma'am, I just wanted to make sure that you were seated properly."

I swear I thought I saw smoke coming out of Yvonne's ears. "You mean you want to make sure that we are in our rightful place which must mean coach."

"No ma'am. I mean, if you are supposed to be in coach them you would have to move, but I wasn't implying that you were in the wrong place."

"Yes, the fuck you were. The other stewardess already checked our tickets."

"Flight attendant."

"What?"

"The proper term is flight attendant."

"Oh is that right."

"Yes ma'am."

Yvonne was unbuckling her seat belt and although I have never been to her home state of Louisiana, I could tell that she was about to get straight up project-like on our white stewardess...I mean, flight attendant. I stopped Yvonne from undoing her restraint and opening a can of whup-ass and showed the flight attendant our tickets.

"Here you are. Are you satisfied?"

The flight attendant looked over the tickets and was satisfied that we did in fact belong in first class. She then spoke rather smugly to me while offering Yvonne a fake smile.

"Thank you sir."

"Can we make phone calls yet?"

"Yes sir, you can."

"What is your name?"

"Sir?"

"Your name, what is it?"

"Kelly, Kelly Millner."

"Thank you Kelly."

   I called the players union. That was an advantage of being a former pro athlete. I got on the phone and told my union rep what happened on the flight. That was my first call. The second was to an ex of mine that was a reporter for channel seven. I then called 3J and let him know how poorly this airline treated his sister. That prompted him to call the front office of the team as well as the front office of the Oregon team. Within twenty minutes, Ms. Kelly Millner was not only going to lose her job, she was going to rue the day that she was born.

The captain called Kelly to the cockpit and had words with her. I don't know what he said to her, but she made a B-line for coach and we didn't see her again until we touched down. She was so apologetic that it was ridiculous. Yvonne smiled a smile of victory. I said to her, "Now wasn't that better than fighting with her and getting arrested?"

Yvonne said, "Nope, I would have rather whipped that bitches ass."

I laughed at how tough this little woman acted. It's hard to believe that she used to whip 3J's ass when he got out of line.

BEAVERTON OREGON

After we landed we took a limo into Beaverton. I had the laptop up and running and poured myself a drink as I viewed the files that I had downloaded earlier.

"How much money did 3J say that he was willing to spend?"

"He said that the house and furnishing should cost no more than a million."

"Did he give you the checkbook?"

"Yes he did. We have a joint account and he deposited a million in there this morning. I saw all those zeros and like to have fainted."

I laughed at Yvonne and told the driver to take us to Murrayhill County. When we got there I think I saw the perfect house that would be a second home to my client and his lovely sister. I found a 5 bedroom 3.5 bathroom that was almost 3400 square feet. It had a fireplace, basketball court, three car garage and a swimming pool. The cost? $549,000. Yvonne and I both looked at the house and thought it was a steal. It looked so good that there was no need to shop further. The house was just 15 miles away from the new stadium where 3J would be playing. Yvonne looked at the outside and took my hand, squeezing it and telling me that this was the house. We told the realtor who met us there that we wanted the house. He looked at us and smiled.

"I think you will find this house to be a treasure. Is this your first home? How long have the two of you been married?"

Yvonne and I blushed a bit as we looked at one another. It was an innocent mistake. Still, there was something about Yvonne's smile that didn't sit well with me.

"We are not married." I told the realtor.

"Yeah, we are just friends." Yvonne interjected.

"Oh, I see…" the realtor said in a very judging voice.

"No you don't see." Yvonne said. My brother is buying this house. His name is JJ Johnson. *This,* is his agent Jamie Kennedy."

The realtor then looked me up and down and came to an epiphany as to who I was, or at least who I used to be.

"You are Jamie Kennedy. You were a wide receiver for the Chicago Bandits, right?"

"That's right."

"And your client is 3J?"

"That's right and this is Yvonne Johnson, 3J's older sister."

"Oh my, I am sorry if I offended either of you. Mr. Kennedy I was a big fan. How is your knee?"

"The knee is fine. Thank you for asking."

The realtor asked us to follow him to the closing agent's office. I had our limo follow him and we closed the deal on 3J's new home. Now all I needed to do was close the deal on his new contract. I knew this was all going to take some time so I told Yvonne that we needed to get separate rooms in a hotel and separate cars to take care of our respective errands.

"That sounds like a good idea. While you are finishing the details at the stadium with the new team, I will work on furnishing the remainder of the house with the 451k that I have left."

"Damn girl, you don't waste any time. Do you even know where to purchase things on Oregon?"

"Nope, but I am betting that the realtor can point me in the right direction. Hand me the keys to 3J's new place."

Yvonne was off on a mission to furnish 3J's new home. I was off to the new stadium to work on hammering out the remainder of the details in 3J's contract. I rented a Dodge Stratus and headed to the new facility where I would have to do business. I got on the cell phone and called Mia to check in, something that I hadn't done in months, but felt right to do after last night.

"Hello?" my wife asked as she picked up the receiver.

"Hey Sexy, how are you?"

"I'm fine baby, how are you?"

"Great now that I am talking to you. Listen, I called to tell you that I am going to be here for a minute. Why don't you fly up here to Oregon?"

"I can't I have business to take care of here with the magazine. How long do you think it will take to finish your business up there?"

"Maybe two or three weeks."

It was Monday now, I don't think it will take more than two weeks to actually finish up this contract, but I have never been to Oregon before. I don't think Mia has ever been here either. I figure I can finish the contract and she and I can go horseback riding or something, or do whatever the hell people do for fun in Oregon.

"I tell you what, I will fly up there Sunday and we can spend some quality time together then. Is it a date?"

"You bet your ass it's a date. See ya babe, I will call you later. I love you."

"I love you too."

I thought about the fact that I hadn't told my wife that I loved her in quite some time, a sin that should never go unpunished between couples. It felt good to confess love for my wife again. Things in my life were slowly getting back on track. Just think, last night I was thinking about divorcing her. A few months ago my frat brothers were trying to kill each other and I was fantasizing at every waking moment about Yvonne. We all need to take our asses back to church and get some prayer.

I checked into the Holiday Inn in town and took a quick shower. I then changed into my Brooks Brothers suit and Sean John shoes. When I was satisfied with the way that I looked, I jumped into the Dodge and headed to the stadium.

Hammering out the deal took all of three hours. All the contract needed was 3J's signature which I faxed to him from the Oregon headquarters. I had 3J on the phone as we finalized the deal.

"Damn man, this is more zeros than the last contract that you inked for me." He said.

"Yeah I know. This contract has more money, more incentives, and I even got you a 3 million dollar signing bonus."

3J asked, "Where is Yvonne?"

"I think she is shopping to furnish your new home."

"Tell her it's hers."

"What?"

"Tell her that the house is hers to keep, and rather than her staying with me, I will be staying with her during the season."

"Wow. I think she will love to hear that 3J but shouldn't you tell her all this yourself? It might mean more coming from you than me."

"Nah, you tell her. Besides, I am going out to celebrate my new contract. I think I am going to throw a party this weekend. Will you be here?"

"No, I still have loose ends to tie up here. I will tell Yvonne about the party though."

"Don't bother. Besides, I need to party some without her around. You know she is just my half sister, but she acts like my mother sometimes."

I told him, "That isn't necessarily a bad thing 3J."

"I hear you, but still, I need to party alone for a minute. Tell her that I love her and to give me a call when you see her."

3J signed the contract and we each had a little bit more than what we had because of it. The team was richer because they got a running back that they needed, 3J got a bigger contract, Yvonne got a new home, and I had a huge pay-day. I phoned Yvonne on her cell to inform her of the news about the contract and her new home.

"You have to come to the house tonight to celebrate."

"What?" I said.

"You need to come to the house tonight to celebrate."

"I don't know Yvonne, I have a lot of loose ends that need to be tied up here."

"Today is the happiest day of my life and I don't know anyone here and the only family I have is thousands of miles away on Chicago. Are you telling me that you can't spare any time for a friend?"

I laughed a little at how pitiful she sounded. I said, "Okay, what time do you want to meet?"

"Come and get me around Midnight and let's find a club or something to party at. See if you can find somewhere nice on that laptop of yours."

Reluctantly, I said, "Okay, I will see you at the stroke of midnight."

THE STROKES OF MIDNIGHT

I went home and took a nice long and hot bath. Afterward, I took a long nap. I didn't really want to hang out with Yvonne this evening, but I could think of a lot worse ways of spending my time in Oregon. Hell, I didn't know anyone here either. After my nap, I asked the girls at the front desk where was a good place to party. They said in all honesty, there was no where that was worth my time considering that I was from Chicago. Rather than debate about which place would be the best to try out, I figured that I would simply grab Yvonne and we would drive around town until we found something that looked appealing to us. At 11:00 that evening, I jumped in the Dodge still only half awake and made my way to the house that we closed on earlier.

The house looked fly as hell at night. It had the running lights on the sidewalk and driveway. The house was huge, but it was not well lit. I rang the bell and waited for Yvonne to come out. I hoped that she didn't overdress. I had on a suit earlier, but now that I was off the clock, I had on Lugz Boots, Sean John jeans and a Phat Farm sweatshirt and cap. Earlier today I was the corporate brother that I needed to be. Right now I was straight Hip-Hop. I rang the bell again and still there was no sign of Yvonne. I started to leave but I had to at least make sure that she was safe. I thought to myself that she must be sleep. I knocked once more instead of ringing the bell. It dawned on me that the electricity was probably not on and that is why she was not answering the bell. Sure enough, the door opened a few minutes later.

When I opened the door, Yvonne was standing there in a turquoise Baby Phat jogger. Her hair was pinned up in a style that I expected her to wear of she had on an after five dress. Her hair was Raven Blue, almost black. I could tell that she found a black hair salon somewhere in Oregon and got her hair hooked up. I flicked the nearest light switch and to my surprise, the electricity was working. She cut the light off and led me up the stairs to see the interior of the house.
"What gives? Why do you have the lights off?"
"Do you see any window treatments on many of these windows? If you cut all these lights on, people can see clearly through the entire house."
"Oh."
She led me upstairs and the first stop was the guest bedroom. In it was a sleigh bed, recliner, and 32 inch TV set. Next she took me to the other small bedroom where the entire place had been set up in an Asian fashion. There was a round mattress on the floor with maroon and gold prints on it. Strewn about the room was Asian tapestries, paintings and ceramic dolls.

I took a gulp as she lead me to the master bedroom. She opened the door and in the room was the traditional King size bed, large fluffy pillows and a color scheme of beige and black. At the foot of the bed was a large Jacuzzi that I didn't see during my initial tour of the home. It had to be there earlier however and I guess I must have missed it. Just when I thought I was going to have to make some hard choices, she led me out of the bedroom and down the rear stairwell of the house. She then showed me the kitchen which was fully furnished, the living room which was decked out in Italian leather and then the den which she opened up to reveal a private picnic, stereo system and two glasses of chardonnay. She then cut off the light and lit two candles.
"I thought you wanted to go out?" I asked.
"There is nothing to do here in Oregon."
"Well you had better find something to do" I said laughing. "You are going to be living here."
"I think I have found something to do."
"With that I became flush. She had taken the game to me and rather than be the pursuer in our *situation* I had become the pursued.
"Come here." She said.
She cut on the CD player and played Chante Moore's Album, Precious. From there we ate Italian food that tasted as if every ingredient was freshly prepared. The next thing that I knew, we had both drank a whole bottle of wine. Wine

doesn't get me drunk. If anything, it gives me a headache. I never understood how many people could use wine as an excuse to do things that they say they don't want to do. I knew where this private picnic was leading. I also knew that neither of us can blame what might be about to happen on a bottle of Arbor Mist brand Chardonnay. The wine gave me a headache, a very slight buzz and a desire to pee.

Yvonne smiled a smile at me that said she was ready to get closer to me. Although she was fine as hell in her little Baby Phat sweatsuit, I was still thinking long and hard about Mia. Things were just starting to get right between us. If I do go ahead and sleep with Yvonne, now it would be me driving the wedge between me and Mia, not her job. Every man goes through what I am going through right now. Every man has experienced that period before an affair where you know that you shouldn't, but you know damn well that you are. A lot of times our dicks get blamed for the pussy that we fall into, that is not the case. Sure we all have primitive urges, sure we get horny as hell some days and when sex is offered to us it becomes *very appealing.* But ask any man that you are not involved with about what really goes on, and he will tell you.

In spite of the urges, in spite of how fine the woman is and in spite of the opportunity, we all think about our woman before we actually have an affair with another woman. We picture our woman's face, we think about the fact that we are *about to* make a poor decision. We then try to justify it by blaming it our dicks, the media, BET, and any other excuse that comes to mind. The bottom line is we make a cognitive decision to cheat. We think to ourselves, "I shouldn't, but wifey/girlfriend doesn't have to know." We think, "I should go home" we justify that with "The pussy is here, why travel home to get more." What is worse, is when we travel home and *turn down other pussy,* and then come home to girlfriend or wifey and *get turned down for pussy at home.* These arguments wouldn't work for me, and I know this.

I can't say that I am not getting any sex at home, I am. I can't say that my wife doesn't understand me, she does. I can't say that we are still having problems, because we are on the road back to reconciling. So why am I about to cheat on my wife? Because Yvonne is looking fine as hell, that ass is fat, and chances are slim that Mia will ever find out. *The truth about the matter if she does find out is equally damning*—Brothers know that sisters will allow them *at least one* indiscretion during the course of the relationship. It's almost like a get sex for free card. Sure the woman will be heartbroken, upset and yell and scream, but when the smoke clears, like most sisters, if she finds out, Mia will take me back.

I tried to act cool and nonchalant as if I didn't know what was about to happen next. I went through the motions and the script so that we could dispense with all the preliminary bullshit and cat and mouse, and get this party started.

"So now what?"

"What do you mean?" She said.

"Are you ready to go out and find something to get into?"

"I think I have something for you to get into."

"Really?" I said seductively.

"Yeah...Really."

"Well, what did you have in mind Ms. Lady?"

Yvonne walked over to me and unzipped her Baby Phat top. She tossed the sweat-suit top into the corner to expose her tight abs and push up bra. Her breasts were already a 36C which most men see as the perfect size. Having them pushed up just made her breasts look even more tempting and juicy.

I licked my lips as I gazed at the vision of Black and Asian beauty that Yvonne was. She had hips that were much smaller than my Mia, and her ass was no where as large, but it was nice enough. I was still seated on the floor. Because she isn't tall at all, I was able to reach up and grab Yvonne's ass with both hands and feel the soft, round contour. I stood on my knees and began kissing her stomach. I kissed the ripples that were there and made my way all over her front. I bathed her in kisses from her stomach, to her naval, to her ribs. I kissed her bare stomach and gave a hard squeeze on her ample apple bottom.

Yvonne didn't wait for me to undress her. She began pulling her tight sweatpants down to reveal a pair of black panties that looked as if they matched her bra. She wiggled from side to side as I continued to kiss her belly as she tried to get out of the tight fitting material. Once out, she stepped side to side out of the pants and grabbed on to my locks as I kissed her stomach some more. She let out gracious moans as I turned her around. I kissed her back and her butt and then slowly rose to my feet. I kissed the back of her neck as I lifted up her long mane of hair. As I worshipped her neck and shoulders with kisses, I cupped one breast in one hand and began massaging between her legs with the other. Yvonne then gave out a primitive moan that turned me on. Once I met with her approval, I reached under the panties and my hand made it's way to her mound of flesh below, where my ring finger searched frantically for her clit.

I continued to squeeze her breast and began running circles around her clit, which was moist. When I started my circular massage, she tongue kissed me deep and began moaning and speaking to me in sweet whispers—in Chinese!

THAT SHIT, BLEW MY MIND! I have had women talk dirty to me before, I have had women speak Spanish to me while making love before. Fellas, fuck that, ladies…speaking any language other than English, talking shit, AND Moaning…is THE BOMB! Yvonne was moaning as if I was already in her. My dick was *so hard* that you could have broke marble with it. I stuck my finger deep inside Yvonne and she was just so incredibly wet. She gave out a guttural moan that told me I was doing a good job. She then began to grind her ass back against me. Her perfectly round ass was giving. She began grinding harder and harder against me and I against her. I continued to massage her clit over and over and over again with her juices running like a slippery slope down her thighs.

I felt Yvonne's legs begin to tremble. She struggled to get off her panties with my still fingering her and her moans became louder and louder. She began swearing.

"Oh…shit…Oh…shit…Oh Jamie damn, Oh…shit…shit, damn….Oh my God, Oh my God….Oh My…my…shit…my….ohh…ohhh…shit—ohhh. Dammit there…right…right….yeah….yeahhh….Oh yeahhh….OOOOOoo-ooooohhhhhh…yeah!

Her legs trembled more and began to quake. Yvonne came all over my finger and shook like a tremor as I began to finger her deeply after her orgasm subsided.

Yvonne turned to face me and undid my belt. She dropped to her knees as I stepped out of my pants. She grabbed my rock hard dick which felt like a table leg. She pulled it from my underwear and examined my girth. She knew that I wanted her because my dick was *so hard* that veins were bulging from it's sides. I thought to myself in that instant, that small fraction of an instant where the cognitive mind gives in to the primitive urges, I thought to myself, "*Here we go…the moment that I cheat on my wife.*" Again, all men have been there. There is a small window where we think about what we do before we go to the point of no turning back.

I did think about stopping her. I did think about saying that this was all wrong. I did think to myself that I am madly in love with Mia. Then I thought about the fact that there was this fine black and Asian motherfucka in front of me, with free flowing hair, nice tits, nicer abs, and a warm inviting mouth that is going to precede a nice warm pussy.

I just have to make sure Mia never finds out.

I have to also make sure that I don't fall in love with Yvonne.

How bad could an affair be?

Yvonne knows about Mia, so she can't be expecting too much. She knows that I am married, so she can't demand a lot of my time. We will just have to agree to be physical and nothing more. We will just have to get an understanding that's all. We will just have to…

*   *   *   *

Warmth. Orgasmic, senusual…warmth. That is what I felt as Yvonne took me in her mouth. All bets were off at this point. There was no turning back now. My head reeled back and I let out a gracious moan as I felt the warmth of Yvonne's mouth on my member. The room was filled with her throaty slurping sounds and also the sounds of her moaning as she gave me head. I became light headed and almost high as she worked me like a calculator in an advanced statistics class. I grabbed a fist full of hair and helped her to help herself to my throbbing invasion. For minutes on end she pleased me orally until I thought that I might fall over from the intoxicating caress of her mouth.

"No more…No…more…"

I pulled away from her to keep me from climaxing. Some twenty minutes had passed and I savored each minute waiting for her to stop. She never tired, never complained and she stopped pleasing me orally long enough to hear my cry of no more, and then she began pleasing me again. She masturbated me with a skill that I didn't even know existed even with my own post-puberty practice of solo love. She jacked me off and gave me head simultaneously while massaging my balls.

"Yvonne…baby you have to stop…I don't want to come yet."

"You won't"

"I will"

She smiled and said, "You can't."

I said, "Shiiiit…wanna bet?"

"Go for it."

She continued this massage on my balls and jacking me off. I figured what the hell, I would shoot my load and blame *not actually having intercourse with her* on my ejaculation. As good as I felt, I went to shoot my load but couldn't. She had me feeling so good that my balls almost went numb. My penis was feeling great, so great that I was now trembling, but I didn't cum.

Yvonne laid me down on my back and continued fellatio just a bit longer. Then, without slowing down, she mounted me. I was laying on my back and she was on top of me, with her back to me. She leaned forward and grasped my ankles. She then began grinding on top of me while I was inside of her. I have never felt sex this good before. Yvonne rocked her ass back and forth and up and down with a rhythm that I had never known before. She moved in a way where her ass moved around in circles, but nothing else did. Then without warning she stopped. She then began slowly rocking forward as if doing Yoga. She brought my penis out all the way to the tip and then slowly allowed me to go all the way back in. When I penetrated her as deep as I could, she tightened her inner vaginal walls. This sent me reeling into oblivion. She did this motion over and over again.

"You like that?"

"Oh shit yeah?"

"You enjoy this pussy?"

"Oh yes baby, damn…what are you doing to me?"

"Shhhh…say my name."

"Yvonne."

"Say it again."

"Yvonne."

"Say it like it means something."

"Oh shit, yeah…Yvonne!"

She rocked back and forth and I swear to God that I was in love with this bitch from this point forward. My toes were tingling, my muscles were tense, and my entire body was vibrating like a personal massager. Then Yvonne spoke.

"Don't Move."

"What?"

"Don't Move."

She repositioned herself by spreading her legs and lowering her head. She then grasped onto my calfs, sat up a few degrees and began to make that perfect ass of hers clap. Back and forth her ass jiggled like something out of a Luke video. She made her cheeks clap up and down as she rocked on my dick and soon the only sounds in the room was that of her cheeks, her moans, and soon after—my moans. Chante Moore's CD is over an hour long, we made love well pass her final song.

"Slap my ass." She said.

I obliged her.

"Slap it harder." She said.

I hit it again.

"Harder!"

I whacked her ass like she was a disobedient child."

"I…I…I'm cumming!"

She screamed, I screamed, she came, I came…she unstraddled me and continued to jack me off. There was my seed—everywhere. I came harder then I ever had before. My seed shot out like a sprinkler system. When no more would come out, Yvonne gave me head again—I passed out.

THE DAY AFTER

Shit. That is what I said aloud and how I felt the next morning after my indiscretion. I awoke still in Yvonne's new house. Just as I was getting up, I heard the lock jingling. Someone was about to walk in the front door. My heart began racing as I thought about the fact that someone was about to see me in my naked glory on the floor of the living room. Yvonne and I started out in the Den, but I don't think there is any room that we didn't end up in. Last night was incredible. When I woke up the first time, I tapped that ass ala Chicago style throughout the entire crib. Now someone was coming in and not only would they see my bear ass, they would smell my personal scent.

I scrambled to gather my belongings as Yvonne walked in the door in yet another Baby Phat sweatsuit. She looked as if she had just finished jogging.
"Are you just now getting up?"
"Er, yeah…I am."
"Call your wife."
"Hunh?"
"Your wife…call her, she has been trying to reach you."
THAT, Fucked my head up.
I promised Mia that I would call her back later. Later never came.
"How do you know?"
"Know what?"
"That *my wife called.*"
"Your phone rang."
"You answered it?"
"No. I silenced it. The caller ID said home."
"Oh."
"Yeah…Oh."
This relationship or whatever it was, was starting off on a very bad note. I didn't mean to sound accusatory, but I was new at this sort of thing.
"I thought that the two of you were having problems?" She said.
"What?"
"I thought the two of you were having problems."
"We were."

"Were?"

"Were."

"So everything is okay now?" She asked.

"Yeah. Well it was...until...now."

"When did things become okay?"

"The day before yesterday."

"That's convenient."

"That's the truth."

"Was it still the truth last night?"

I could feel the tension in the room rising.

"Yeah, and it's still true today."

"So why didn't you say something?" She asked.

"Would that have changed anything?" I replied.

"Are you calling me a hoe?"

"Where did that come from?"

There was a short silence between us.

"So where do we go from here?" She asked.

Where do we go from here? I was hoping that she would say that last night was a mis-take. I was hoping that she would be the strong one and put an end to things. I was maybe even hoping for anger, tears, or some sign of closure. She is putting the ball in my court. I have to be the one to end it, I know that I need to, I know that I should, but I can't bear dealing with her feelings if I should shun her. I am not ready to deal with the consequences of her snapping out. Shit...why couldn't she just say that we are through? Damn. I'll try putting the ball back in her court.

"Where do you want this to go, I mean...what do you think?"

"I think that we can try this out and see where it takes us. First we need to estab-lish some ground rules. Why don't you go upstairs and shower, I'll join you in a minute and then we can go to the grocery store."

That was not the right answer.

Like an obedient child coming in from playing outside, I went upstairs and show-ered. I thought long and hard about my next move.

"Shit, I still haven't called Mia back."

I thought about all that has transpired as the water hit my body.

I love my wife.

Damn, the sex with Yvonne though, was all that I imagined and more.

What the hell am I going to do?

"Weak ass men." I heard Michael's voice say in my head.

"I'm not weak." I whispered to myself.

Just then, Yvonne stepped into the hot shower, butt ass naked and looking good enough to eat. She kissed me deeply on the mouth and grabbed for my dick.

"What the fuck did you do to me last night?" I asked her.

"I put you under my spell."

We made love again.

Maybe I am weak.

LORETTA

Keith and I made love last night like God commanded us to do so. I swear I thought Moris Chestnut himself was in the bedroom of the timeshare last night. That man, that man. He was all over me like a cheap suit and I loved every minute of it. My first time making love in three years should have been with my husband, or rather ex-husband. After last night though. I have no complaints.

We have been up here in Beaverton for about three days already. Keith has been the perfect gentleman this whole time. At first, I thought I was losing my girl appeal and was a little disappointed. On day three, or rather night number three, that man didn't disappoint me one bit. Since our arrival here we have gone horseback riding, climbing, walking in the woods, visiting ranches and just taking in the green scenery here in Oregon. When we went places he held my hand. When something made me smile, he smiled. He treated me like a lady...his lady, and he listened to my every word. This man asked me about my dreams, my aspirations and what I wanted out of life. He listened attentively as if to say to me whatever I wanted he would provide, if only he could be near me while doing so.

We did some corny white people things while we were up here. We picked apples, we went to the zoos and aquariums, and we even went to a restaurant that was supposed to have been a five star place, but a place where we had to make our own food. We have places like that in Chicago, but I have never been to one. I guess I am going to have to try to get used to *new things*. Keith not only cooked *for me*, he fed me also. Later that night, he rubbed my feet in lotion as we listened to Boney James on the radio by the fireplace. He pampered me yall, and I enjoyed every minute of it. After he rubbed my feet, I laid back in his arms as he told me things like how special I was and how beautiful I was to him. He told me sweet things that made me feel good to be a woman. I laid back in his 42 inch chest and relaxed as he wrapped his muscular arms around me. I felt like Whitney Houston's character in *Waiting to Exhale*. I wanted to lay in that man's arms and pretend that he was all mine and that we were both secure and in love, and secure in that love enough where relaxing in one another's arms, meant connecting on a totally different level.

I lay in his arms and I *did pretend.* That lasted a good twenty minutes. It felt so good that I fell asleep in that man's arms. When I awoke, I allowed myself the fantasy a bit longer before hearing the words of my therapist in my head. *Seeing the world with new eyes and seeing men for what they truly are as opposed to what you want them to be.* I let out a gentle sigh and reminded myself that although Keith came here with the best of intentions, his primary goal was to sleep with me. I had warmed up to the idea a great deal. I made up my mind yesterday, that if he played it right, he would get some. He played it right yesterday all through last night.

The day began with Keith and I going to breakfast at IHOP. We ate breakfast and then walked off breakfast by going further into town to the local bookstore. Oregon had a Borders and a Waldenbooks and the other large retailers, but it also had a mom and pop bookstore. Of all the things it could be called, it was named *Mom & Pops Bookstore.* We went in and were greeted by a nice elderly black couple that had owned their store some fifty years. Inside the store were pictures of the owners and Malcolm X, Marcus Garvey, Dr. King and other famous black people. There were books by Fredrick Douglas, Dick Gregory and Sojourner Truth.

Every few minutes, the elderly couple would change the tune on the record player. That's right—a record player. They played everything from *Moms Mabley* to *Richard Pryor albums.* They also played speeches that were made my famous black voices over the years from Dr. King to Louis Farrakhan to Elijah Muhammed himself. I had no idea that these recordings were ever placed on wax. We bought quite a few books there from the store. The couple was so appreciative of the money that we spent, they gave us a book that had been autographed by Dr. King. I really enjoyed Oregon. Not only did I enjoy it, I was bringing home a piece of history with it.

We walked back to our car with bags of books and placed them in the trunk of the car that we rented. We then took in a movie, and then went for another walk at lunchtime. We had a private picnic in the park where Keith *read to me.* As he read words from books prophesying about our future, I heard passion in Keith's voice as I listened to stories from our past. We then saw a stage play that night, and hit a small reggae club outside of town.

At the reggae club, we danced the night away. I had a single long island iced tea, and Keith had about three seven and sevens. After we got a buzz from the drinks in the small dive, someone lit a joint and began passing that bad boy around. I hadn't had a hit of weed since my battle with cancer. Even then it only helped to calm my stomach from the chemo, it never really did get me high. It also helped with the pain. Today, I was feeling no pain and the sweet hit of the joint on top of the long island, and I was feeling better by the minute. Someone began shouting Anna Mercy, and the next thing that I knew, one of the vocalist broke out into a version of *I shot the sheriff.* Next it was a rhythmic rendition of *What's going on* and *Mercy, Mercy, Me.* I remember saying out loud, "I didn't know that *Marvin Gaye* was Jamaican. I also remember people laughing at me also. That was when I knew that I may have had too much.

The band then began to play *No, No, No.* Upon hearing it, there was a small roar from the crowd in the tiny little place. While sweating and feeling no pain, I hiked up the skirt that I had on and began grinding my backside against Keith's front. We danced the dance of sin and forbidden love as we kept grinding against each other like teens at a Catholic school dance in the Midwest.

Midnight fell upon us and it was getting late. Keith led me back to the car and walked with his hand around my waist. He opened the door for me, led me in the car, and kissed me softly on the lips as he closed the door. When we got back here to the time share, he took me into the master bedroom, peeled off my clothes down to my underwear, kissed me on the forehead, and tucked me in. Somewhere during all that, I came to the conclusion that he was special. This was at 12:35 AM.

I had a quick nap. At 3:00 I was back up again ready for my second wind. I thought about the wonderful night that I had been having and I decided what the hell. I called out to my host and asked him to come to me.

"Keith? Keith could you come here for a minute?"

I saw the light come on from underneath my door and heard the sound of soft and heavy footfalls as they came to my door. Keith knocked and then stuck just his head in the door. If he wasn't Morris Chestnut's brother, than I have no idea who he was.

"Did you call me?"

"Mm hmm" I said.

"You okay?"

"Unnh Uh, Nope. I am not okay."

"You sick?

"It was only one long island."

"So…you are…"

"Horny." I interrupted.

Keith smiled a bright, oscar winning performance smile.

"Really?" He said.

"Really." I responded.

"So what do you want to do about this condition?"

"Come here and find out."

Keith opened up the door. My room was dark but I could see him clearly because the light was still on across the hall. He had on beige slippers, white linen pajama bottoms, and a white linen pajama top that buttoned up—no buttons were done. His mahogany brown skin was banging on that white linen.

His abs, oh my God, his abs were tight.

He walked over to the radio and turned on a custom CD that I watched him burn earlier this week. It had everyone from Teddy to Luther, to the Isleys on it. He then took me in his arms and we began to slow dance.

He looked deep into my eyes and asked, "Are you sure about this?"

I smiled a smile that said I was happy that he asked and was concerned. I said, "Yes."

"No more games?" He asked

I told him, "Your window of opportunity is closing."

He smiled to himself and then kissed me deeply on the mouth. He rubbed the back of my head skillfully with one hand and lightly caressed my ass with the other. Back and forth we danced as Teddy sang, *Turn off the lights.* Keith's body was hard and chiseled. I felt his chest as we kissed and it felt like stone with flesh over the etchings. I kissed him lightly on the lips and felt secure in his arms as he held my shoulders. He then kissed my neck and we nuzzled and danced for a long time. He then kissed my shoulders and collarbone. All the time, we never stopped dancing. A light breeze made it's way into the bedroom as if the elements themselves were jealous over us and decided to get involved and caress both our bodies with the delicate touch of a west coast wind. My nipples began to harden. I kissed this Mahogany Adonis deeply as I began to squeeze his biceps and feel the strength of a man coursing through his arms. Keith then kissed my chest, ran circles around my nipples with both of his thumbs, kissed my belly beneath the bra, and then my nipples over the bra. He then held me firm and hugged me—and we returned to our dancing. He smiled at me and I smiled back. I felt like a young girl again in his arms.

Keith undid my bra. I trembled with fear and my bottom lip began to quiver as he slowly pulled the bra away from my body. No one had seen my bare breasts other than Michael for many years. I felt like a virgin all over again, wondering if my thirty-something body would still look attractive to this young virile man. I wondered if my thirty something breasts had any appeal at all. Just when I began to have doubts and question my own self esteem, Keith spoke.

"My God you are beautiful."

I smiled. I smiled a smile that was so big my face was sure to crack. I wrapped my arms around this beautiful man and danced with him, grinding with him, I cupped his ample ass and laughed a little as we swayed back and forth in one another's arms.

Keith then began kissing my neck again. He then cupped both my breasts and began running circles around them with his tongue. I became light headed and let out a soft moan of approval. He then kissed my stomach, my hips and my thighs. My nipples were now erect and pointing north. While on his knees, Keith bathed my entire front with kisses and I closed my eyes and enjoyed him as he worshipped my body from head to toe. He then stood up, took my hand and led me to the bed.

He said, "Wait here."

He left the room and then came back with body lotion.

He then laid me down on the bed, stomach down. He slowly removed my panties. Again I was scared, and again I heard the words, "Damn you are beautiful." He took a minute to look at my thirty something ass which in his words, was perfect. I closed my eyes as Keith gave me a full body massage. He began with my hands, rubbing my hands within his. He then moved to my forearms and shoulders. I then felt him on top of me. He must have lotioned himself up some, because he was grinding against me and I felt his massive girth from behind. He then worked some lotion in his hands, sat up, and slowly massaged my back. He then massaged my butt, my thighs…my calves…and my feet. Just when I thought that I might drift off to sleep, he bathed my backside with kisses.

"Turn over." He said.

I turned over to meet his gaze and looked at a man with the perfect smile, perfect chest, and arms that looked like they had been carved out of granite. I reached out to touch his six pack and just for me he flexed each and every muscle in his stomach. I touched just beneath his chest and let my hand slide down every ripple in his midsection. I was breath taken with the incredible shape that he was in. I licked my own lips and continued to run my hands *past the abs and onto his manhood*. I was *quite impressed* with what I grasped in my hands. So impressed— that I used two hands to make sure that I wasn't dreaming.

Keith was still smiling at me.

I told him, "That's something to smile about."

We shared a laugh. Keith then went back to showering me in kisses. He kissed and teased my breasts. He sucked them, licked them and took his time with each one, giving them the attention that I had been craving for. He then kissed my ribs, my stomach and my thighs. His attention continued southward and yet again I began to tremble. No man had been down there in some time, my hus-band—ex husband hadn't even been there. I went to try and stop Keith I placed my hands down there as if to stop him. He locked his hands within mine and held firm. He began to please me in ways that I thought a woman should only be pleased by a man that she was in love with. My guilt quickly passed as Keith took me to that special place that every woman longs to be. He tongued me there as if my kitty and his face were age old lovers. I felt my nipples point straight up, my back arch and my ribs become pronounced as minutes later I came. I had the big O in Oregon. I again knew a pleasure that I had long since forgotten, a pleasure that I was going to treasure for a long time all these hundreds of miles away from Chicago. I came so hard that I was ashamed of the loud moaning that I did. I was ashamed, but I was satisfied.

I was almost praying that Keith did not expect me to return the favor. It had been years since I had given a man head. I didn't want to seem selfish, but I was not going to return the favor. You know what? He didn't expect me to. As I fin-ished with my waves of orgasms, Keith reached for the Magnum condoms and slipped one on. He entered me slowly and I let out a gasp. Though I felt full upon his entry, I was able to work with his large member. With the skill of a patient and skillful lover, Keith made love to me again and again and again last night. I got up at 9:00 this morning to relax alone and savor the feeling that this man has given me. I haven't been this satisfied for some time. It's almost noon now and he is still sleep, or at least he was.

I heard footfalls walk down the stairs and there was Keith in all his glory, just waking up.

"What's the plan for today Pretty Lady?"

"Get dressed. Let's go to the store and get some groceries."

"I will go jump in the shower now. You wanna join me?"

"I will be right there."

CHAPTER 6

▼

MEANWHILE...BACK AT HOME.

MIA

Jamie hasn't called me. I hope that he is okay. I have been paging the hell out of him since last night. I bet he got up early this morning and something didn't go right with 3J's contract. I bet he is locking horns with the team owner right now over some small detail in the contract. If he doesn't call me in a few hours, I think I am going to lose my mind. I am not going to be able to get up there to Oregon Sunday as I thought. I am going to tell him that my mother is sick. I hate lying on mama, but I do not want to tell him that I am canceling on him again in order to do some work at the magazine.

Sonja has her own ideas about how next month's issue should go, and Wanda is thinking that next month's issue should be a fashion extravaganza. The last thing that I need right now is either of these two heifers getting back in one another's faces at the office. Why can't these two divas ever think about the word compromise? Sonja wants to spotlight Chicago's top businesswomen. Wanda wants to target Chicago's most beautiful women. I am thinking that we need to spotlight Chicago's most business *and* fashion savvy women. I can think of quite a few women that would look great on the cover including the brat (minus the braids), Lisa Raye, Bonnie DeShong, Diane Burns or virtually any of the corporate sisters working downtown.

I am taking that idea to the office with me and I am hoping that it does not take me all week to get them to warm up to the idea. I know that I am the boss, but I don't want to stifle their creativity either. I walked into the nice downtown office where already I could hear the loud shouts of Wanda and the sharp wit of Sonja in Sonja's office that overlooked Michigan Avenue.

"These corporate hoes that you are suggesting have no fashion sense at all!"

"The dumb broads that you are suggesting for the cover lack CFS."

"What's CFS?" Wanda asked.

"*Common Fucking Sense.*" I said as I entered the room. Sonja laughed.

"You know, I can hear you two from the elevator." I said "Wanda, how did you two get in this conversation anyway, your office is on the south side. Why are you down here?"

She said, "Ms. Thing here sent me an email telling me that she was sending over some women this weekend and asked me to hook them up with some fashionable clothing for a photo shoot this weekend. I agreed, but I asked her what story were they going to be featured in. She said next month's issue on fashionable black women in Chicago."

I asked her, "So?"

"So? So? So I am looking at these heifers and there isn't one redeeming quality about them. Most of them didn't wear makeup, they had little to no body to begin with, and all they seemed to be concerned with was their cell phones and calculators."

"PDA's dear. Get it right. You see the level of competence that you have me working with here?" Sonja said.

I put my head in my hands and began massaging my temples.

"We three agreed that next month's issue would be about fashionable women in Chicago."

They both nodded their heads.

"We agreed that they should be both fashionable and have business savvy, right?"

Again they both nodded in agreement.

"So Sonja, I know why Wanda doesn't like your picks, why don't you like hers?"

Sonja said, "I interviewed the women that **she** sent over. Only a handful of the women were educated. The rest were big bootied, fake breast having, weave wearing wanna be little Kim types. It was like having the video booty bitches union from BET right here in my office. None of them have *any business savvy.*"

Wanda said, "That's just not true. Laquisha and Yvette both have side businesses."

Sonja said, "Tell Mia what type of businesses they have."

I said, "Okay, I'll bite. What type of businesses?"

Wanda said, "Laquisha had a beauty salon in her basement and Yvette is a motivational speaker."

I turned to Sonja and asked her, "So what is wrong with that?"

Sonja said, "Laquisha has an *illegal* salon in her basement and hasn't paid taxes in like ten years. I asked her. Yvette—spells her name E-V-E-T. That's not Yvette, that's evit. You can top that off with the fact that she does motivational speaking during breaks in rehearsal on the sets of music videos. What the fuck could she be saying that is motivational? Could she be saying, 'We won't always have to shake our ass and suck the occasional dick to get paid.' Give me a break. The women she sent give the rest of us a bad name."

Wanda mumbled, "Bitch."

Sonja said, "Don't let that word get your ass whipped again."

I let out a sigh. I could see that it was going to be a long day.

MICHAEL

I have been leaving all types of messages for Loretta on her answering machine. Initially, I thought that she was still mad at me. That is, until I came to her job with flowers in hand. I felt like shit when I walked in with my regular bouquet from 1-800-FLOWERS. I swear, these days I had them on speed dial. When I got to Loretta's job to surprise her, the receptionist told me that she was not in.

"I'm sorry sir, she is on vacation."

"How long has she been on vacation?"

"I'm sorry sir. I can't give out that information."

"Even for her husband?"

"I'm sorry sir. And no disrespect, aren't you her ex-husband?"

Her words cut deep. This broad was obviously new. Just then, Loretta's assistant, Bonnie walked by.

"Excuse me Bonnie, could I have a word with you?"

Bonnie said, "Sure Michael, how have you been?"

"Fine. Listen, I'm kind of in the doghouse with Loretta, how long has she been on vacation?"

"Just a few days."

"Where did she go?"

"She didn't say."

"Damn. She left no forwarding information?"

"I'm sorry Mike, she's the boss, She isn't required to leave any."

"So where do I put these flowers?"

"I guess you can put them on her desk with all the other ones that you sent. Maybe you can help me clear all the old ones away while I put your fresh ones on her desk. She is never gone from the office more than a few days. She may even be in tomorrow. Won't she be surprised when she sees that even while she was gone you were still sending flowers. I wish someone loved me like that."

I was at a loss as to what the fuck Bonnie was talking about. I had only sent one other bouquet prior to this one to her office. There were other deliveries, but they were sent to her place. My confusion was lifted as she opened the door to Loretta's office. Someone—had been sending my woman dozens and dozens of red roses. I felt my heart tighten in my chest.

"We will keep the vases, but we can toss all the old flowers." Bonnie said.

I held back tears as I helped to immediately toss the roses into the garbage. Bonnie suggested that I leave the flowers on her desk. I attached a separate note to her desk in my own handwriting:

Loretta,

*I am sorry for our last argument. I love you. I would give anything to take back the words that were spoken that night. Given the chance, if I could redo that night, I would take you in my arms, tell you that everything is okay, and make love to you. We both have to sit down and talk and make a conscious decision as to whether or not our marriage or rather our relationship—is worth saving. I hope that you still find this bouquet warms your heart rather than the many **ROSES** that were strewn about your office. Do you know why I send you these flowers instead of roses? When we were in college this was the first bouquet that I had ever bought you. Remember how broke we were in college? I always sent you these flowers from 1-800-FLOWERS to remind you...and me, of how far we come. I'm sorry that I hurt you. I hope that hurt hasn't pushed you in the arms of another. If it has...All I ask is that you come back to me.*

—Michael.

I finished writing my note and gave a wry smile to Bonnie. I might have lost my woman forever with my foolishness. Rather than act a fool, I will have to just pray on the matter. In the meanwhile, I have a city to run and an election to win. Even if I win, it won't be the same without her by my side.

WINDY CITY POLITICS

My opponent's name in the primary is a woman named Leslie Allen. When the Mayor decided that he was not going to seek a second term, oppositions against me began coming out of the woodwork. This began with Ms. Allen, a Harvard Grad that had every intention of making me look like an idiot at every opportunity. Had she gotten wind of the fight that I had with Don, my career would be over now.

I had a distinct advantage over her with the fact that I was already in office as the Deputy Mayor. The other advantage that I had was the fact that she kept talking about what changes she wanted to make in Calumet City. One thing that I have come to learn over the years was the fact that many of my constituents hated change. There was no need to drastically begin changing the way people have lived, especially when the people are confident that the people presently in office will do their jobs. People in the city feel comfortable in the fact that they can call city hall and actually talk to either their alderperson, or me and sometimes the Mayor. People in the community can visibly see the changes that our administration has made, and they expect more of the same from me. Many of my constituents come to the bi-weekly meetings at city hall. Many bring their concerns to these meetings and I make damn sure that their concerns are my concerns. That is the trust that the people have had with the present Mayor, and that is the same trust that they can have in me.

I love Loretta. I want her back more than I want anything in life, but sometimes when you love someone, you have to let them go. It hurts, but I need to take a step further.

MIA

I finally got Wanda and Sonja to agree on the selection of women for next month's layout. Wanda agreed to help all Sonja's "stuffy" selections with their styles, fashions and appearance (including push up bras, lace, and theatrical makeup). Sonja agreed to help the women that Wanda sent over, with their articulation and public relations skills. Wanda even suggested throwing together a benefit such as a fashion show that presents Chicago's elite women and Chicago's women of music videos. I will have to sleep on that one. The two of them have both worn me out.

Since the magazine started, I have paid myself a decent salary of 100k. I plan on giving myself a raise when the budget allows. 100k is nothing compared to the salaries that CEO's of other magazines are making. In the meanwhile, I wish to hell that Jamie would call. In order to pay for the promotional party for the magazine doing as well as it was doing, I needed to front the money for the Hotel, Ballroom and Entertainment until I received the check from the bank for the fiscal year spend down. I had half the money in my account. I got almost the rest that I needed out of mine and Jamie's joint account, and I needed to take the remainder that I needed out of his credit union account. Jamie gave me a debit card to his account for cases of emergency (he so sweet). Still, I had no idea how to tell him that I went through all my money, our joint account and part of his account just to pay for a party. I will get the money back at the end of the week, but I know I should have at least talked to him prior to taking the cash. *If he would call me back,* I could discuss it with him. He is really pissing me off with not calling. I am so mad right now that I could spit. If it goes any longer that I do not hear from him, my anger is going to turn into worry.

I can't sit here and wonder what is going on with Jamie all day. I need to hit the gym, get some work done tonight on the computer, and watch *The West Wing* on *NBC.* I have been trying to call Loretta lately, but I can't seem to get in touch with her. I keep getting her answering machine.

I began flipping channels on the digital cable. I have to admit that the picture on my TV screen is a lot clearer, but there still seems to be nothing on all these damned channels. Thank goodness for *TNT, Lifetime and A & E.* I was just going to flip the channel to BET to watch some music videos to help motivate me to go to the gym, when I saw Leslie Allen, Michael's Mayoral opponent on public television dogging Michael the hell out.

The anchor said, "So you think that Michael Carter is the wrong choice for Mayor?"

"He is the worst choice for Mayor. The city does not need a man with all his issues." Ms. Allen said.

"And what issues would those be?"

"He graduated in the middle of his class. He and his first wife were living in sin all through college, and he reportedly broke up with her, for a younger woman. His first wife, Loretta, stood by his side through all his endeavors and then he dumped her like a bad habit for a woman that he was having an affair with."

The news anchor asked, "Are you sure about this? I mean, Michael Carter seems to me, to be an upstanding guy."

"He married his *second wife* just months after his divorce, now you tell me what does that sound like?"

I got on the phone and began looking for Michael's cell phone number to see if he knew this bitch was dogging him out on TV.

The anchor said, "I can certainly see your point, but the people of the city admire the work that Mr. Carter has done and they can see the work that he has done. What is it that you have to offer the city that he doesn't."

"I am a Harvard Grad, I have a loving husband and two wonderful children and stability. I graduated in the upper ten percent of my class, I have a long positive tenure in politics, and I am not going to be doing who knows what while in office. I will not just be the Mayor between the hours of nine to five."

The anchor said, "That sounds nice, but what does Mr. Carter's social dealings have to do with his being Mayor?"

"I think the way he carries himself outside of the office has everything to do with how he will act while in the office."

"And how does he act outside the office?"

"Well, let's take a look and see."

The monitor began showing footage of Michael's home in Calumet City where what looked like fifty scantily clad women were seen going in and out of Michael's home. Most of them came in one at a time. Some two at a time and others, as many as four at a time.

"You see? I think that the Deputy Mayor enjoys the company of prostitutes and may even be engaging in group sex."

I looked closely at the TV set. I know that Michael is not that type of man. The footage that they showed had to be from Jamie's bachelor party. Even still, I am not to sure that I am happy about how many hoes he had at his bachelor party. He told me that it was going to be a small affair. There had to be at least fifty of these high priced hoes going into Mike's house. I am going to have to make a mental note to kick Jamie's ass later.

"Here is yet another video feed of the would-be mayor, drunk at his best friend's wedding. Mr. Carter, is best friends with a womanizer that used to play for the Chicago Bandits named Jamie Kennedy."

I almost spit out my drink when she said that. No this bitch didn't just front my husband off, use footage from *my goddamned wedding* and say some foul shit about my man. I have kept Jamie's ass on a *real short leash,* so there is no way in hell that he ever fucked around on me. This must be just more media hype.

"Finally, I would like to show you some still shots that were taken by a neighbor of a man in Hyde Park in Chicago. Here are photos of the Mayor drinking in his car outside the man's home, walking up the man's walkway, and assaulting the man in his front yard.

The fight then reportedly went into the house and lasted for some time. Minutes later, the Mayor's womanizing friend showed up, and simply walked into the man's house. Minutes after that, the Mayor returns to his friend's car, and then the womanizer comes out twenty minutes after that, and takes the man to the hospital.

If this woman calls Jamie a womanizer just one more goddamned time, Michael won't have to worry about her. I will drive down there and beat this bitch down myself! I cannot believe that this shit is going down like this.

I dialed Mike's number after finding the phone book. Mike picked up the phone and sounded like his world had shattered.

"Yeah. Hello."

"Mike are you watching this shit?" I asked.

"Yeah Love, I'm watching."

"What are you going to do about it?"

"Hold a press conference tomorrow. I guess it's on with me and this broad."

"You damned right it's on, and if you need me to, I will kick this bitches ass myself."

"That's sweet Mia, but not necessary. I have a team of people working damage control right now and preparing a written response to tonight's telecast."

"How bad do you think this is going to be?"

"No clue love. No clue."

We both sat and watched as Ms. Allen went on berating my husband's best friend and going on about the fight that Michael had with Don.

"Did the man that was assaulted give you a statement?" The anchor asked.

"No. he refused to be interviewed. I think that the womanizer threatened him. I think Jamie Kennedy is one of those gang members turned athlete like that boy in Philadelphia, Allen Iverson."

"Imma hurt this bitch." I said.

"Relax Mia, I will take care of this, I promise. Look, I need to let you go. When Jamie calls home, tell him to hit me up."

"If he calls home."

"What?"

I know that Michael was going through his own little thing with the way he was being made to look bad on TV, but I had to tell him that I was worried about Jamie. He hasn't called me all day, and I have been worried about him. Months ago, I wouldn't have even noticed his comings and goings, but now that we are on the road to saving our relationship, I am concerned. He might be somewhere hurt. I beared my soul to his best friend and told him of my concern. That was the thing that I liked most about Mike and Loretta, no matter what they were going through, they always made time for others.

"Mia, I am sure that Jamie is okay. He probably was negotiating the deal well into the morning hours. You know how stubborn that brother can be. Let me call the Oregon front office and have them get someone to have him call you back."

"You can do that?"

"I sure can, R-H-I-P."

"What's R-H-I-P?"

"Rank has it's privileges. Talk to ya love."

"Thanks Mike."

Mike hung up the phone and I decided to put my clothes on and get ready to go to the gym. I am taking my cell with me so I do not miss Jamie's call. I could not bear to watch the remainder of the interview.

JAMIE

Yvonne and I finally got dressed and stopped screwing long enough to go to the grocery store. We were both starving, and let little Ms. Louisiana tell it, I was about to have the meal of all meals cooked for me in her brand new kitchen. On the way to the store we had a strange conversation in the car.

"I want one day per week and the occasional holiday."

"What?"

"You heard me, I want one day per week and the occasional holiday."

"I thought that you said that you were not going to make things difficult for me."

"I'm not."

"Yes you are."

"How?"

I didn't answer her. I thought about Don and how he would respond if he were me. I then thought about Mia and the wonderful night of making love that we had the night before I came here to Beaverton. Finally, I thought about how mind blowing the sex was with Yvonne last night. Mind blowing or not, that does not change the fact that I love my wife, I am not ready to get a divorce, and as good as the pussy was with Yvonne, if caught, I know right now that I would spend the rest of my life pursuing Mia. That is my heart. She is my soul mate. I know it's hard to picture a man cheating on his soul mate, but in my mind, it can happen. That doesn't make the shit right, but it can happen. It's like DMX says, "It is what it is. Love one—fuck another."

I pulled into the grocery store and got out. Yvonne got out on her side and we were both obviously going to give one another the silent treatment. I was not in the mood for that shit. I hate it when my wife pulls that shit at home and I am not about to put up with this shit from my mistress. Damn—did I just think of her as my Mistress? Two months ago she was my client's sister, a month ago she was my fantasy, now she is my mistress...damn this all happened fast. I grabbed Yvonne by the hand and made her face me. We were going to talk this shit out before going to the store. Otherwise I am driving her ass home and going back to my hotel room.

"Yvonne, we need to get an understanding. I like you. I think that you are a strong, beautiful and amazing woman. I think that you have business savvy and have the looks of a supermodel. When I thought that my wife and I were going to split, I could think of no one else that I wanted in my life besides you. For a while there, you were my fantasy. For a while there, you were everything that I ever wanted in a woman. As amazing as last night was and as amazing of a woman that I find you to be...I love my wife."

Tears began to well in the corner of Yvonne's eyes.

"Did you love her last night when you stuck your dick in me?"

"Yes I did. And I loved her still when we had sex before coming here."

"Don't you mean make love?"

"I think the two terms are interchangeable."

"They're not."

"Okay then, maybe I need to clarify the difference between making love to you and making love to my wife."

"Maybe you do."

"Okay...[sigh]...When I make love to my wife, I am making love with someone that I am in love with, someone that I know that I want to spend the rest of my life with. When I have sex...er, make love to you, I am making love to someone that I like and admire, and someone that is very giving of herself, but someone that I am not in love with."

"How can you not be in love with me?" she asked.

"Yvonne, I don't even know you. I mean I kind of do, but not really."

"Would you like to get to know me better Jamie?"

"I would, but that would not change how I feel about my wife."

"I don't understand. How could you be ready to leave her just a few weeks ago, and do a full reversal in just as many weeks? What the fuck happened that made her so important again and made me a passing fancy?"

"I don't know. I am at a loss for words to explain it."

Just then a familiar voice said, "Jamie? Jamie is that you? Who is this?"

JAMIE/LORETTA/YVONNE AND KEITH

I turned around and my chest tightened as if I was having a heart attack. I also became light-headed. I tried to gather my composure, but I am sure that the look I had on my face had given me away. Here in Beaverton Oregon, was Loretta, my best friend's ex-wife and some brother that looked like Morris Chestnut. I was scared and at a loss for words. The first thing that I thought was who else is up here? Had Mia come up here with Loretta and surprised me? Would Mia be walking out the door next to greet me? Jesus, what have I done? What have I done to my marriage? What will I say? What can I do? I love my wife. I don't want to lose her. I felt heartache, lightheaded, numb and cold all at once. I stood there with my mouth open and was so out of it that I didn't understand the words coming out of Loretta's mouth, nor could I hear her.

"Jamie? Jamie? Jay-me? Aren't you going to introduce me to your associate?"

"Er, Um...sure. Loretta Carter, this is...Yvonne. Yvonne Johnson. Yvonne is the sister of my client 3J, you know, the running back for the bandits? He is um...being traded to the Oregon team, although I am not supposed to say anything for two weeks."

"So why are you saying something?" The dark skinned brother asked.

I said, "I'm sorry...just who in the fuck...I mean, I'm sorry brother, what's your name?"

He responded, "Keith, my name is Keith Bryant brother. I caught your name. Jamie, right?"

"Yeah, that's right."

There was a long uncomfortable ass silence between the four of us. I made the mistake of breaking that silence.

"Loretta...I am um, surprised to see you here—with someone."

"I'm not married."

That shut me the fuck up. Her words stung. Her words also signaled me to walk a fine line.

"Yvonne is...the sister of a client of mine."

"Yes, you said that."

Yvonne interrupted with, "I'm sorry [to Loretta] you are whom to Jamie?"

"His best friend's ex-wife and a friend to his wife, Mia. I was in their wedding."

"So you were Jamie's friend first...before what's her name."

"Her name is Mia."

"Oh right...Mia. And your gentleman friend here is?"

Loretta responded, "None of your business."

I could feel the conversation going south quickly. So I decided to take the initiative to put out the embers before they became a full blown forest fire.

"Yvonne, I will meet you in the store. Loretta can I have a word with you?"

Keith said, "I'm not sure how I feel about that."

I responded with, "Mother fucka, I didn't ask you!"

It was Loretta's turn to put out a fire.

"Keith, please go to the car. I will be there shortly."

Reluctantly, Keith went to the car that he and Loretta arrived in, which was good because I was just a few seconds from whipping his ass into a coma. I turned to Loretta and began to speak.

"What are you doing here with this guy?"

"What are you doing here with this tramp?"

Silence fell again between us.

"Mike loves you." I said.

"Mia loves you." She responded.

Again silence.

I said, "This isn't what it looks like."

"Jamie this is exactly what it looks like. There is no way that you can tell me that you are not having an affair with that woman. She has that I fucked him last night and this morning look on her face."

That threw me off. Did she actually have such a look? And if it's that transparent to Loretta, Mia would see through it even faster.

"Look, Loretta I am staying at the Holiday Inn. Where are you staying?"

"I am not comfortable sharing that information with you Jamie."

"That's fair...I guess. How long are you going to be here in Beaverton?"

"I am going home tomorrow."

"Can you meet me at my hotel? I am in room 1107. I'd like to talk to you about what I am doing here. I know it's none of my business, but I would like to talk to you about why you are here as well. I don't think we should discuss this here in a grocery store parking lot. I also do not think that we should discuss it with our mutual friends present. Can we meet as two longtime friends and have a conversation?"

Loretta thought long and hard before saying, "Yeah, I guess we can do that. I will meet you in the lobby of the Hotel at 7:00."

"Cool, I will see you then."

I went into the store and gathered a few things for this meal that Yvonne planned on fixing. The truth of the matter though, is I am not in the mood for anything now.

"What the fuck was that about?" Yvonne asked.

"Yvonne—not now. Get what you need and let's go. We need to finish the conversation *that we started.*" Just then, my cell phone rang.

Shit! I STILL haven't called Mia. I checked the caller ID and it was Mike. I had to answer it although I was not sure at all as to what I would say after seeing the love of his life all they way up here in no man's land.

"Yeah, whaddaup" I said, trying to sound cool.

"Dude, where the fuck are you at? I called the Oregon office and asked them where you were and the GM said that you finished negotiations yesterday and that as far as they knew, you were on your way back home to Chicago."

"You checking up on me Mike?" I said laughing.

"No, but Mia could have made the same phone call and come to the same conclusion that I have. You are up there with some broad ain't ya?

"Something like that. You spoke to Mia?"

"Yeah and she is bugging the fuck out about your not calling her. I told her you were probably wrapped in all night negotiations. That is the story that she is most likely to buy. Get your shit together and call your wife."

"Thanks for looking out. I am going to call her at 6:00. Do me a favor, tell her that."

"Why the fuck can't you call her to tell her?"

"Dude, I have major drama up here in Oregon. Dawg, call her for me and tell her that you didn't speak directly to me, but someone in the front office. Tell her that I promise I will call her at 6:00 on the dot on her cell or at the house."

Mike let out a sigh, but agreed to call Mia for me. All The time that I was sitting here talking to Mike, Yvonne was looking at me with eye daggers. I gave her a wry smile and picked up some snacks off the shelves of the store as I hung up the phone.

"Who was that?" She asked.

"Mike."

"Whose Mike?"

"My best friend."

"Oh you mean that bitches ex-husband."

"Watch your mouth."

"What?"

"Watch your mouth. She didn't call you out of your name, don't you call her out of hers. Let's go"

We drove back to her home and unloaded the few groceries. I explained to her that although last night was wonderful, as was this morning, we will never share another embrace like that. I explained to her that I was wrong in leading her on, wrong in approaching her in the first place, and wrong to have shared what was going wrong in my marriage with her. Yvonne was as fine as baby's hair, but I didn't know her from Adam. We had a few conversations, some obvious chemistry, and 24 hours of passion. I explained to her that none of that changed the fact that I loved my wife, and was going to go back home where I belonged.

"You led me on!" She screamed.

"I might have." I responded.

"You took advantage of me."

"I might have, if I did it was because I was taken in by your looks. If I hurt you I apologize. It's too early into this for you to have any real feelings for me, so I am hoping that the damage is minimal."

"I will tell your wife everything that happened."

Again, there was a long silence between us.

I took in a long sigh and said, "So be it. You will tell her, it will hurt her, hurt me, and damage my relationship. But it will not *end my relationship.* If you feel that you need to tell Mia, then do so. In fact, if you like, we can do it together. That only means however that I will spend the rest of my days if need be, pursuing my wife and begging her forgiveness."

Yvonne asked, "Why are you doing this to me?"

I responded with, "I am trying to hold on to the single greatest thing that has ever happened to me. My marriage was never in trouble to begin with. I was just too stupid to see that. There was a great deal of distance between me and my wife a few months ago. It wasn't until just now that I realized that I am the one that put that distance there. Mia was there for me when I was no one. She was there when I became someone. When the money was gone, she was still there. When we began doing well again, she was still there. No matter what crisis, or chaos comes my way, I stand strong against it because of her. She is my rock. She is also my fantasy."

"Why can't I be your fantasy?" Yvonne said with tears in her eyes.

"Yvonne, all I can say is...I'm sorry."

"We can't just keep going on like we are going? We can't just have a little something every now and then?"

The offer was tempting. I never knew a woman to make love to a man like Yvonne did. But I never knew a love like the love Mia had for me either. Yvonne was admittedly better in bed, but sex fades...love...is forever.

"I'm sorry Yvonne. Goodbye."

And with that, I turned down my fantasy girl, and walked out of her life.

YVONNE.

I thought that Jamie was the man that I wanted to be with. I thought that maybe he was the one. I knew that he had a woman, and I have to admit, I was happy when he shared with me that he and his woman were having problems. All my life I have been dogged by men. All my life men have tried to run through my credit, finances, and get in my pants. All my life I said that my baby brother was not going to be the type of man that I always fell for. That is why I tried to raise 3J to be an honest, hard working and god fearing man. As his sister, I thought that was the least I could do. I got him into sports mainly to keep him from these streets. I was so happy when he got drafted to play pro football. After he got drafted, I always wondered what would then happen to me.

3J has always looked out for me. I was not surprised that he gave me the house in Beaverton. I was surprised that Jamie was willing to turn me down for his wife. She looked like *she used to be cute back in the day.* There is no way he should have been able to turn me down for her. If not by looks alone, I would think the nagging and all the time that she refused to give him, would have been enough for him to leave her. I knew that he loved her, I was hoping that his love for her was beginning to wane.

I think that Jamie led me on. Granted, I flirted with him that night I first saw him in the mansion. Not once did he stop the conversation. Not once did he say that we needed our "friendship" to go in a different direction. I think he knew damn well what he was doing and I think he knew damn well that one day we would end up in bed together.

I started to play the whole cat and mouse thing, but I wanted Jamie from the moment that I saw him and figured there was no need in making him wait or play any games. I pulled out all stops when we made love for the first time. I did that in hopes to get him to leave Mia and start a new life with me. I know many people would think that doing so makes me a ho. Well, I have quite a few girlfriends that have been able to steal *their men* from their wives. I know a lot of women that were able to break a man off so good, that the man would generally leave his wife anywhere from 30–90 days later.

I can't believe that Mia would put herself in a position to almost lose Jamie in the first place. You see, that is where a lot of women make their mistake. They take their men for granted and think that not only is there man not going anywhere, they think no other woman would want him anyway. Too many women think that because their man is overweight, underweight, poor dressing, not making enough money and all that other shit, that their men are not marketable.

Shit, those bitches are as wrong as the day is long. If your man is a *Good Man,* I wouldn't give a fuck if he had one leg. I will take him any day of the week. Good men with a few flaws are an untapped market. Women like me and white girls will snatch another woman's man up in a heartbeat and look that woman in the face like, "Bitch what?"

There are too many men out here that work long hours and treat a woman right just for that same woman to not ask about his day, not cook for him and not give him some coochie on the regular. Not me. I'm on top of my man from the moment he hits the door so he is too tired to think about another bitch. There are a lot of women that complain that their men work *too hard,* "what the hell is that?" Let me get a man that works a job with long hours or two jobs, or works and goes to school. I will feed him, fuck him and tuck his ass in to bed each and every night. I know men out there that take care of their women; *Especially the pro athletes,* all these women have to do is keep themselves up. I would love to be in their shoes. So when I found out that Mia was neglecting Jamie, not properly loving Jamie and picking up weight? I jumped right on the opportunity while it was there.

I am not the only one at fault in this. Jamie is just as wrong as I am. He wants to go back to his wife, that's fine. She better not fuck up. I am sure that he is not apt to forget my number anytime soon. I have my own place, no kids, no drama and my own money to boot? Shit, he will be back. No man can turn down free sex with no strings attached. He will be back.

JAMIE

I called Mia at 6:00 and got cursed the fuck out. I hadn't called my woman in 24 hours and she was mad as hell. I lied to her and told her that the negotiations ran into the wee hours of the morning. I told her that the next day I slept in late and then, went right back into negotiations. Being the wife of a pro athlete, she fell for it and I was most grateful to Michael for the idea. Mia told me what was going on with Mike and the interview that his opponent had on channel 11. I was shocked to hear that there was footage of me on TV. I was also shocked to hear that I was being referred to as a womanizer. I explained to Mia that saying so was defamatory and I told Mia that I was going to sue the TV station as well as go after Ms. Allen.

"You need to." Mia said. "By the way, exactly how many hoes did you have at your bachelor party?"

"What?" I said.

"Jamie you heard me."

"Um…five, maybe."

"Jamie youz a lie! I saw footage of your party and I counted at least fifty women in that motherfucker!"

"If you knew, then why did you ask me?"

"To see if you would tell the truth."

"Oh. Well, I am never going to intentionally tell you something that might hurt you so I guess I am guilty as charged."

"What else have you lied to me about?"

"What?"

"What else have you lied to me about?"

"What have you heard?"

"Jamie that's not funny. You lied to me about how many women were at your bachelor party. If you lied about something as small as that, you are apt to lie about anything."

I took in a long sigh and said, "Mia, if I ever lie to you it's because I love you."

"Jamie what kind of backward bamma shit is that?"

"I'm serious, if I ever lie to you it's because I love you and I don't want to hurt you."

"That's bullshit, you know that's bullshit and it sounded like bullshit when you said it. What else have you lied to me about?"

"I love you Mia."

"Don't start that."

"I do. I love you."

"Jamie we need to talk about this."

"Not long distance we don't. Let's take this up when I get home. I am betting that this conversation is costing me like three dollars a minute or some shit."

Mia said, "You are full of shit."

"I know. We can cover that too when I get home. I will be home tomorrow."

"I thought you said it was going to take more than a week?"

"That is why I stayed up until the wee hours of the morning and didn't call. I worked around the clock while I was up here just so I could hurry up and get hone to your sexy ass."

I could practically hear Mia smiling on the phone.

"You think I'm sexy?"

"Shit I know you are sexy."

"I'll see you when you get home."

"Any chance of you wearing that red outfit tomorrow?"

"Nope."

"No, what do you mean no?"

"You ain't getting no nookie again until I find out what else you have lied to me about. You ain't slick Jamie. We have been together ten years. You can't just distract me with a little sweet talk."

I began laughing. Yep, things were back to normal again in my life.

"Bye babe"

"Bye. Be sure to watch Mike's press conference tonight at 8:00."

Breaking things off with Yvonne was easier than I expected. I was expecting a lot of tears and drama, but I guess it was too new in the relationship for any of that anyway. Now I had to head over to my hotel and see if Loretta has made it there yet. I don't know what I can possibly say to her to get rid of that other guy, but I know this, Mike deserves another chance.

I was early getting back to the hotel. It was 6:30 but I could already see Loretta in the lobby having a glass of wine with what's his name. Why did she bring him here? I thought we agreed to meet without the baggage. I walked up and he extended his hand for me to shake. I ignored his hand and gave him the universal head not and sat across from Loretta.

"I thought we agreed to meet alone."

Loretta was put off by my ignoring what's his names hand. She frowned as she began to speak.

"Could you act a little more like an adult and acknowledge Keith's handshake?"

Put off myself I said, "Keith—isn't supposed to be here."

Keith said, "I drove her here."

I told him, "I am sure Loretta can drive and she doesn't need her big strong, insecure ass boy toy to drive her around and baby-sit her."

Keith was pissed off now as he said, "I was just keeping her company until you arrived."

"Whatever Nigga."

"Yeah, whatever back to ya...brother."

Keith was in peak shape, but I have stiff-armed lineman and safeties bigger than him. I was just about ready to pimp slap his ass when Loretta spoke.

"Keith, Jamie will bring me back to the house, or I will phone you. In either case, I will talk to you later."

Loretta kissed him on the cheek and Keith looked at me like a little bitch as he walked off. I turned to Loretta and began to speak.

"So really, what's with Buckwheat?"

"The same thing that is up with your little miss me-so-horny bitch. Jamie I didn't come here to justify my situation with Keith."

"Is it a relationship or is it a situation?"

"Not that it's your business, but it's a situation."

"And when does this situation end?"

"Jamie, my father has long since been dead. Don't let me have to tell you that again."

"Okay. I'm sorry. But listen, you and Mike are the envy of every one that I know, in spite of the fact that you are divorced. You guys are the ideal couple and it hurts us all to see you guys hurting and it hurts us all to see that you guys are not together."

Loretta responded with, "Jamie, Mike and I have problems. We also didn't ask to be the lead couple for the clique of friends that we have. We are no different than anyone else. We have problems and like everyone else, getting past those problems is no easy task."

"He loves you."

"Sometimes love isn't enough, especially if that love is not unconditional. Loving me, means accepting me with all my faults. Loving me, means accepting me and my past. Loving me, means ignoring my past, trusting in the present, and looking toward our future. Loving me means that I come before everything else, including the political career of the great Michael Carter. Loving me is not always easy, but loving me is the task that he swore to undertake the day that he said I do."

"Loretta that is a two way street."

I know Jamie. I didn't say that I didn't play a part in this too. But Michael and I need to take a long hard look together at the part that we both played. He hurt me Jamie. Just when I began to forgive him for that hurt, he throws my past in my face; a past that I was very much aware of and trying to forget."

I said, "That which doesn't kill us, is supposed to make us stronger."

"Yeah well if that is the case, then I am the most powerful bitch on the planet."

We shared a laugh when she said that.

"So tell me Loretta, what is really going on? What happened and what prompted you to take up with this guy Keith?"

Loretta explained to me that Keith has always paid attention to her and was always giving her compliments and he seemed to be the only person these days not judging her. She explained that he was the only man right now that accepted her for her and seemed genuinely interested in her. She explained that she has been in therapy for some time and that she and her therapist thought it would be a good idea for her to test the waters a little. She said that she knew that Keith was only interested in taking her to bed. She admitted that she wanted to take him to bed as well to see what he was like. She said that she regretted doing this because Keith turned out to be a gentle and attentive lover and while she thought that being with a man might confirm her love for Michael, it really only confused her even more.

"So does it look like this relationship with Keith could turn into something serious?"

Loretta gave pause with my question; after some thought she said, "No, I don't think so. But that does not mean that I am ready to forgive Michael either. I understand that he was upset when he found out about me and Don. What happened with me and Don was before Michael's time. At least I didn't mess around while I was married."

She said that in a tone that almost led me to believe that Mike might have taken on a lover and cheated on Loretta. I never did find out why they divorced. Mike was really tight lipped about that one. I wanted to ask but it was not my place. As if she were reading my mind, Loretta asked me the million dollar question.

"Jamie, did Mike ever tell you why we got divorced?"

"Uh...naw. Actually, that is one of the few things that we do not discuss when we are kicking it or playing Playstation-2."

"Do you want to know?"

"Mike doesn't want me to know."

"Do you want to know?"

"Uh...yeah. I guess."

Loretta told me the whole story about how she left Mike for almost getting some pussy. I mean, he got some head, but she had every opportunity to stop him. I felt so bad for him losing his wife and lifestyle all over some pussy that he would never get, or actually ended up getting later anyway. Loretta told me the story and after thinking about it, (and after having a few drinks) I laughed at the expense of my best friend.

"What is so funny?" Loretta asked.

"I'm sorry. Had you stopped them, stayed with Michael and just went off on his ass a little, you would probably still be together and he might not have ever gotten with old girl. But **you let him get his dick sucked,** and then punished him for it. I mean you didn't separate; you didn't even fight with him about it. You went straight to divorcing his ass after a blowjob that he didn't even initiate. It sounds to me like you were willing to leave him at the drop of a hat. He was in a lose/lose situation."

Loretta said, "he would have been in a win/win situation had he not let her give him head."

"Bullshit." I said.

"What?"

"Bullshit. Listen, Loretta. I love you and Mike, and that's my boy. But you figure, he didn't even ask for the blow job. Let you tell it, old girl offered him the head and the sex on a silver platter. No man, and I mean No man would have turned that fine young thing down. It's like Darrin Lowery said in his book, *Handling the Truth,* "Many an affair began with a blowjob?" Shit. You're my boy's woman, and I see you like a big sister, but if you dropped to your knees right now, my friendship with Mike becomes negligible. I'm just keeping it real with you. You looked at it from the wrong angle."

"So what is the right angle Jamie?"

"That man was working hard and giving all his love to you. That man didn't initiate the intimate contact. By your own words, you said that he told her point blank that he loved you and that he did not want to have an affair. He told this broad that he had a woman, was in love, and he didn't want to do it."

Loretta interrupted with, "But he did it!"

"He's a man! I mean give me a break with that shit. Women always talk about how weak we men are, but guess who we are fucking? We are sleeping with other women. We cheat sometimes because it is simply so easy to. We cheat other times because we want variety or because there is opportunity. Other times that we cheat, is because we were offered sex or a blowjob on a silver fucking platter. I know too many men that get all the head and sex they want from their baby's mommas. Then there are the men who are seduced by their ex girlfriends. There are also men that are taken in by aggressive women. That doesn't include gold diggers, women that are into married men, *some* white women, and cliques of women that are out there looking for good men, married, engaged, committed or not. If you ask me, you gave Mike a raw deal."

"What about my cancer?"

"What about it? It wasn't Mike's fault that you got the big C. Had you let him, he would have been with you every waking minute of that ordeal."

"He was too busy being Deputy Mayor."

"That's not fair Lo. You know that's not fair. Given the chance he would have put the very universe on hold if it meant being by your side. He loves you. That is not to say that he doesn't have issues, all men do, but he loves you more than he loves himself."

On and on we talked about Loretta and Mike's issues. A while later Loretta switched gears on me and asked me about Yvonne. I explained to her all the problems that Mia and I had been having with her giving her full attention to the

job rather than to me. I explained to her that I was at 3J's house when I met
Yvonne and how I was just taken in with her beauty. I explained that yes, I was
going to leave Mia for Yvonne; that is, until I gave careful thought to the history
that Mia and I have with one another. I explained to her that the key reason that
I decided to stay with Mia was because one, she came back to me and was actually
working on keeping our relationship and two, when I saw Loretta in that parking
lot, I thought my world had ended at the very thought of losing Mia.
"So you are done with Ms. Thang?"
"Yeah, I'm done."
"How did she take it?"
"There were tears."
"They were fake."
"How can you tell? You weren't even there."
"She hasn't known you long enough to cry over you. Either that or she is one of
those insecure women with emotional and boundary issues."
    Loretta and I talked for another half hour until it was time for Mike's press
conference. We then went up to my room to watch the telecast. I turned on the
TV set and they were just setting the podium up for questions. Mike read a
speech that stated that he had no intention of dropping out of the Mayoral race.
He then took the time to field questions.
A reporter asked, "Is it true that you have been bedding almost fifty women?"
Laughing, Mike said, "I wish. At my age I would need both Viagra and No Dose.
That footage that was shown was of a bachelor party that I threw for my best
friend Jamie Kennedy."
Another reporter asked, "What about the rumor that your best friend is a wom-
anizer or at the very least a gangster?"
"Jamie is no more a gangster or a womanizer than I am white."
"What about the fight that ensued with you and the other man that Ms. Allen
alleges is afraid to testify."
"That man and I did have a physical altercation; the reason for that altercation is
between me and that man. I will not comment any further than that."
"What about the rumors that you cheated on your first wife with your second
wife?"
"Those rumors are unfounded untrue and unimportant; next question."
"Is it true that your ex wife Loretta Carter is seeing another man and you are still
doggedly pursuing her?"
There was a long pause at the podium. Mike took in a deep breath. He smiled the
smile that men give when they are at a loss for words but still have their pride.

"I do not know about the social activities of my ex-wife, hence the title, **ex-wife.**"
Another reporter asked, "Are you still in love with your ex-wife?"
Mike said, "Very much so, I am not however sure that she is still in love with me.
At any rate, this will not interfere with my duties as Mayor if elected."
I looked at Loretta and I could see the hurt in her eyes when Michael stated that
he still loved her and suggested that her feelings might not be reciprocal. Loretta
began crying. I put my arm around her and told her that everything was going to
be okay. The questions continued.
"Your second wife who is now divorced from the Governor, stated that she would
love to have you back. Are you interested?"
*That seemed to throw everyone off including Michael who had a surprised look on his
face.*
"My only interest at this time is running the city and addressing the concerns of
my constituents."
"Did you know that your first wife is in Beaverton Oregon with her new Beau?"
*Loretta dropped her wine glass and gasped for air. The camera focused in on a white
female reporter who was obviously on a cell phone with someone.*
Mike said, "No. I was not aware of that, nor is it my business."
"One final question Mr. Carter. In what city and state is your best friend Jamie
Kennedy in right now?"
There was a silence as the reporters looked to Michael to answer the question.
Then there was a wave of lights as the reporters took hundreds of pictures of the
would-be Mayor.
With a tears welling up in his eyes, Michael said, "Beaverton…Oregon."
There was another wave of flashes as the reporters bathed Michael in photo light.
Mike stepped down from the podium and left the press conference.
I dropped my glass.
"What the fuck just happened?" Loretta asked.
"Someone set us up nasty."
"Did you see the hurt in Michael's eyes?"
"Yeah, but he couldn't possibly think…"
"He does."
"Are you sure?"
"I know my husband."
Just then, both of our cell phones began ringing off the hook.
"There was a knock at the door. I looked out the peep-hole, there were at least
four reporters outside my room.
Loretta was *in my room.*

This was not looking good.

"Looks like you are going to have to spend the night in here."

Loretta said, "Do you know how bad this looks?"

"Leaving will only give them confirmation."

"Who would do this to us?"

"Either your guy Keith, or my girl Yvonne."

Loretta said, "Hell hath no fury like a woman scorned. It had to be that tramp ass bitch Yvonne."

I said, "Shit."

Our cell phones were flooded with messages, and still ringing. Loretta's caller ID said MICHAEL'S CELL my caller ID said, MIA'S CELL.

It was a tight vice.

CHAPTER 7

▼

PICKING UP THE PIECES

MICHAEL

I could hardly breathe at the prospect of my best friend bedding my wife. My head was reeling and my chest was tight as if I was going to have a heart attack. Whom Loretta was with was not my business, but my best friend? Jamie was the type to send a woman a dozen roses. In fact, I remember Jamie commenting when we were younger how, "If you send a woman 100 roses, she will remember you the rest of her life." How far fetched could it be? After all, Loretta slept with Don, what was to stop her from sleeping with Jamie as well; especially of she wanted to hurt me. I just can't see Jamie doing it though. I mean, we're boys. Boys don't do that to one another. It's like a cardinal sin among guys that are close to do such a thing. I mean, don't get me wrong, we have passed a woman or two around in our time, but they were loose women to begin with. We have never been through something where one of us slept with the other's woman. I mean, damn!

I heard the familiar voice of a woman pushing through the crowd of my supporters trying to get to me. She had two other women in tow.
"Let me through, I need to talk to Michael, goddammit let me through!"
It was Mia, and two of her girlfriends from her wedding party.
"Let her through, it's cool."

I was expecting her to give me a hug and tell me that we were both going to get through the infidelity of our partners. Apparently Mia had a little more faith in her spouse than I did in mine.

"I know that you don't believe that shit, right?" Mia said.

Wanda said, "Why not? I believe it."

Sonja, Mia and I looked at Wanda like she was just—stupid.

"I don't know what I believe Mia."

"Jamie is your **best friend**."

"I know, but...well, there was the thing with Don and..."

"That was different. Don is a low life motherfucker that will never grow up. He will fuck anything that moves and what happened between Loretta and Don was what happened between her and her *ex boyfriend*. That is totally different from what you think is happening now. Besides, we know for a fact that Jamie is up there working on 3J's contract. After all, you talked with the Oregon office and Jamie is supposed to make the announcement on ESPN this weekend. Jamie has been up there better than a week. You mean to tell me that you think Loretta just decided out of the blue to fly up there and rendezvous with Jamie?"

I thought about it and said, "So you don't think anything is going on?"

"Knowing my husband, something's up, but it's not that!"

Just then a member of my staff walked up and said something that stunned the hell out of me and Mia.

The staff member said, "Rumor has it that the local press in Beaverton is outside of Jamie's room. They haven't confirmed it yet, but they think that your ex-wife is in the room with him."

There was a long silence as Mia and I looked at one another.

Mia finally spoke, Sonja you are in charge of the magazine. Wanda, don't give Sonja any shit while I'm gone. [to Michael] I'll drive us to the airport."

I said, "I will have my limo drop us off that way we don't have to pay for parking."

We caught the first thing smoking out of Midway Airport. Both of us were frantically calling Loretta and Jamie to get some type of understanding as to what the fuck is going on.

JAMIE (On the phone with Mia)

"Yeah...Yeah she is in my room but, Mia look...what I am trying to tell you is...goddammit if you let me get one word in edgewise...No I didn't lie to you...I am trying to fucking tell you but you won't listen! Look, if you love me babe you have got to shut the fuck up for a minute." *That is how my conversation was going. Loretta's was a bit different and she was more in control.*

"Yes I am in Jamie's room. No, I did not, would not and have never thought of messing around with your best friend. I am offended **once again** by your words....Well, I guess you are going to have to trust me...I am sure that is hard for you, but let me remind you of something, we are no longer married...I am explaining things to you only because I still love you...I don't have to tell you anything the only reason that I am telling you now is to help clear up how this looks. What's really going on? What is really going on is that the truth of the matter is that I came up here with someone else...Who—is not important. Jamie saw me with this other person and asked me could he and I talk. We talked in the lobby of his hotel and came upstairs to his room to watch your speech...I don't know where the reporter got her info from. I know that she had to be on the phone with someone, I suspect that the someone was either the person that I was up here with or the person that Jamie was up here with...Don't play dumb with me Michael Lawrence Carter. Jamie was up here with another woman and there is no way that he didn't tell you that...So he didn't tell you who and you automatically assumed that it was me?"

This is how our conversations went for the next hour. I explained to Mia that Loretta was in fact there with someone else. I of course didn't tell her that I was there with Yvonne. I explained to her that Loretta was there with another man and because they were such good friends of ours, I felt compelled to speak to her about her seeing someone else. I explained to her that when I realized the time, I told her that we could watch the speech from my hotel room.

Mia was mad. I could tell, but she eventually came to the conclusion that we were set up either by Loretta's new beau, or Mike's opponent. I explained to Mia, that if Mike's opponent could misconstrue my bachelor party, it only made sense that she would set us up and make Mike look crazy at his own press conference. Mia was *not pleased* at the fact that Loretta had to spend the night in my room. I explained to her that the press had no proof that she was in my room, but if she left out now, it would look worse for Mike and we would have a hard time living this down. As a sports agent, I also didn't need any more negative press. Mia was not the only one calling me on my cell, so were my clients.

Mia told me that she and Mike were on there way to see us and they would be in my room in a few hours. It was only 8:30 PM. So it was looking like we would all be spending the night in my room. After I hung up the phone with Mia, a few minutes later, Loretta hung up with Mike. We both looked at each other with a worn look that said that we both knew no matter what transpired this night; it was not going to be an easy night for us or our relationships.

"So what do we tell them?" I asked.

Loretta said, "We tell them the truth."

"*All of the truth?*" I asked.

"Jamie I will not expose your relationship with Ms. Thang. But I have to tell you as a woman, if you do not tell Mia and she finds out later, it will be much worse for your relationship."

"I can't…I won't tell Mia about Yvonne unless I am cornered about it."

Loretta said, "Typical Male Mentality."

I know that Loretta meant well by telling me to tell Mia, but no matter what rationale women give you for telling the truth, they know damn well there is nothing that we can say to them that will cushion the blow for our cheating on them. I thought *briefly* about telling Mia the truth, and then I decided, "Oh hell no. I won't."

HOURS LATER…

Mia and Mike arrived at 12:30 to Oregon's airport. At 1:30 AM, there was a knock at my door. I looked through the peephole and there was my best friend and my wife, neither with a look of joy on their faces and they both had reporters in tow. I opened the door just wide enough to let them both in. My eyes met with Mike's, which looked bloodshot and worn. His eyes looked as if he hadn't slept, but he also had an inviting look to his eyes that told me he did not suspect me of sleeping with his ex-wife. His eyes also told the story that he was ashamed of the fact that I had seen his wife with another man.

Reporters were leaning in and trying to force their cameras in the room to take random pics, hoping to get a shot of Loretta. I pushed them out of the small opening and all they got were pictures of the palm of my hand.

Mia sat on the bed.

Mike grabbed one of the chairs in the room and sat across from Loretta.

I took a seat on the bed next to my wife.

We each sat there in silence for some time.

Mike broke the silence first. He took the hands of his ex wife and said, "I'm sorry."

She looked deep into his eyes and said, "So am I."

Mike said, "Where do you want to go from here?"

Loretta said, "I don't care, as long as it is with you."

Mike said, "So you mean?…"

Loretta said, "I'm not promising anything, but I am saying...Let's try."

Mike began weeping and hugged and held on to his wife for dear life. He had been to hell and back recently, but none of that mattered. What mattered was the fact hat he was given a second chance—at love.

I placed my hand in Mia's, but felt some resistance from her. She didn't push my hand away, but she did not freely accept my invitation either. I was scared that perhaps she knew more than she was letting on. *But how could she?*

We watched our friends embrace as if they were newly in love again. We both looked at each other knowing that what we were seeing was true love and hope. If Michael and Loretta can find one another again, then surely there is no reason for Mia and I to lose our relationship to begin with.

Mike looked at me and said, "So dawg, how are we going to get out of this mess?"

I said, "I have a plan."

Mia looked at me in an odd way and said, "Liars generally do."

I dismissed her comment like it meant nothing; the truth of the matter was it meant everything. She had no evidence of my messing around, but I get the feeling that her women's intuition was beginning to kick in. I hate women's intuition. That shit is like spider sense.

SWEET HOME CHICAGO

We waited twenty minutes and I had Loretta and Mia change clothes. I then ran out of my room at top speed and ran down the hotel stairwell. Mike was on my ass as if he were giving chase. There were only four local reporters in the hall. Three of them gave chase to me and Mike as we tore down the stairwell. The one reporter that waited to see if Loretta was there was surprised as Mia, (who had a scarf on her head) briskly walked out of the room and she also went down the stairwell. The reporter followed her asking her questions the entire way. Mia kept saying that she had no comment. The reporters that followed Me and Mike were surprised as we hugged once we got to the bottom of the stairs. The reporter following Mia was surprised when she got to the bottom of the stairs and took off her scarf.

Loretta went down on the elevator unnoticed, where she got into the limousine that was waiting in the front. Mike told the press, "There is no story here." Then without warning, the three of us walked off after I checked out of the Holiday Inn. Mike and Loretta got in the limousine and took off. I had to take my Dodge back to the rental house so Mia and I got in the rental and told Mike and Loretta that we would see them either on the plane or back in Chicago.

MIKE AND LORETTA

Mike asked Loretta, "Do you need to pick anything up from this guy's house?"
Loretta said, "I do still have a few things there that I need to pick up."
Loretta gave the driver directions to get back to Keith's time share.
As the limo pulled up to the big beautiful house, there was a dejected look on Mike's face. Loretta took Mike's hand and gave it a squeeze.
Mike said, "Do you need me to go in with you?"
Loretta thought about it and said, "No."
Mike said, "Okay then…I guess I will wait here."
Loretta said, "I might be a while."
"But not too long…right?"
"Not too long baby, I promise."
With that, Loretta walked up the long walkway, and was met at the door by Keith whom had a puzzled look on his face.

LORETTA AND KEITH

"I thought you were going to call me to pick you up?" Keith said.
"I was, but then there was some drama at the hotel."
"I see." Keith said. "What's with the limo?"
"My husband is in the limo."
"Ex-husband, and what do you mean he is in the limo?"
"There were reporters at the hotel and…"
"Yeah, I know about the press conference and all the drama, why is Mike up here?"
"Because he loves me and he wants me back."
"And do you want him back?"
"I do."
"You do? What about us?"
"There is no us Keith. I had a wonderful time, but that is the extent of our situation."
"Situation? Wait a minute, I have been spending all this money on you, kicking it with you and flew you out here just for you to go back with your husband?"
"Keith, I didn't mean for things to happen *this way,* but I never said that we were going to be in a relationship or anything."
"So you used me?"
"I didn't use you, I simply thought that we were each satisfying one another's mutual needs."

"So are we going to get together again later? You know, after we get home?"

"No Keith."

"So you fucked me and are now leaving me."

"I wish that you wouldn't make it sound like that."

"How else is it supposed to sound Loretta?"

"Keith I really don't see what the big deal is."

"What do you mean you don't see what the big deal is? There is nothing that Mike can give you that I can't. I am a few years younger, better looking and better in bed."

"You don't know that." Loretta said.

"The hell I don't. What the hell happened that you are so high on your ex-husband all of a sudden?"

"I can't explain it. All I can say is that I love him and what we did was a mistake."

"A mistake? So you were having problems in your marriage, you then decided to come down here with me where I have been the perfect gentleman, *you* initiate sex with me, and now you are walking out of my life."

"Okay, maybe it does sound bad, but I don't see what the big deal is, I mean, cut the crap, you brought me down here with every intention of having sex with me. You might have been a gentleman, but that was with the hopes that I would give you some. Well Keith dear, you got some. It was great, I enjoyed these past few days, but the bottom line is, I am going back to my husband."

Keith said, "But that motherfucker has issues!"

Loretta said, "Who doesn't these days? Mike and I are going to need to go to counseling, of that I had no doubt. God knows that I have quite a bit to talk about in therapy as well. But the bottom line is it's over between you and me."

Loretta began packing.

"That's fucked up." Keith said.

Loretta kept packing her belongings.

"So no pussy even when I get back to Chicago?"

Loretta kept packing and shot Keith a cold glare.

"Well fuck you then. Fuck you and him."

Loretta stopped packing for a second, and then thought better of it. She could hear the words of her therapist again saying, *seeing men for what they are, rather than what you want them to be*. After thinking about what she learned in therapy, she kept packing.

"That's why I dropped a dime on your boyfriend."

That got Loretta's attention. Keith then walked out of the room.

"What the fuck did you say?" Loretta said.

"I'm the one that called the reporter and told her that you were here with Jamie."
"Why would you do something like that?"
"I did it to solidify what *I thought we had,* and to make that punk ass guy Jamie look bad."
Loretta said, "You stupid motherfucker."
Keith said, "What?"
Loretta said, "Motherfucker you heard me. You are a stupid motherfucker. Why would you ruin people's lives like that?"
"That's nothing. Wait until I find out who Jamie's wife is and tell him about that broad Yvonne."
"You do that, Jamie is going to bust a cap in your ass."
"We will see."
"Yeah, okay."
Loretta finished her packing and walked toward the door. She just knew that it was Yvonne that had talked to the reporter and not Keith. She wanted to tell Jamie, but she had enough on her mind right now. Telling Jamie would have to wait until later. Keith blocked the door.
"Loretta, I'm sorry. Can we talk about this?"
"No Keith."
"Loretta, can I call you some time?"
"No Keith."
"But we work together."
"Not anymore. I am going to tender my resignation once I touch down in Chicago."
"What are you going to do for a career?"
"I'm going to be the first lady of Calumet City."
"Not if I begin singing like a Canary to the press."
"Keith, you do what you feel you have to do, but let me tell you something. I have powerful friends in powerful places, and I know niggas in these streets. If you fuck with me, my husband, or my friends, I swear I will bury you and spit on your grave afterward."
Keith thought about saying something witty, but decided at this time the best thing for him to do would be to simply step aside and try to hook up with Loretta later, when she wasn't so mad. Her leaving the agency also meant a promotion for him.
Loretta tried to walk past him and Keith took her gently by the hand.
He said, "Loretta, what would you say if I told you that I loved you?"
Loretta responded, "Goodbye."

She got in the long black limo and took off for the airport with her husband.
"Is everything okay?" Mike asked.
"It is now."

MIA AND JAMIE

I dropped the rental off at the dealership and dropped the keys off in the lockbox.
I then called a cab to take Mia and I to the airport. Mia was unusually quiet so I
asked her what was going on.
"You are awfully quiet over there."
"I am just wondering what else you might have lied to me about."
[sighing] "Why does there have to be something else?"
"Why didn't you tell me that you saw Loretta here with another man?"
"I had other things on my mind."
"Other things? You mean to tell me that after seeing your best friend's woman
with another man that was not the first and foremost thing in your mind? What
had you so distracted that you didn't mention that to me when you talked to me
earlier? I mean for you to have Loretta in your room *during the press conference,*
that means that you knew you were meeting with Loretta *while you were on the
phone with me,* yet you didn't mention it at all, why?"

Mia had a damn good point. I didn't think that any woman would be this
analytical. Hell, I hadn't even thought about how things looked to Mia. I
thought again about coming clean, and then totally dismissed that idea.
"Mia, things are just starting to go right between us, can we please not have an
argument today? I love you, that should be all that counts."
"I love you too Jamie, but honesty and integrity are also important components
in a relationship."
The cab pulled up, we got in, and headed home.

MIA

I was still upset with having caught Jamie in quite a few lies lately, but he was
right, things had been good between us so I figured there was no need to press.
We went home went to bed and turned the pagers and cell phones off for a few
days. Mike and Loretta I imagine, did the same. I let Sonja and Wanda handle
things at the magazine, and Jamie didn't leave my side again until Sunday, when
he made the announcement to the world that 3J had signed a seven year, forty
million dollar deal with Oregon. He made the announcement in Orgeon. He
asked me to go with him, but I had my full share of the state of Oregon. It was
where a good friend of mine's marriage almost ended and where I believe *some-*

thing happened with my husband that he is not telling me about. I have that gut feeling that a woman has when her man has been unfaithful. A woman knows, a woman always knows, but I can't quite put my finger on with whom or exactly what happened. For a brief moment *I did suspect he and Loretta of messing around.* After careful thought and having lunch with Loretta today, I know that it wasn't her.

Loretta and I had lunch together and talked about all that happened the previous week. She confessed to me that the man she was in Beaverton with was a colleague, a colleague that was sweating her about giving him another chance. She told me how built he was and what a tender lover he was. She also told me what an asshole he turned out to be.

"Loretta, do you think Jamie was up there fooling around with another woman?"

"Mia why would you ask me that?"

"I don't know. I have just caught him up in so many lies recently. I mean, I haven't caught him in anything serious. He lied about how many women were in his bachelor party and he has had two or three other inconsistencies in stories that he has told."

Loretta said, "Two or three lies don't add up into an affair though girl."

"I guess you are right. Maybe I am just flipping out."

We continued with our lunch and then went shopping.

The election campaign was going crazy. Things were about even between Michael and Leslie Allen. The white, red-haired, freckle faced Harvard Grad was leading Michael in the popularity poll 51% to 49%. The actual election was in nine days. The two opponents took shots at each other the entire way and the fact that Michael and Loretta were back together seemed to solidify things. Loretta and I were walking into the Nordstrom mall downtown when we saw a breaking story on Leslie Allen.

This just in, Carl Allen, husband of Calumet City Mayoral candidate, Leslie Allen, was arrested today on charges that he assaulted his mistress. The woman who was identified as Wanda Williams, said that she and the potential mayor's husband were meeting for their usual rendezvous, when Carl allegedly threatened to kill her if she ever slept around or cheated on him. Reportedly he slapped Ms. Williams around, prompting her to flee the room and flag down a police officer.

"Wanda Williams!" I said.

"Loretta asked, "Mia girl, what's wrong?"

"We gotta go!" Mia said.

JAMIE

I hadn't seen Yvonne since I left her home in Oregon almost a week earlier. I made the announcement to the world that 3J was playing for Oregon and I had 3J and Yvonne on either side of me at the press conference. After talking about what a painstaking ordeal the negations were, I explained to the world that Chicago would be given two high draft picks, and the Oregon team would be getting the running game that they have desperately been in need of for past few years. 3J then took the podium and began fielding questions from reporters. I took a step back so he could get to the podium and I could feel Yvonne looking at me. I couldn't look in her direction out of fear and the possibility that Mia might be watching me on TV and may see right through me. I knew that there was a chance that she might be watching. If she were, there is a good bet that rather than watch 3J's speech, she would be looking solely at me. I had to play things off at least until I was off camera.

After 3J finished with his questions, he gave the press a tour of his house. I told him that I had a call to make and headed for the Den. The truth of the matter was that I needed to get my head together. I walked in the Den and in there was three bookshelves stocked with books, a large oak desk, and the fireplace where earlier that week Yvonne and I had made love. The room looked totally different from the last time that I was here, but the sin was still ever so present.

"Why haven't you called me?" Yvonne's voice interrupted.

She startled me. I was hoping to elude her, but I guess this conversation could not be avoided.

"And what would I have to say to you?"

"After all the drama that you stirred up here, I thought you would have at least said goodbye or wanted to talk to me about how you wanted to play things."

"What do you mean play things?"

"I mean…I just thought that you might want us to get our stories straight so that Mia didn't find out about what happened up here."

"I thought that was the whole purpose of you telling that reporter that Mike was up here cheating on his wife."

"What?"

"Wasn't that your motive for dropping a dime on Loretta, to get back at me somehow?"

"Me? Wait a minute, you think that it was me that told the press? How dare you!"

I was thinking to myself…oh shit, it must have been Keith.

"It...It wasn't you?"

"Hell no it wasn't me! What would I have to gain by telling the press?"

"I thought it was some sort of ploy to get at me or to get me back."

"You arrogant son of a bitch! First of all I am not a desperate women that needs to chase your trifling ass. Secondly, if I wanted to get back at you I could just tell your wife."

"Yvonne, I'm sorry. I had no idea, you have to admit that it looked like it could have easily been you or Keith that told the press."

"Yeah, and I would have thought that you would have thought of Keith first rather than point the finger at me. What is stopping him from telling your wife?"

"I don't know."

"So what then is stopping me from telling your wife."

"We have been through this, no matter what happens, if you or Keith opens your mouth, that is not going to change things between me and Mia."

"Even if I tell her that I am pregnant and carrying your child?"

"What?"

TAKING ONE FOR THE HOME TEAM
MIA/LORETTA/SONJA/WANDA

Loretta and I got to the police station in Calumet City and we arrived at the same time that Sonja arrived.

"You saw the story too?" I asked Sonja.

"Yeah, I figured I would come down and see what was really going on." She said. Coming out of the station with a rape counselor was Wanda. Wanda said to the counselor, "My friends are here, I will be fine, thank you."

I asked Wanda what happened, and why was she messing around with Ms. Allen's husband to begin with.

"Mia, don't you know that you should never ask a rape or assault victim that question? You should never ask a question like that. It places the blame on the victim!"

"You are right, Wanda girl, I am sorry."

Wanda began laughing.

"What is so funny?" I said

"The look on your face when you thought that I was serious."

"You aren't serious?"

"Girl no, I just decided to take one for the team."

"Take one for the team? Wanda what the hell are you talking about?"

"I made the story up about Carl assaulting me."

Sonja said, "So you didn't have an affair with him?"

Wanda said, "I didn't say that. *I did fuck him.* In fact, I fucked him quite a few times. But I made up the story about the assault."

I asked, "Why would you do something like that?"

"To make a scandal about old girl the way she made one about your man. And to get the story into the press."

Sonja said, "You can't just go around lying about the sexual misconduct of men. When women do that, they take credibility away from real victims."

Wanda said, "It worked for that girl in Colorado. Besides, I plan on dropping the charges against Carl *after he has tried to explain all this to his wife, Or after he has offered me a nice settlement.*"

Loretta laughed.

Sonja said, "I'm confused about something, you said that you slept with him a few times. You only needed to sleep with him once to get the story in the press."

"I didn't say that he was bad in bed, did I? I guess with some guys, once you go white you discover that it's right."

I said, "So I guess you aren't lesbian anymore."

Wanda said, "Nah…I think I am into white guys now."

Loretta said, "You need therapy."

Sonja said, "She needs Jesus."

I said, "She definitely needs some prayer."

Wanda said, "**I need a cheeseburger. Shit, I'm hungry.**"

MRS. ALLEN

Mrs. Allen was coming out of the gym when she was accosted by a number of reporters. She didn't even know that the story had broken. She tried to get to her Lexus Truck but was hit with a barrage of questions.

"Mrs. Allen do you have a comment on your husband's affair?"

"How does your husband's affair compare in contrast to Michael Carter's dogged pursuit of his wife?"

How doe it feel to know that your husband cheated on you with an African American Woman?

She resonded, *"An African American Woman?"*

Another reporter asked, "Is your husband leaving you for his black mistress, and if so, will this affect your running for office?"

Mrs. Allen's head was reeling in confusion. She ran back into the gym to get away from the reporters. Female reporters followed her into the women's locker room where they filmed her breaking out in tears.

We didn't tell Michael the truth about the allegation until after the election…which he won of course.

Leslie Allen dropped out of the race.

I saw her once leaving my therapist's office.

CHAPTER 8

▼

TWO YEARS LATER

JAMIE

Yvonne had my baby. I never told Mia. Yvonne and I had a private court hearing where we agreed on support, visitation and we each agreed to place a gag order on the other as well as never talk negatively about one another in the media. We eventually told 3J about us and he was not pleased at all. The only reason I am still his agent is because we have a contract. We didn't tell 3J until my son Jerry, was a year and a half. Prior to that, 3J was lead to believe that the father was one of Yvonne's ex boyfriends. I began living a *double life* as I traveled back and forth to Oregon *playing daddy* to my son Jerry, whom I had allowed to keep Yvonne's last name.

The scariest part about all this is the lies that I have to keep telling to Mia in order to keep my secret safe. Lying is the one thing that Mia hates more than anything else, and I lie to her almost every other week when I make some excuse to go to Oregon. If I am not lying to her directly, then I am living a lie each day that I don't tell her. The problem is, lying has become so easy, that I have dug myself in such a deep hole that I see no light at the end of the tunnel. I have snuck off for birthdays, illnesses, vacations and special trips to be with my son. How do I tell Mia that I now have a son that is two years old?

Yvonne has a new boyfriend now that is thinking about adopting my son Jerry. His name is Travis and he is a really great guy. But I love my son, and I have a hard time simply letting go and letting another man handle what is supposed to be my responsibility. The thing is, I told Mia that I never wanted children. I have known for years that Mia has wanted quite a few. We have been together ten years and whenever the topic has come up in the past, I would tell her that having kids was out of the question. Now, how do I tell her that I have had a child with another woman? I had the paternity test done when Jerry was born. He is definitely my kid. I went off on Yvonne for not being on the pill and she reminded me that there were two of us making love that night two years ago in Beaverton. That first time that we made love, we hit it about five times that night and once that next day. I shot my load each time. I did so thinking that she was on the pill. Yvonne told me later that she doesn't believe in contraception and whatever happens, happens. I could not believe this shit.

I would love to say that Yvonne and I have never slept together again after that night in Beaverton. The truth of the matter is, somewhere along the way of my coming to Oregon to visit, we have been back in one another's embrace quite a few times. The first time this happened was when I was supposed to pick Jerry up and I got to Yvonne's house to find out that 3J had picked up his nephew and took him to Texas. When Yvonne answered the door, she was in nothing but a sheer black teddy. I was mad that my son wasn't there. That anger later turned into swears of passion as I screamed, "I'm cumming!" This time however, I was wearing a condom.

It made sense for me to have to go to Beaverton often because my client was there. It was becoming more and more difficult for Mia to buy this when she saw many times at events that 3J and I seldom spoke to one another. In spite of all the money that I brought 3J's way, he was furious at the fact that I fucked his sister, had a baby out of wedlock, and never even offered to marry his sister. 3J even offered when he found out, to help me pay for a divorce from Mia. I explained to him that I loved my wife, and I planned to stay with her. From that point forward, 3J and I kind of just fell off.

Yvonne and Jerry stayed at the co-op that Don helped me to get in Park Forest. When they were in Chicago, they lived there. I loved this because Mia had never been to Park Forest and never had a reason to go to Park Forest. I could easily sneak off and be with my son without fear of being caught. Park Forest had its own mall, its own theatre, and everything that my son might want to do, we could do in peace. They also stayed with 3J in the mansion from time to time, but of course I was no longer welcome there.

Everyone knew about my son but Mia. I put her in the same position that Mike was in when he knew nothing about Loretta and Don. Because of this, I decided to give Mike a call and talk to him about my son, his godson and ask him what should I do.

"Dude, I think it's crazy that you let all this time go by without telling her. In either case, she is going to snap. You might as well tell her now, get it all over with, and spend the rest of the year (it's January now) trying to make it up to her." Mike said.

"Bruh, I am scared as hell of telling Mia about Jerry. I mean she hates being lied to. If I tell her there is a good chance that she may never speak to me again."

"I don't think she will take it that far. You will be in the doghouse. You will just have to get used to it and wait until she is ready to take you back. She may want time apart after not telling her that you had a child with another woman."

"But dawg, that's exactly what I am trying to avoid."

"There is no avoiding it Jamie. Having the kid is a problem, how the kid got here is another problem, *lying to your woman for the last two years is even worse.* You need to just man the fuck up and deal with it."

"There is another option."

"What option is that Jay?"

I told Mike about Travis and what an upstanding guy he was. He had been bugging about adopting Jerry since he was born. He had no idea that I was periodically tapping that ass on Yvonne. I told Mike that if Travis adopted Jerry, I could slowly transition out of my son's life.

Mike said, "You could do that, but then the child is wondering what happened that drove daddy away. If you were going to do that, you should have done that when he was smaller. At this point, he knows that he has a daddy and all of a sudden he doesn't anymore. The boy may blame himself."

"He might also just forget about me as well."

"Maybe, then again, maybe not."

I had a lot to think about. I was scared as hell at the possibility of being left alone. Mia and I were doing great since our reconciliation. We went to Greece shortly after Mike won his election, we went to the Cayman Islands last year, Las Vegas and a host of other places. Her magazine, Black Woman Chicago was turning into a dynamo. Wanda was the fashion editor and making a name for herself in the entertainment industry, and Sonja was noted to be one of the top female executives in Chicago. Between the three of those sisters, there was nothing that could stop them. Mia had a vision and she ran with it, and her girls had her back in every capacity. Wanda and Sonja even learned to get along with one another better.

The New Year brought new vision, new ideas and for Mia, new love. I was miserable at the thought that sometime soon I was going to have to break my woman's heart with my deceit. There was no easy way to tell Mia that I had a baby with another woman. So I decided that I was not going to tell her. The next time that I go to Oregon, I am going to sit down and have a long talk with Travis and Yvonne and let them know that I have decided to let Travis adopt Jerry. I then plan to transition out of the boy's life.

The night that I made up my mind to let Jerry be adopted by Travis, Mia came home in a great mood and was scaring me with baby talk.

"Jamie, we have been together for eleven years now. We have been married for two and a half years. I love you. You have been doing well as a sports agent, and I have been doing great at the magazine. Baby, isn't it time that we began talking about adding an addition to the family?"

Her timing was incredible. Or mine was just lousy. I never really wanted kids, but I have to admit that we are in a good position to have children. Mia had been trying to get me to bend on this issue for years. After the bullshit that I pulled with Yvonne, having a child with Mia is probably the least that I can do. I know that is no reason to decide on creating another life, just because I feel guilty about my indiscretion, but the way that I see it, one thing might help to cancel out the other.

"Yeah baby, I think it's time that we had a shortie."

"Really Jamie?"

I know that she was surprised as hell that I had finally given in.

I told her, "I love you. I want to spend the rest of my life with you and I would love it if our love could live on through a baby. [smiling] So when do you wanna begin trying?"

"Later this week!" She kissed me and raced up stairs.

I was a little confused. I yelled up to the stairs, "Hey! I was thinking that we would start now!"

Mia yelled downstairs, "You just want some ass, I got plans to make and some errands to run."

I said, "Just want some ass? Isn't that how you make a baby?"

She yelled, "Yeah smart ass, but that's not how we are going to make a baby." She changed clothes and was coming back downstairs so we wouldn't have to yell so loud.

"We [kissing me] are going to make things special. I want our baby to be conceived on any number of planned nights of passion [still kissing me all over]. I want the house to be nice, the music to be nice, and the moment, to be the bomb. I want you cumming so hard that dammit you high five me and say that you know, that was the seed that made our child. This is a special time for us Jamie. I want you to block out Saturday, and Sunday and Monday for just me and nothing else. In the meanwhile, I am running to the mall to meet Sonja and Wanda."

Still confused, I said, "Baby, how do you go from talking to me about creating a life, and teasing me with that perfect ass of yours, to going shopping with your girls at the mall?"

"I just told you. I got plans, and who better to help me with those plans then my girls?"

"Are they going to help you in the bedroom too?"

"You got jokes. Don't make me cut your ass."

"Okay, Okay [kissing her] have fun. I will see you later."

Mia went to the Mall and met her girls. I got on the phone and told Yvonne that I needed her and Travis to come to Chicago if possible so we could talk about the adoption. I was due to visit Oregon this weekend, but I have to make sure that Mia takes priority first. If she wants Saturday through Monday, she gets Saturday through Monday.

Yvonne and Travis said that they would meet me Wednesday at Lawry's downtown. I was nervous at the prospect of giving up my son, but at least this way, I could do things right with Mia. Besides, Jerry will be taken care of the rest of his life with 3J as his uncle. Yvonne is now working as a sports agent/manager herself, so she is making a nice piece of change. Jerry will grow up with two loving parents and doing things my way means that no one will be hurt.

THAT WEDNESDAY

I met with Yvonne and Travis at Lawry's and we each had a grand meal as we talked about 3J, Jerry, Yvonne and Travis' wedding plans, and life in pro sports. After we dismissed with all the preliminary talk, Travis figured that it was time for us to get down to business.

"So, Jamie, I hate to rush into this, I mean there is no easy way to do this. So what ideas did you have about my adopting Jerry?"

"Well Travis, I am all for the adoption and I think that Jerry will be in good hands with you and Yvonne. I am ready to sign the papers whenever you say so."

Yvonne said, "Why did you change your position all of a sudden?"

"I was never closed to the idea to begin with." I said.

Yvonne said, "No you weren't *but* you seem sure of yourself all of a sudden. I want to know what brought you to your decision."

I said, "What difference does it make?"

"It makes a difference." Yvonne said.

"Well, I think we can both agree that we did not plan on having Jerry, and I have my own life to lead and I am sure that you have your own life to lead, so I am trying to make this decision based on what I think is in the best interest of our child."

Yvonne sat silently and thought about whether or not my answer was sufficient.

Travis said, "I'm glad that you decided to let me adopt your son, Jamie. I love him as if he were my own and I am going to try and give him all the love and support that he can stand. Of course visitation and things like that will never be interfered with, it's just that I can also officially call him son as well."

"Well, that is something else that I wanted to talk to you two about." I said. It was time for the other show to drop. "I think that I am going to stop coming around Jerry and slowly begin transitioning myself out of his life. You all aren't hurting for any money, but I will still contribute whenever you need me to. In the meanwhile, I think that it is best that I simply remove myself from the picture."

There was silence at the table.

Travis said, "Wow…Man, Jamie. When I said that I wanted to adopt your shortie, I wasn't trying to imply that you not be a part of his life or anything."

"I know Travis, this would be my decision. Your wanting to adopt him has no bearing on that decision. Your wanting to adopt him is a godsend, because I know that you are a good brother that will in fact take good care of my kid."

I could tell that Yvonne was pissed. Breaking things off with my son also meant breaking things off with her entirely.

"Did 3J put you up to this?"

"No."

"Then why?"

"I have had to make some difficult decisions in my life, and this is one of them."

"What about the co-op in Park Forest?"

"I plan to sell it."

"What about child support?"

"I will still continue to pay it."

"College?"

"I already have an account set up in his name, it will be provided for."

"So in other words, you want out of our lives?"

I let out a sigh. "In so many words—yes, I guess so."

Travis was sitting in shock. Yvonne was shocked and mad. I don't know how I felt. It was hard to describe. I was acting like all this was cool and as if it wouldn't bother me one bit. The truth of the matter was it was tearing me up on the inside. I was in effect, giving up a part of me.

"You guys okay with this?" I said

"Sure...why wouldn't we be?" Yvonne snapped.

There was a short silence before Travis spoke.

"Well...okay then...Jamie, I will send you the adoption papers to be signed Friday. They will come by messenger, or my assistant. And then, I guess everything will be final. I just have one final question."

"Shoot." I said.

"What happens if."

"What?"

"What happens if. The question that I am asking is what happens if you change your mind later. Or what happens if your son is drafted into the NFL or the NBA. What if he discovers the cure for Cancer? Should we look for you to come into the fray looking for credit? Do we have to worry about you challenging the adoption? Do we have to worry about you going to the press? The reason that I say all this is the decision that you are making has life long consequences."

Wow. Travis was a smart brother and insightful as hell. None of that had come to mind. I was blown away by his questions. If I played pro ball, there was a chance that Jerry might play pro ball. I would want to be there for that. I would want to be able to help him make these decisions. I would also wasn't to be there to cheer him on. I had not thought this through. I couldn't tell them that. So I lied—again.

"I have taken all this into consideration, and I have decided to admire Jerry from afar."

Yvonne, who was still pissed, was on 10. She looked to Travis and said, "Let's Go."

She then looked at me scornfully and asked, "Are you going to at least say good-bye?"

I thought about my response and decided against it. I said, "No, sorry Yvonne."

She said, "Don't be sorry to me. Be sorry for yourself and your son. Just like being a father means more than being there, for the trifling niggas that call themselves daddy in the hood, being a father is more than the financial part and signing a support check. You ain't shit. I expected more from you Jamie. I will respect your decision, but I damn sure don't like it. When Jerry asks me what happened to his daddy, I am going to tell him that his daddy died when he was a little more than two."

Yvonne walked out of the restaurant.

Travis asked me, "Did your wife put you up to this decision?"

"Travis, my wife doesn't even know."

"I see. That's why. Are you trying to start fresh?"

"Yeah."

"I feel you. I will send over the papers, but at anytime you change your mind…just holler at me, we will work things out."

"Thanks Travis."

"No problem, Peace."

MIA/WANDA/SONJA

I met my girls at the mall and we made a B-line straight for Lovers lane. I planned on breaking Jamie off a little something proper every day this weekend. All I needed was three outfits, but instead, I bought about seven. Wanda and Sonja helped me to pick out all my outfits and we talked the usual trash that we do when we get together.

Wanda said, "What about this outfit?" It was a black bustier and garter made out of leather. It also came with optional crop or whip.

"Nah, I can see the leather, but not the dominatrix stuff. Besides I am trying to make a baby, not bring slavery back."

Sonja held up a plaid skirt, bobby socks and a white blouse. She said, "What about this Catholic School uniform?"

I said, "No, that is just too perverted."

Sonja said, "I don't know, I think it's kind of cute."

Wanda said, "Look at the closet freak. Sonja I knew you had some freak in you somewhere."

Sonja said, "Please, I have a lot of freak in me, I'm just not the exhibitionist that you are."

Wanda veered off to the toy section of the store and started loading my cart up with all types of stuff. I scolded her.

"Wanda, I am not buying all that stuff!"

Wanda said, "I'm getting it for you, my treat."

Sonja laughed. I walked over to the cart and inspected the gadgets and things that Wanda placed in my cart. I began throwing things out.

"We don't need this, this, this and especially not this!" It was a jar of KY jelly.

Wanda said, "Why especially not this? There is nothing wrong with a little KY."

"There is when you don't do things that *require* KY." I said.

Wanda said, "Please, you and Jay have been together more than a decade, I know you give him some ass every now and then."

I said, "No the hell I don't. *That opening* is exit only."

Wanda said, "So you never give him any ass?"

I said, "He can hit it from the back, but that's all. I think that men that like anal are closet homosexuals. Besides, I did that shit in college once and it hurt like hell."

Wanda said, "That's why you use the KY."

Sonja interjected with, "Or you learn how to relax those muscles."

We both stopped when Sonja said that. Neither of us thought that Ms. Conservative was getting any dick, let alone taking it up the backside.

I whispered, "Girl you take it up the butt?"

Wanda said, "Sonja girl you are a freak, shit, we might have to hang out some time."

I said, "Sonja…so?"

Sonja said, "I've done it before. It's not may favorite thing, but I believe in compromising from time to time."

Wanda said, "Compromise my ass, I bet this bitch has a butt plug on now."

I laughed at that one. "So Sonja, you are okay with that sort of thing?"

She said, "Sure, why not?"

I said, "Fuck that. Jamie gets no back door action. My ass is big enough and jiggly enough for him to hit it from the back and pretend."

I picked out a few more outfits, grabbed flavored oils, feathers, handcuffs and a few multi-speed dildos. I wanted to hit Bakers next to get some stiletto heels, pumps and some thigh-high boots. I had a lot of freak in me. I can suck, fuck and talk dirty to my man and make him think that I am Chicago's biggest freak—without compromising my beliefs. Me and my girls hit the mall—hard.

JAMIE

I did it. I am officially no longer a father. I called the association in Park Forest and told them that I was selling the co-op. I gave all the contents to Don who had just moved out of his step mother's home into his own place. I then took a lump some of money and dumped it into a money market account. I then set the account up to continue to make scheduled payments to Yvonne. We agreed that $1,000 was fair. The remainder of the funds would go into a trust for Jerry when he was eighteen. I figure that he will think before his father "died" he left and made appropriate arrangements for his future, a gift that I wish my father had left for me.

I felt really guilty that I was shirking my responsibility to my first born. I tried and tried to shake it, but I couldn't. I again called Mike to let him know what it was that I was going through. At first I thought that he was going to lecture me, but being friends for the last fifteen years or so has taught him when to just listen. "Mike, I am at a loss as to what to do. I mean, what have I done? I love my shortie, but I also love Mia. But I can't betray Mia like that. I just can't let her know that I have a child. I know for sure that she will leave me."

"Jamie you are not the first brother to surprise a woman with a baby. Other couples have been through this sort of thing. You are going to have to exercise some faith in your woman and tell her."

"Mike...I...I can't."

"Then Jay, you are going to have to live with the consequences of your actions. I don't have the words or the answers to this brother, all I can tell you is to pray on it. Maybe you and Mia can go to couples counseling or something."

I hung up the phone with Mike and poured myself a glass of Bacardi and Coke, sat down and massaged my temples as I tried to figure out what I was going to do.

FRIDAY NIGHT

Friday night at about 6:00 PM is when Mia decided to give me a pleasant surprise. She put on a purple silk teddy, with a gold silk robe over it. She looked like a Que sweet from back in the day. She had on purple pumps to match and no stockings. Her legs had been shaved smooth and girlfriend looked good enough to eat. She walked over to be with a plate of fruit and began slowly feeding me grapes. I was in purple boxers, I had on Omega Psi Phi slippers, an Omega Psi Phi Robe, and had my dreads pulled back into a ponytail. My pecks were rock hard, as were my biceps. I took my beautiful bride in my arms and began planting slow wet kisses on her neck and collarbone as Floetry began singing *Say Yes* from our stereo system.

About 6:20 our doorbell began ringing incessantly. Mia told me to ignore it and whomever it was would go away. At 6:30, the bell was still ringing. It had to be the messenger waiting for me to sign the papers. I had been home all damn day waiting for the papers to arrive while Mia was out running her last minute errands. The moment that I think that the papers are not coming, they arrive.

"I am expecting some papers in the mail. I have to run and get that real quick."

Mia looked a little miffed, but she decided against starting an argument. She kissed me on the lips and said, "Make it really quick."

I ran to the front door and there was Travis' assistant, Ms. Richardson.

I said, "Hey...Ms. Richardson, I was expecting a messenger."

She said, "This is too important to be left with a messenger."

"So you know what this contract contains?"

"Yes sir."

"Great."

"Is there a problem sir?"

"No problem."

Ms. Richardson was a fine ass Asian lady that I thought Travis must be sleeping with. She was Asian with long black hair, hazel eyes and smooth almond skin. She was built like Kiana Tom from ESPN. I led her to my den and noticed as she took a seat across from my desk, that she had a *nice little body on her* for an Asian chick.

"Okay, where do I sign?"

She said, "There are 32 places that you need to sign."

"We need to get this done quickly."

"Mr. Kennedy, I am supposed to explain each clause."

I closed the door to the den. That was something that I had never done before. When I closed the doors Mia came in to the office on 10. She didn't care about the fact that she was in a teddy and although she looked elegant to me, she had to look ghetto as hell to Ms. Richardson.

"What is all the damn secrecy about?"

"There is a Confidentiality Clause in the contract dear. I'm sorry."

"Make it quick."

"You should tell her." Ms. Richardson said.

"Damn, how much did Travis tell you?"

"Mr. Kennedy, I am his attaché that means that I have his full confidence. There is nothing that I do not know about any of his private or public dealings or transactions."

I was thinking to myself that if I had an assistant this fine, I wouldn't keep anything from her either. I signed the document in all 32 places without reading one damn clause. I then escorted Ms. Richardson to the door.

She said, "You are supposed to keep a copy for your records."

"Send them to my office."

"You don't have an office, you work from home Mr. Kennedy."

I was like *Oh yeah.* "Mail them to me tomorrow then Ms. Richardson."

"You really should tell your wife."

"That will be all Ms. Richardson."

I let her out the front door. The whole ordeal took all of twelve minutes. Fortunately for me, Mia was still in the mood. I called out to her and already she switched into a totally different outfit. This time she was in leopard skin. She also had on a mask.

"Are you ready for the cat woman?"
I was like, "Hell Yeah."
She pounced on me.
After the first session of making love, I have no problem saying *Forget Eartha Kitt.*

ROUND TWO

After that first session of making love I laid there in bed beside my wife. I came so hard that I curled up I the fetal position and drifted right off to sleep. I had the most pleasant dream. I dreamed that my son grew up to be one of the top high school prospects in the nation. The NBA wanted him as well as the NFL. Like Bo Jackson, my son played two sports. He was trying to decide if he was going to be a power forward for the Chicago Bulls or a quarterback for either the Chicago Bears or Bandits. I also dreamed that my son would indeed discover the cure for Cancer and win the Nobel prize for his efforts. Finally, I dreamed that my son became the first black president of these United States. In each of the sequences my son was smiling. In each sequence his mother was beside him. In the back with his chest stuck out and smiling proud was...Travis.

I had another set of dreams where I flashed forward to things that have yet to come. The first time my son tries to ride a bike, the first time that he tries to play organized sports, the first time that he kisses a girl, drives a car, or goes to prom. All these things will be milestones in his life. I won't be there for any of them. What if he grows up resenting me? What if he thinks that I have abandoned him? I have, haven't I? What if he goes down the wrong path simply because he had no father there to guide him? He has Travis, but how much do I really know about this brother? For all I know he could be abusive, he could be a child molester, he could...kill my son!

I awoke sweating and every muscle in my body was tense. Why was I bugging the fuck out? Jerry will be fine. He has a loving mother, a rich uncle and a man that I have come to know and respect. I have to get my head back into the game and let him go. Someone once told me that sometimes when you love someone, you have to let them go. I always thought that was referencing relationships, but I guess that can also apply to father-son relationships also. I am doing what is best for my son.

Just then, a voice in my head said, *"No, you are doing what is best for you."* The voice was child-like, almost angelic. I looked over to Mia, and she was dead sleep. I called out to her over and over again, but she wouldn't stir from her slumber. "Hello?" I said aloud.
"Daddy don't leave me."

"Jer...Jerry?"
"Daddy Don't leave me, I need you."
I was wildin the fuck out. I looked over to Mia and she still hadn't moved. Here I was sitting up in bed and speaking out loud, and Mia didn't fuckin move. I started shaking her, but she still didn't stir. It was like she was dead or catatonic. *Daddy Don't you leave me! Do you here me Daddy? Don't you leave me!*
I awoke sweating and shouting my son's name.
"Jerry!"
    Mia was up. I was dreaming—again. She was looking at me strangely and I looked back at her with fear. *What did I say in my sleep? Shit, I am hoping that I didn't say much. Why is she looking at me like that?*
"Baby, it's okay, you are juts having a bad dream, relax, it's okay."
"Right...I...um...I'm sorry."
"It's okay Jamie. What were you dreaming about? Do you want to talk about it?"
"Uh, naw, that's okay. I would rather forget tonight's dream."
"Okay."
"I'm going to get a drink of water, do you want anything?"
"No, I'm fine."
I got up and threw my robe on and headed to the door to go downstairs to get some water.
"Jamie?"
"Yeah Babe?"
"Whose Jerry?"
"No one. It was just a dream. I mean...I don't know."
I went downstairs and got myself a Rum and Coke. I was thinking water, but my body needed a stiff drink. A few minutes later, Mia came downstairs. She still had on the leopard outfit. With that big juicy ass of hers she looked like a ghetto thundercat.
"I can take your mind off the bad dream that you had." She said smiling.
"Oh? And how do you propose to do that?"
"Come here."
I walked over to my wife in my maroon silk pajamas and robe and she undid the silk belt. I felt my member stiffen as she touched it ever so lightly through the light smooth material. She kissed my rock hard chest and ran the backside of her hand up and down my six pack. She kissed both my pecks, then my stomach, and then back up to my mouth where she tongued me deeply. She then dropped to her knees right there in our newly remodeled kitchen and began to please me orally. I threw my head back in ecstasy as I felt her warmth. In just a few minutes,

she began working me with a familiar rhythm. I was just about to reach out for her long free flowing hair when I heard as clear as day,

"Daddy don't you leave me!"

My dick went limp. In just a matter of seconds, I went from hard to limp.

Mia was not pleased.

In fact, she looked disappointed.

"Baby, I'm sorry." I said. "Another time?"

She stood up and looked at me with a look of confusion, I saw her look and she saw that I saw her look, yet I offered no explanation. I went upstairs and took myself to bed. Mia stayed there in our kitchen. I didn't hear her speaking to herself.

"I wonder is Jeri a woman?"

CHAPTER 9

▼

WHICH WAY IS UP?

MIA

Jamie must think that I am a goddamned fool! No man in the world goes from rock hard to limp in the middle of having his dick in a woman's mouth unless that man has problems with impotency, or that man is preoccupied with a another woman. I might be wrong, *I might be.* But in the same token, he has been acting strange as hell lately. I should have known something was up when he agreed to have kids all of a sudden after my begging his ass for years. Something is wrong in my marriage again, and I will be damned if I am going to come up on the short end of things this time. I worked to goddamned hard to see my shit go in ruin. He had better not be cheating on me, I swear to God he had better not be cheating on me or I am gonna fuck around and be on the news! People think Lefteye and Blu Cantrell have tempers, they ain't seen shit if I find out that Jamie is messing around.

All weekend long I have been dressing up and trying to keep a positive mood between us. All weekend long I have tried everything short of Viagra to get him hard and now all of a sudden he has a problem. Something is wrong here and I know damn well it ain't me. He had better not be having second thoughts about us, I will cut his balls off first. I cut back my hours at the magazine, we have been to couples therapy, and I even dragged his ass in the church a few times to meet with the pastor. I have done everything to keep my marriage in tact and to hold on to my man. Now all of a sudden it seems like he has taken his interest somewhere else.

I called Loretta and asked her what did she think of the situation? After all, she is a little older and she and Mike have been through hell and back in their relationship. She is the most controversial woman in City Hall as the first lady, but at least she has her man.

"Mia I think you are jumping the gun on this a bit. He might be having penis problems because of the pressure you are putting on him to have this baby." Loretta said.

"Pressure? What Pressure? All Jamie has to do is get laid?

"You know what I mean. He may be afraid of fatherhood, or having doubts. What was his relationship with his father like?"

"Terrible, so terrible in fact that I don't even want to get into it. Jamie is carrying more baggage than both Midway and O'Hare airport."

[laughing] Well then, there you go. Jerry doesn't have to be a woman, Jerry could be anything, an old friend that was killed, something from his past, it could be anything."

"Yeah, well…I guess you might be right." I said.

"I know that I am right. Girl don't put so much pressure on yourself, and try to put less on him. The baby will come, in time. Just go with the flow and let things happen naturally."

"Sounds like a plan to me. Loretta girl, thanks. You might have saved a life today."

"Really? How?"

"I was ready to wake Jamie's ass up with hot grits this morning"

We both laughed and talked the talk that girls talk when they are going through a thing with their men.

LORETTA/MICHAEL

After I hung up the phone with Mia, I was a bit pissed at Michael. There was something going on with his boy and Mr. Mayor hadn't told me anything. I wasn't in the mood to argue with him. He and I have been reconciling fine of late and I was hoping that we may remarry one day soon. Granted we were married before, but I have been sexing Michael like crazy and with all the nookie that he is getting, he needs to marry a sister—again. I walked into the bathroom where Michael was brushing his teeth and getting ready to go play ball with his boy, when I started in with the questions.

"Michael do you love me?"

"More than anything."

"Really."

"Yeah, of course."

"So do you keep things from me?"

"Aw shit, what's wrong?"

"Nothing—between us."

"Then who?"

"Your Boy and his wife."

"Lo, I am not getting into Jamie and Mia's relationship, whatever it is, we need to stay out of it."

"I'm not in it. I just want to know what's going on at our end of things."

"We have no *end of things*."

"Well, I have a question."

"Okay, shoot."

"Who is Jeri?"

Michael let out a long sigh.

"Shit, does Jamie need a place to crash? He can stay in the spare room until things blow over...Please say that he can stay here."

"Stay here? Michael...what...So there is another woman!"

"Woman? What the hell are you talking about woman?"

"Jeri, J-E-R-I. Mia thinks that is the name of your boy's new mistress. I tell you, when the hell are you all going to grow up and stop fucking everything that moves? Jamie should know better by now!"

Michael started laughing.

"Exactly what the hell are you laughing at?" Loretta said.

"Jerry is spelled J-E-R-R-Y. It's a male name."

"So Jamie isn't messing around on Mia?"

"Not as far as I know?"

"So who the hell is Jerry?"

"His son."

"His Son!"

"Aw, shit...maybe I shouldn't have said anything."

"Michael, this motherfucker had a son with that tramp ass bitch Yvonne?"

"You knew about Yvonne?"

Long Silence. They both remembered that that name reminded them both of a time they would each like to forget. For a minute, Mike stopped brushing and Loretta stopped pressing. Then after more time, Loretta broke the silence.

"Mia doesn't know that Jamie has a son?"

Mike looked at Loretta with a look that said what do you want from me? He then said, "No, Mia doesn't know."

"So how does Jamie plan to get out of this one?"

Mike told Loretta Jamie's plans for letting Travis adopt young Jerry. Loretta shook her head in disgust.

Mike said, "What's the big deal?"

"What's the big deal? Children are not defective toys or merchandise that you return when you are bored our through playing with them. Jamie can't just have a baby and decide that he no longer wants to be a father and make a fucking exchange!"

"Why are you fussing at me like I had something to do with this shit?"

"Because that's your boy!"

"Jamie being my boy has nothing to do with what is going on with him and Mia. That is their business and we are in no position to judge."

"So you don't think what Jamie is doing is fucked up?"

"I didn't say that, but Jamie is a grown ass man capable of making grown ass decisions. You can't hold me accountable for what he does, in the same token you can't judge him."

"Why not?" Loretta asked.

Mike said, "To be honest with you Lo, It's not your business."

There was a short silence between the two of them.

"Sometimes I wish that the two of you were not friends."

"TFS."

"What's TFS?"

"Typical Female Shit."

"Excuse me?"

"When a man and woman get together each holds the other responsible for the behavior of their friends. Women especially do this and come to loathe and hate most men's best friends. Why? Because they think that the single friend or the one that they come to not have so much respect for is influencing their mate, rather than accepting that their mate is grown and if that mate should step out, cheat, steal or do any wrong, they did it because they were going to do it anyway, *not because of the no good friend.* Jamie is a good man. To not want me around him because you don't approve of things he is doing in his life is TFS—Typical Female Shit."

"Wait a minute brother. The same applies for men. If I had a best girlfriend that was a hoe, you would think that she was influencing me. So why is it TFS instead of TMS, which rhymes with PMS but would stand for Typical Male Shit? Why isn't that a two way street?"

"Because I'm a man and we are hypocrites." Michael laughed and walked off.

Loretta yelled behind him. "Your boy is fucked up."

He yelled back, "That's between that man and that woman, get dressed. I am taking you out to dinner tonight."

Loretta shook her head in disbelief and got undressed in the bathroom. She began running bathwater and sat on the toilet to pee. She felt abdominal pains that were knifing her midsection. It felt as if someone were pushing knives through her from the inside out. Before passing out she screamed Michael's name. Michael rushed to the bathroom and found his ex-wife unconscious, in a pool of her own blood. The blood was running from between her legs.

JAMIE

I had to get Mia's mind off making a baby and I had to get her mind off of it soon. I was unsuccessful as of late in not only making a baby, but maintaining an erection. Psychologically I was going through something. Each time that we tried to make love, I would go limp. I know that part of the problem was the fact that I have just given up my parental rights to my son. I think that the other reason is that I really don't want a baby. I never wanted children. I am too selfish for children. I have no desire to change my lifestyle or deal with all the drama that comes from having kids. I am betting that the minute we have kids, Mia will stop keeping herself up and that slamming ass body that she has will quickly disappear. Then there is Christmas and my birthday to consider. Kids are so expensive, that the majority of the money in the house will go to them, plus if things don't work out between me and Mia and we ever get divorced, I will get raped financially in court. Nope, I don't want kids and that has got to be part of the problem and the reason that I can't function physically.

Mia was mad as hell initially, but after she got off the phone with Loretta, she seemed to calm down some. To get her mind off the bedroom and our immediate problems, I decided to take her to *Bandits Day* at the stadium. Bandits Day is a day for family and friends. It is a day when present players, former players and their families get together for a week of fun. New movie releases were shown in the theatre on site, celebrities and their families showed up, and the wives all got a chance to get together to bitch and complain about what was going on with the men in their lives. Mia loved getting together with the other wives of Pro athletes. I guess it was therapeutic for her to see other women that were going through similar problems with their husbands or worse. Generally after talking to the other women, Mia was grateful that she and I didn't have the problems that other women had. Believe it or not, there is a lot of domestic violence that goes on behind the scenes in pro football. There are other issues as well. You have guys on psychotropic medication, guys in therapy, steroid use, drug use and a host of emotional problems.

The men of course do not discuss all the drama that we are each going through. Mia seems to learn more about what is going on than I do. She said that last year she found out that one of the biggest and meanest linebackers in the league had a three inch penis. This threw me off because his wife had to be the finest woman I have ever seen. Their sex life is non existent. He just keeps her around for show. Another defensive player in the league that is rumored to be one of the most vicious hitters to ever play the game, is gay. His wife gets paid 20,000 a month just to pretend to be his bride. He brings young men home all the time and although the two of them live together, they are in separate wings of his mansion.

Mia comes back with a new report each year on guys that I used to play with and new members of the team. I wonder some days what the women say about me behind my back. I don't have to worry about Mia telling anyone our business, she is too proud for that. I let Mia have her time with her friends and I walked down the stadium's walk of fame. While in the great hall I looked at the photos and busts of great players for the Chicago Bandits. My heart was swollen with pride when I saw their newest exhibit. Right next to a photo of 3J, who broke the rookie record for rushing yards, was a number of photos of me. My section of the display said, "See the Flash, the great Jamie Kennedy." I only played five full seasons, but I left my mark on the league. I sat on the bench in front of the display, with a tear in my eye as I wondered what could have been. Just then I felt familiar arms hug around me and give me a kiss on the cheek. I could recognize Mia's Halston perfume anywhere.

"I thought that you were out gossiping with your friends?"

"I heard about this new exhibit from one of the other wives and thought that I might come and check it out."

"No new dirt on anyone yet?"

"Not yet, but I intend to get lots of juicy gossip when I get back to my crew."

"Your crew? You guys a gang or something?"

"Yeah, it looks like we are all going to call ourselves the ex-wives club."

"Really?"

"Yeah, half the women that were here last year are divorced from their husbands. What's worse is that a lot of the new wives are here."

"So their might be a catfight later?"

"Maybe."

"So whose side will you be on?"

"The ex-wives. I hate most of the new wives. They are all younger, skinny, and full of themselves."

"TFS"

"What's TFS?"

"A Private joke between me and Mike."

Mia and I stood there hand in hand and in awe of my photos. It was a proud moment for our little family. She had been with me when I was no one and stood by my side when I went down with my injury. She has helped me to keep my head above water by helping me to budget the remainder of my contract money. She was willing to downsize to a smaller house just to be by my side. Hell, I could have said, "Baby, we have to move into a shack on the west-side of town." Mia has always been down for me. I know if the bottom fell out, she would be there for me. I owe this woman my all.

As I sat there with my arm around my lady, I thought about all that we have been through and how good she has been to me. I then thought about the fact that Mia has only asked three things of me.

1.   Love her unconditionally

2.   Don't cheat on her

3.   Don't lie to her

In the past two years, I have broken all three of her rules. I said a silent prayer to myself as I told God, *"Just give me one more chance, and I will never lie, cheat or question her love for me again."*

God wasn't listening today.

The Devil however, I think had me marked on his calendar today.

I heard another familiar voice while I had my arm around Mia looking at my photo.

"Daddy! Daddy, Daddy, Daddy!"

I thought that I was imagining things again.

I prayed that I was imagining things.

As I turned around, Jerry was running at me full speed. 3J was behind him.

Although 3J played for Oregon now, he came back to Chicago to see his exhibit right next to mine. He brought his nephew…my son, to see the exhibit.

I was scared.

I looked over to Mia, who was holding back a well of tears, and hate. She looked at me with a scornful gaze that shook me to the very bone.

I didn't have the words.

She didn't move and neither did I. Jerry jumped up in my arms and I picked him up as he kissed me on the cheek. All the time, I never took my eyes off Mia nor did she take her eyes off me.

"Daddy, you have a picture right next to uncle 3J."

Still looking at Mia, I acknowledged my son. I said, "Yeah little man, I do."

I slowly put my son down.

Mia had a look of terror on her face. She looked at 3J and looked back at me as if putting things together as far as who Jerry's mother was. She then looked back at me and if looks could kill…

…"Daddy who is the pretty lady?"

I didn't say a word.

[To Mia] "Hello, my name is Jerry, what's your name?"

Mia knelt down to look at my son. He had his mother's eyes which made him look almost Asian, but he had my smile, my lips, my nose, and my cheeks. With tears in her eyes, she said, "My name is Mia."

Being the little gentleman that he was, Jerry said, "Nice to meet you."

Mia said, "*Nice to meet you too…*"

Jerry asked Mia, "Why are you crying?"

Mia said, "Because I am getting a divorce."

Mia gathered her purse and all of her belongings. She looked at me with a look that said that this was the final straw. Tears began streaming down my face.

"Daddy now why are you crying?"

"No reason son."

I asked 3J, "What are you doing here?"

"The same thing that you are doing here, seeing my exhibit."

"Why didn't you or Yvonne tell me?"

"As far as I know, we don't have to consult with you about anything anymore. You signed away your rights, remember?"

"Yeah, well now that Mia knows, I guess that part is over."

I walked down the hall to see if I could catch up to my wife.

3J yelled out to me, "Yo Jamie?"

"Yeah?"

"You are no longer my agent, you are fired."

"See you in court 3J."

I knew that my termination was coming. 3J and I had a contract though. For every commercial, every endorsement and every TV interview, I was going to be paid. My contract is very specific about these things. 3J could hire a second agent if he wanted, as long as he continued to pay the both of us. I made my way to the parking lot where Mia was pulling off in our BMW truck. Just then my cell phone rang. I hoped it was Mia, it wasn't. It was Mike, Loretta was in the Emergency Room at Mercy Hospital. The Cancer had returned. My problems with Mia would have to wait. My best friend needed me.

MIA

I can't believe him. I cried all the way home. That bastard. Now I know what Cheryl Pepsi Riley's song *All cried out* was about. I cried over Jamie's ass until I was out of tears. I loved that man. Scratch that, I loved that nigga. I can't believe that he did this to me. All this time I have been *begging him for a baby* and this MF has a baby with another woman. That means he fucked another woman and had unprotected sex. That means that my mouth has been where another woman's vagina has been. That means that I have slept with whomever this other woman has slept with. This also means that he could have exposed me to any STD including HIV. Jamie cheated on me. Not only did he cheat on me. He cheated on me and had a baby with another woman.

I got back home to our place and thought about my next move. I planned initially on tearing the house up, but that's not really my style. A baby was living proof that he cheated on me. The fact that his son looked two or three means that he intentionally kept this from me and that means more deception. Rather than go off on him, I got on the phone and called a lawyer. There are plenty of lawyers in Chicago chomping at the bit to hook up a professional athlete. I was doing fine at the magazine and now bringing in more money than Jamie was. That being the case, I had enough capital to spend on crushing his ass in court. I was going for half of all his assets and suing him on top of that for mental cruelty. He will rue the day that he stepped out on me.

When I finished talking to the attorney, I began crying uncontrollably. I was so hurt that I began tearing shit up anyway. I found everything that was of value to Jamie in our home and destroyed it. The hurt that I was feeling was unbearable. I thought that I would feel better after I tore the place up—I was wrong. Nothing could take away the hurt of the betrayal. I upset myself so that I ended up throwing up two or three times over the next few hours.

I expected Jamie to be home to beg my forgiveness, but he hadn't come in and it's been over three hours. He is such a fucking coward. Why isn't he here begging to get me back? Why isn't he here explaining himself? Then it dawned on me that there is nothing that he could say to make this right. I guess he accepted things for what they were just as I need to, our marriage...is over. I poured myself a strong drink and sat down on the couch, the same couch where we made love most evenings. When I thought about all of the lovemaking that we made over the years, I became sick in body. That man touched me after touching another woman.

What about Yvonne? I have met that tramp on more than one occasion. She knew, she had to know, and here she was all up in my face smiling, knowing damn well that she had my husband's child. Things are starting to make sense to me now. His son looks like he is a little over two years old. That means that when Jamie had that drama up there in Oregon, doing 3J's contract, that is probably when he got her pregnant.

I went to look at Jamie's scrapbook. Even though he was no longer playing ball, he kept every article and every photo of him that was in a newspaper or magazine clipping. There was one that I remember in his scrapbook that I needed to see again. It was like I knew in the back of my mind, but my thought patterns kept me in denial. I looked at the photo of Yvonne on the day that she had the baby. The article said, *Former Running Back an Uncle!* I read the article. It said that she (Yvonne) was having a baby and that the baby was conceived through invitro-fertilization. I remember Jamie saying that he had to be there because it was a good PR move to support women's rights and it would be a good promo for 3J. As I look at the picture now, I see things much more clearly. The article was on 3J which is why in the photo he is all smiles and cheesing for the camera. When I look at Jamie in the background of the picture, he is looking adoringly at the baby and oblivious to the camera. In the photo, *Yvonne is looking up at Jamie adoringly,* she too is oblivious to the camera. I threw up again. That bastard. I looked through Jamie's phone book and found a cell number for Yvonne. She was written in the phone book as 3J's manager, Yvonne. I was mad as hell and decided that I needed to call her. She picked up on the first ring.
"Hello."
"Hello is this Yvonne?"
"Yes it is. Who is this?"
"This is Mia, Jamie's wife."
There was a long silence on the phone.
"Hello? Are you there?" I asked.
"I'm here."
"We need to talk."
"I always knew this phone call was coming…how do you want to play this?"
"Can you come to my house the next time that you are in town?"
"I'm in Chicago now."
"Can you come over?"

"Sure…give me the address."

"I'm sure you know the address." I snapped.

"I don't. Mia, I have never been to your house before."

That comforted me some. I gave Yvonne the address.

"Is Jamie going to be there?" She asked.

"I doubt it."

"Okay, then I guess I will be there in twenty minutes."

My stomach was all tied in knots. I didn't know what I wanted to say to Yvonne, but I knew that I had to talk to her and find out exactly what the hell was or had been going on.

I cleaned my face up and put my makeup back on. I didn't want to look like I had spent the last few hours crying. I also threw on my snakeskin tan boots, Levi blue jeans, and a Tommy Hilfiger top. I pulled my hair back in a ponytail and threw on a cap just in case I had to put in some work on Yvonne's ass. I also called my girls to let them know everything that happened. Wanda wanted to come right over, but I told her to stay home. Sonja said that she wanted to come over as well. I started to let Sonja come over just because I knew that she had no problem with helping me stomp Yvonne's ass if need be. I told Sonja to stay home too. I was going to handle this myself. I told them both to keep their cell phones with them in case I needed their support later or a place to stay. I still hadn't heard from Jamie which bothered me a little.

CATFIGHT

Yvonne arrived at my house about a half hour later. She was dressed in an after five dress, pumps and black stockings. She was dressed as if she was headed to the Grammy Awards. She had on a diamond necklace, Diamond Phat Farm Pin, and a Gucci watch. I noticed that she had the distinct smell of Chanel number five on. I had to admit to myself that Yvonne was a damn nice looking woman. She looked as if she were Black and Asian mixed. She had the best of both worlds. She had the long free flowing hair, the beautiful almond and caramel mix of skin, and an ass like mine, but smaller and curvier. She was working the hell out of this dress that she had on and she walked into my home like she owned the place. I could tell that this overconfident swagger of hers was just part of her personality. She looked over our home as if in awe to finally be allowed in this part of Jamie's world. The look that she had on her face told me that she had not been in my house before.

She looked at the walls and seemed surprised at all the photos of me and Jamie everywhere. We had a beautiful condo downtown that was three levels. When you first come into our home, there is a long hallway. On both walls for as far as the hall stretches, are pictures of me and my husband. There are pictures of us in college, pictures of us in France, Greece, Africa, the Cayman islands, Brazil and all over the U.S. In each photo we are holding hands, smiling and very much in love. I could see the hurt in Yvonne's face as she saw the love that was in our embrace.

"Come in, please sit down. Can I get you anything?" I asked.

"No I'm fine. Let's just get this over with."

Yvonne threw me off with her comment. I was not going to be dictated to *in my house,* so I ignored her comment and continued to be pleasant.

"And what is it that we are trying to get over with?" I asked.

"Look Mia, I know that if you called me over here it is because you found out about my son, now the question is, what do you want to do about it? I need to know, if there is going to be animosity, then as long as you and Jamie are together, my son cannot come over here. If you are cool with everything, then let's just agree to be civil and draw up some type of agreement."

I was ready to choke this bitch. She had obviously been around Jamie too long. I didn't just jump into business. That was a Jamie move. I liked talking about things, processing them, so she was going to have to slow her role.

"That's not how I operate. Now, Yvonne, let's talk about what brought us here in the first place. Let's talk about the affair that you had with my husband."

"What difference does any of that make? It was a long time ago, it was a one night stand, and quite frankly, it's old news."

"It may be old news to you, but it's new news to me. I am the one that was cheated on. I am the one that was disrespected here, and I would appreciate it if you kept that in mind while you are in my house."

"I am in your house at your invitation. You figure Jamie has never had me here, not even once."

"Nor should he have."

"Okay, is there a point to this exercise?"

"Yes, now please...I'm asking, start at the beginning."

Yvonne told me that she met Jamie at 3J's house at a party. She explained that at the time, Jamie and I were having serious problems and all I seemed to care about was work. Yvonne explained to me that she had a thing for Jamie from the first moment that she met him. She explained that the first night that she approached Jamie, he declined, telling her that he was married. She said that shortly after that, a friendship developed, one where when he and I were having problems, he would turn around and give her a call. She admitted that their friendship alone was inappropriate. She also admitted that she had been flirting with him since day one. I interrupted her.

"So you knowingly went after another woman's man?"

She said, "Like I said, you all were having problems. At the time you were acting like you didn't want him. At that point, I felt that he was fair game. No disrespect, but had been on top of your business at home, I would have never had the opportunity. He turned me down on more than one occasion. But the conversation, just being there for him, was how I was able to snag your man."

She said it so smug as if I were nothing. She said it as if working and seeking independence was a bad thing. She acted like she was perfectly justified in pursuing my man. I was ready to fight, but instead of going off, I listened. She then told me that it was 3J's idea that they go to Oregon together and pick out a house. She told me that Jamie seemed uninterested in her when they got to Beaverton. She then told me how while he worked on 3J's contract, she worked on ways to seduce him. She explained to me that she went after him that first night in Beaverton and things sort of just—happened. I held back tears as she told the story. She then went on to tell me about how the next day he regretted everything.

"So why didn't he or you use a condom?" I asked.

"He assumed I was on the pill, and I chose not to say that I wasn't."

"So you got pregnant on purpose?"

There was a long silence in the room.

"Yes, yes I did."

I felt light-headed all of a sudden. The room seemed like it was getting smaller and hazy at the same time. I poured myself a drink and then asked her to continue. She then went on to tell me that things were cool between she and Jamie that next day until she began to make demands of him. She then told me that the two of them got into an argument and then drove to the local grocery. She then explained to me that they were arguing in the parking lot when the two of them saw Loretta and Keith. Her words stung. I now know that Loretta knows or has known for the last two years. I asked her while we were up there if she thought Jamie was fooling around and she said no. I can't believe that Loretta covered up for Jamie. Not only had my husband betrayed me, my friend betrayed me as well. I would have told her if Mike had been cheating on her.

Yvonne told me that she and Jamie then had a long conversation that ultimately ended up with Jamie breaking up with her. She said that she heard that Michael and I flew up to Oregon, so she kept a low profile, She told Jamie weeks later that she was pregnant.

"Had the two of you even discussed the possibility of an abortion?"

"We discussed it, Jamie even offered to pay for it."

"But you decided against it."

"Yes, I did."

"Why?"

"One, I do not believe in abortion. Two, I guess at the time, I was trying to hold on to Jamie in any capacity. I know I didn't know him very long, but I loved him. Even after we went our separate ways I kept on loving him. That is until I met Travis."

"Who is Travis?"

"My fiancée"

"Fiancée?"

"Yeah, he is the man that adopted Jerry."

"Adopted?"

"Yeah. Jamie signed over his rights to Jerry Friday night. My fiancée sent his personal assistant over Friday with contracts to sign."

I am betting that this is why he couldn't function recently. Now everything makes sense, Jerry of his dreams was his son. He had a nightmare the same night that he signed over the rights to his son.

"Mia, Jamie is not a bad person. You are damned lucky to have him."

"Don't tell me how fucking lucky I am! You don't know me, you don't know us and you don't know shit about it!"

"I know that he loves you. You know what he said when I once threatened to tell you about us? He said go ahead, he said that it might hurt your relationship, but it just meant that he would spend the rest of his days pursuing you. I wish I had someone that loved me like that."

"Yeah, well how would you feel if that same loved one cheated on you?"

"It was a one night mishap, when things were bad between the two of you."

"You and I both know that doesn't make a difference. Besides, the night that he went to Oregon, I went all out for Jamie. He and I slept together. That means that he slept with *both of us in a 24 hour span.*"

"Well, I don't have cooties, if that is what you mean." Yvonne said.

"You are so young acting." I snapped.

"Look Mia, it was a mistake, It was looked at as a mistake from almost the moment that it happened. You can let this shit mess up your relationship with Jamie, or you can make the best of it. At any rate, any woman would be glad to get Jamie. So make him walk over hot coals or whatever it is that you have to do to make yourself feel better, but when you have…get over it and get over yourself. There are plenty of women, myself included that will take your leftovers any day of the week."

"That sounds pathetic."

"Does it? Well check this out. There is a percentage of good black men that are often overlooked by us. There are also plenty of no good ass men out there. There are a lot of men out there that are incarcerated, unemployed, and others still that are perfectly content with the little that they have in this world and have no dreams or aspirations. You have a man that is fine, wealthy, and independent and has a world of potential. I know that you are mad at him right now, but I mean damn, he fucked up! If you can hold on to him, hold on to him. If you think there is no coming back from this, the pass him on."

All this, from the woman that was supposedly, for one night…my man's mistress. I was mad as hell and ready to kick this bitch out of my house. She obviously still held a torch for Jamie. She also had no idea what infidelity meant in a marriage. Maybe she was okay sharing bodily fluids with both Jamie and me, but there is no way in hell I can forgive his transgression. I told Yvonne exactly what I thought of her.

"I think that you are a whore."

"That's fair, I guess I deserve that one."

"Aren't you even going to get mad at my insult?"

"Why should I? Look Mia, I didn't come here to fight or to argue. I came to see if my son would be welcome here now that you know he exists. Jamie gave up his rights on Friday, but I see no reason to honor the contract when I know that he is a good man and I know that he will be a good father. I can't let him come over here though if you are harboring animosity toward him. Now that the secret is out of the bag, I don't have to sneak around and facilitate visits and such. Bedsides, I hate Park Forest."

"What's in Park Forest?"

"The co-op that Jamie owned. That is where Jerry and I stayed when we visited Chicago."

"He bought a home for the two of you?"

"He actually bought it to have a place to cheat on you in peace without worry of being caught. Like I said, you all were having problems. He never used it though. That is where I stayed when I was here."

"Why didn't you stay at 3J's mansion?"

"After 3J found out, he and Jamie stopped speaking. In fact 3J fired Jamie today as his agent."

I tried to hold back the tears. This whole story was riddled with lies that Jamie had told me. I am sick and tired, and you know what? I am tired of being sick and tired.

"Thank you for stopping by. Your son is welcome here. I have nothing against him. The pain, the betrayal and the hurt, comes from you and Jamie. You all are the ones that I have the problem with. I will never mistreat your son *if I am around.* For now, please leave."

Yvonne gathered her things and headed toward the door. As she opened the door, Jamie was coming in. There was a look of terror on his face as he saw Yvonne walking out of his condo. He went to mouth something as if to ask what was going on, and then he thought better of it. Yvonne gave him a look that said he had his work cut out for him.

Jamie walked into the living area where Mia had her legs crossed, had obviously been crying and where she was finishing off the last of her drink.

MIA

"Where have you been?"

Jamie responded, "The Hospital."

"You sick?"

"No. Loretta's Cancer is back. She is in ICU at Mercy."

My heart jumped out of my chest at the thought of losing Loretta. I was salty with her for keeping the truth from me, but I still loved her like a big sister.

"I had better get over there."

I grabbed my purse and my keys and walked past Jamie. He grabbed my hand and spoke,

"Mia, I'm sorry."

My eyes met him and I said, "You are always sorry Jamie."

I headed to the door and left him standing there. I stopped short of the door and spoke again. "I'm divorcing you. I have already talked to an attorney. I don't want you here when I get back."

Jamie said, "Where am I supposed to go?"

I said, "Go to your little love nest in Park Forest."

AT THE HOSPITAL

I walked into the ICU and still there was Michael. He had a worried look on his face and he looked as if he had been ill.

"How is she?"

"The doctor says that it was a minor relapse. She is supposed to recover, but she is so weak, so decimated. I'm scared for her."

"Can I see her?"

"Sure, go right in."

I walked in and saw my friend of the past few years laid up in a hospital bed looking weak and helpless. This was hard for me because Loretta was such a strong woman that had overcome so much in her life. To see such a powerful woman helpless like that, chilled me to the bone. She had tubes in her nose, and in her arms and she was also being given blood. As soon as I saw her tears began streaming down my face. I understood what Michael meant when he said that he was scared for her. I was scared for her as well. The doctor said that she would recover, but to look the way that she looked...I just don't see how. Loretta was already a woman of a fair complexion. After the blood lost, she was so pale that she was almost white. Her eyes had a light blue tinge to them. She was sweating profusely yet her body looked cold, almost lifeless.

She looked at me and smiled. When she smiled I began to cry even more. I was no longer even salty with her for not telling me about Jamie. I was too preoccupied with all that she was going through physically. I walked over to her bed and sat next to her. I gently took her hand and we both were tearing for a while.

"Hey You." I said.

Loretta just smiled.

"I know, you are too weak to talk, that's okay. I just came to say that I love you girl and we are all pulling for you. The doctor says that you are going to be okay." Loretta nodded her head slightly saying yes. Michael walked back and forth outside the door but didn't come in. He was tearing something awful and didn't want to come and be with his wife until he could get himself together. No matter how hard he tried though, the tears just kept coming. When he did step in the room it was just to look at Loretta. Each and every time that he entered the room he mouthed the words I love you. Each time, Loretta gave him a smile. I rubbed my friend's head and wiped away her perspiration with a cool damp cloth.

"He loves you a lot." I said to her regarding Michael.

"Jamie loves you too." She whispered.

I gave a half smile that indicated the last thing that I wanted to talk about was Jamie's trifling ass.

"Sshhh, Loretta you need to save your strength."

"You...need...to...forgive him." She said, slightly sitting up.

"Is it that obvious that something is wrong?" I asked.

"Looks…like…you…have been crying…a lot…then put on makeup. Plus…a woman knows another woman's pain. Sorry…I…didn't tell you…wasn't my place."

"It's okay" I said.

Loretta reached out to me and placed her hand on my stomach.

"New life." She said.

"Huh? Oh…um…no, not me…Lo, you need your rest."

Loretta looked up at me and said, "A woman knows."

Tears streamed down my face. *She had better be wrong, I don't want a baby, not now, not like this. Not after all that Jamie put me through.*

Loretta spoke again, this time with more strength in her voice. "Let it go."

"What?"

"The pain, the betrayal, the hate…let it go."

I began crying. Here was this woman that I have known as a friend and a mother, a woman that I have come to love as a member of my own family, here she was decimated by this illness and still she was consoling me. When God created Loretta, he had Eve in mind. A sister like this is truly one of a kind.

"Mia…Let it go."

"Lo…I…I can't."

"Mia, look at me. Look at where I am. Life…is too short. Jamie has a seed. There is no sense in your taking your pain out on that life, especially with you carrying new life."

"He betrayed me Lo."

"He…made a mistake. One that he was willing to hide…to keep you from feeling any pain. [smiling] what he did was stupid…but not unforgivable. He was ready to give up his child for you. He loves you. Give him another chance."

"I'm tired of giving him second chances. When do I stop granting him second chances?"

"You stop giving him second chances when you stop loving him."

There was a small silence in the room.

"Do you still love him?"

"Yes."

"Then Mia, hold on to him. Don't think about the past, Hold on to the present…Baby, look to the future. Is this how you are going to raise your little girl?"

While crying and laughing I said, "So not only am I pregnant, but it's a girl? You just know this?"

"When you are this close to death…you see things."

That moved me to my very soul. My smile was gone. Her Statement was a sobering moment for the both of us. I felt her grip on my hand get tighter.

The doctor came in and began talking to Loretta and Michael. He asked me to leave, but Loretta said that it was okay for me to stay. The doctor said that he had some good news and some bad news.

The doctor said, "The good news is that like I said, Mrs. Carter, you are expected to make a full recovery. The bad news is that the Cancer has spread some. It is uterine cancer. The good thing about this, is that the Cancer looks like it is indeed going back into remission."

Loretta asked in a whisper, "And the bad news?"

The doctor sighed and said, "The bad news is that you will have to have a hysterectomy. You and Mr. Carter will not be able to have children."

Loretta and I looked at each other. She gave me a look that told me to be grateful. No woman ever wants to hear that she cannot bear children, even a woman that never planned on having any. Psychologically it makes you feel like you are empty, or not complete. Emotionally it pains you because you can never know a mother's love for a child. Mentally, it drains you and makes you question your partner's reaction. My problems with Jamie, no matter how large they seemed to be a few hours earlier, pale in comparison to what Loretta was going through.

The doctor continued with, "We can harvest your eggs and there are a lot of amazing options that are available through technology. Having children the traditional way, is out of the question."

He went on explaining all the various procedures and possibilities that were available through modern medicine. Michael sat there still tearing. He sat beside the bed of his ex-wife and put his head down as he wept. Loretta comforted him by rubbing his head. It was her body that was barren, her body infected with the cancer and still she was the strongest person in that room. If nothing else, Loretta was a nurturer.

Michael said, "If I had my shit together, we could have had kids earlier. Baby this is my fault…can you ever forgive me?"

Loretta said, "There is nothing to forgive."

"Michael said, "I love you."

Loretta said, "Prove it."

Michael said, "How?"

Loretta said, "Marry Me—again."

"If you have me again as your husband, I will forsake the world for you."

"Even though I can't have kids?"

"If you can't have kids, we can't have kids. All I have ever wanted in this life was you."

Loretta began crying.

I made my way to the exit.

She whispered something in Michael's ear. Before I could get out of the door Michael stopped me.

"Mia?"

"Yes Michael?"

"Loretta told me to tell you…New Life. I have no idea what it means but…"

"…I understand. Tell Girlfriend I hear her. Tell her that she's right. But tell her…in time."

Michael said, "Listen, I heard from Jamie about everything that happened and I just want to say that I'm sorry. Jamie loves you though."

"I know."

I walked out of the room and headed home.

BACK HOME
MIA

When I got home, Jamie was gone as I had asked. He left me a note stating that he would be staying at the Red Roof Inn. My heart sunk as I was alone in our home for the first time. I had been alone in our condo before, but I always knew before that Jamie would eventually be home. Once again, I threw myself in my work and began busting my butt at the magazine.

MONTHS LATER

Loretta made a full recovery in the months to come. In the meanwhile, I began to get bigger and bigger. She was right, I was pregnant. I moved out of my home and Jamie and I separated for a few months. I spoke to Loretta sparingly as I had a world of things on my mind. I kept her in my thoughts and prayers often, and I also sent her flowers. I left word with Jamie that he could have the condo and that I was not divorcing him—yet. We talked on the phone, but for months that was the only contact that I would allow Jamie to have. Then one day, I invited him to take me to lunch downtown at Bennigans. I told him to meet me at the magazine and to clear the remainder of the day so that we could talk.

Jamie arrived at the magazine with flowers in hand and looking good as hell. He had on black tuxedo pants, a black tuxedo jacket, and a cream colored mock turtleneck. He had on his face, trimmed two-day old stubble and had his locks pulled back into a ponytail. He also had on a pair of 300.00 sunglasses that made him look every bit of the celebrity that he was. He looked good from his head to his Italian leather boots. He had his Movado watch on, his Drakkar cologne (my favorite) and his superbowl ring. He had been working out all the time that he have been apart like he was back in training camp or something. He came here with the idea of leaving an impression with me. I invited him because I wanted to leave an impression with him as well.

He walked up to my assistant's desk and asked to see me. My assistant told him, "She is a meeting sir, just one moment. I will let her know that you are here. In the meanwhile please take a seat." Jamie sat down and I made him wait 10 or fifteen minutes before I came out.

When I came out of my office I was dressed in gym shoes, and a blue jean jumper—A maternity jumper. Jamie's mouth dropped to the floor.

He didn't know that I was expecting.

He gave me the flowers and kissed me. "We're having a baby?"

"Who said that it was yours?"

That sent him reeling in shock and in pain.

"Are you serious?"

"Let's go."

I had Jamie help me with my jacket. His mouth was still open with shock as I casually dismissed how he might be feeling. We walked from my downtown office on Madison Avenue to the Bennigans on Michigan Avenue downtown, the entire time I said nothing to him and Jamie was still in shock.

We arrived at the Bennigans a few minutes later and because I was pregnant we were immediately seated. Our waitress stopped by our table and asked if we wanted anything to drink.

Jamie said, "I'll have water."

I said, "I'll have a Bacardi and Coke."

Both Jamie and the waitress looked at me like I was out of my damned mind.

Jamie said, "The rum and coke I am assuming is for me."

"Maybe."

"But you are pregnant."

"Why is that your business?"

"I'm sorry Mia, am I missing something here?"

"Are you?"

"Whose baby is it?"

"Why?"

"Goddammit because…" Jamie lowered his voice and tried to compose himself. "You are fucking with me right? The Bacardi is for me and the baby is mine…right? Right!"

The waitress arrived with the two drinks. She sat them down and asked were we ready to order. I told her no and to come back. She walked halfway away almost as if she were waiting to see if I was going to drink the rum and coke. Jamie had a look on his face that said that he was just as curious.

I reached out my hand to grab a drink. Jamie reached out instinctively at the same time and he reached for the run which was close to me as I reached for the water which was closest to him. He looked down and realized his error.

Of course the rum and coke was for him, that was his drink. *I knew this. I knew this because I loved him and I was his WIFE.* He had reached for the Bacardi to stop me from drinking it. He did so without even looking to see where my hand was going. He did this because *he doesn't know me like he should. His reaching for the rum out of concern, was a mistake, a mistake he realized as he picked up his drink.*

"Was there a point to doing this?" He asked.

"There was. You don't know me like you should. There is no way in hell I would risk drinking while pregnant. You should know me better than that."

"And the baby?"

"Do you need to even ask?"

"No."

"Okay then."

We ordered our food. There was a silence as we looked out onto Michigan Avenue. The Art Institute was across the street. There were many people passing by the window going to their respective jobs, shopping and taking in the beautiful sight of downtown Chicago.

"So where are we going. I mean, what is the plan for us?" Jamie asked.

"I haven't decided yet." I said.

"Are we getting a divorce?"

"Do you want a divorce?" I asked.

"No, hell no."

"Then leave that word out of your vocabulary."

"Done."

There was another silence.

"How does it feel seeing me pregnant?"

"Surprising. A pleasant surprise, but surprising."

"How did it feel when I suggested that the baby wasn't yours."

"It hurt."

"But only a little, right?"

"Yeah Mia, only a little."

"What did you think about when I said that the baby might not be yours? What was the first thing that came to mind?"

"I don't know, I guess the first thing that I was concerned with was your health and your not telling me and…"

"Wrong! That is not the truth. You see, this is where we have a problem. You like to sugarcoat shit, conspire and hide things from me to spare my feelings. You think that you are doing all this to help me, when in fact you are sabotaging our relationship. I can't start over with you again if you can't be honest with me about little shit Jamie. If I can't trust you to tell me the truth about little things, how can I trust you in a relationship? How can I trust you in a marriage? How can I trust you to raise a child with me? Now, my question is simple. I already know the answer. All you have to do is tell me the *truth* and we can start all over again and give another shot at being husband and wife. You fuck this up Jamie, I am walking out of this restaurant and out of your life forever. Now, when I suggested that the baby might not be yours, *what was the first thing that came in your mind?*"

Jamie said, "The first thing that came to mind was *who had you been fucking other than me.*"

I said, "Very good. Now was that so hard? Now, when you thought that I might have slept with someone else, what were the first couple of things that came to mind?"

Jamie thought long and hard and gave out a sigh as he said, "First I tried to figure out who else you might have slept with, then I thought about how many times, where that other persons hands have been, whether or not you loved them, and how could you be carrying another niggas child."

"And how did that make you feel?"

"Mia look…I…"

"How did I make you feel!" My voice was loud enough to get the attention of people at the bar. People from other tables looked over at us, but my attention was on Jamie.

Jamie said, "I felt…worthless, betrayed, and *hurt.*"

I let him digest his food and his words again before I spoke.

"Imagine that same hurt, that same feeling of betrayal, and the hundreds of thoughts *at once* of not knowing and *imagining* the worst over and over again in your head. Imagine being so hurt that you are sick. Imagine being so hurt that your very world has been shattered. Then, take that same hurt and multiply it by 100. That is what a woman feels each and every time that one of you brothers steps out on us. Top that off with a hundred I'm sorry's and all the lies and promises of relationships past and you have what it means to be a black woman in today's society. Now, top that off with work, adversity, racism, disease, and siphoning through the next man's bullshit, and you have a very confusing situation known as dating in America. When I married you, we were supposed to be beyond that hurt, beyond that chaos and beyond all that bullshit. I love you Jamie, but you hurt me and you betrayed me. Granted, it was almost three and a half years ago, but the wound is still fresh. I just wanted you to understand that."

Jamie sat there nodding his head in agreement. Finally, I think he understood the depth of my pain.

"So where do we go from here?" He asked.

"From here, I think we go for a long walk down Michigan Avenue. I have some things that I need your help with."

"Things like what?" Jamie asked.

"Names for your little girls."

"Girls?"

"Yeah, we are having twins."

I smiled at my husband. He smiled back.

"I am thinking that we should name one of the girls Loretta."

Jamie said, "I think that would be a great start."

Like Loretta said, "New Life."

EPILOGUE

▼

Loretta waited until Mia had the twins before she and Michael remarried. Mia named the twin girls Loretta and Daryn. That following March, Loretta had made almost a full recovery. She and Michael were married—again. Yvonne Married Travis. 3J had a paternity suit against him from a twenty something year old white girl from Colorado that lied about the entire affair in an effort to extort money from him. Jerry, seems to be adjusting fine to the fact that he has two mommies and two daddies. Loretta and Michael have decided that when time permits, they are going to have children. Mia has agreed to be the surrogate mother and Loretta's eggs will be harvested in Mia's womb.

END.

AUTHOR'S NOTES

If I do more with this storyline, it will be either a rewrite, or I will create a sequel that deals primarily with Sonja and Wanda's characters. I finished writing this book on 12/15/03. I took the day off from work to finish it. My ex-wife thinks that it is too short (as are all my books) but I have come to the conclusion that my books should be quick reads. I would like to call them "weekend books" or start a company called weekend books.

I enjoyed writing this book and I look forward to the feedback of all the people that happen to come across it. This is yet another "underground joint" that will probably do well in the beauty shops across Chicago and in the hands of my regular readers. I am hoping that this book or my last one, *Divorce Him, Marry Me* will get me a large publishing deal. I would really love to write full time. I love my work in social services, but it is wearing me out also.

I am sure that a lot of people are wondering why these books are so small. The truth is, I do not always have the words and at times, I love the storyline, but get bored with writing. I love my books for the first hundred pages or so, but then I am ready to write something totally different. These books are actually not *that small.* Before print, this one is at least 300 pages. Once they are made smaller and double sided, it comes out to like 150 pages or so. The manuscript in my hand however is about two inches thick.

BIGGEST CHALLENGES WITH THIS BOOK:
The biggest challenge with this, or any other book that I have done is two-fold. One of the chief concerns is that there is too much graphic sex in my books. Well, I'm a guy. That's how we think, or at the very least how I think. I have

tried to tone it down. Suggestions in the past have included using the word penis rather than dick. The word penis just sounds so damned odd to me. The second thing that I hear most is "Women don't think like that." I also hear, "A woman would never do _____." I have a lot of female friends and a lot of the stuff that other women say they would never do, many other women say that they would. It is my experience that women think just as we do and at times are just as graphic in their thinking as men are.

My ex-wife (who is instrumental in my work) has tried to get me to write more like a harlequin romance, but that just is not in me (yet). She (the ex-wife) listens to the storylines and the characters as they develop and she critiques me virtually every step of the way. An example of this is the fight scene in the wedding in the first chapter. Leslie (the ex-wife) thought that instead of Loretta giving direction at the wedding and saving Mia's big day, Mia should have thought of everything on her own and simply asked Loretta to participate. That *did make more sense,* but I did not feel like going back and rewriting that whole sequence.

For those that are interested, there are other nuances in this book that you might take note of. If there are typos and grammatical errors I apologize. I can't afford paying for editing, I just can't. When I blow up (If I blow up) these books will be collectable items. For those that don't know me, I was a high school drop out, I ran the streets and though I was a decent student, I was not an English major. People might also notice that where I should have used contractions, I didn't. I am sure that changes the pulse of the book and makes me sound really proper. Well the reason for that is I am in Graduate School to get my M.S. in Counseling. <u>You are not allowed to use contractions in Grad School.</u> That sort of carried over into my writing.

BOOK CLUBS: I am hoping that book clubs will pick this one up. That being the case, I have conveniently written questions for book clubs across the nation to consider while they are reading my book. I would also like your feedback on my website at <u>www.dlsmith.net</u>

CHAPTER ONE QUESTIONS:

1. Should Jamie have gotten married in the first place when from the very beginning he seemed to have doubts?

2. What do you think of Michael's statement that today's black women, "call you, fuck you and dismiss you?"

3. What do you think about the fight between Sonja and Wanda? Do you have friends that can't get along or hate one another?

4. Should Loretta have stopped Michael from getting head from Denise? What might you the reader have done in her place? Is it realistic that she would watch and wait to see how far things would go?

5. Do we get so preoccupied with our work/dreams/aspirations that we sometimes neglect our partners?

6. Should Loretta have gone through her ordeal with the Cancer alone?

CHAPTER TWO QUESTIONS:

1. Did Mia put too much time and effort in her new job? Explain your answer.

2. Was Jamie unfair in his approach to Mia's weight gain?

3. Doesn't sex naturally taper off in relationships?

4. Is there too much sex in this book?

5. Why do men cheat?

6. What do you think of Jamie demanding that Mia quit?

CHAPTER THREE QUESTIONS:

1. Jamie does a lot of flashing back in this book. Why is it so hard for him to see that he has a good woman at home?

2. Mia just wants Jamie to be as loyal to her as she has been to him. Is she asking too much or to little from him?

3.   Loretta and Mike seem more like parents than friends, is this normal in relationships with other couples?

4.   Should Loretta have accepted flowers from Keith to begin with?

5.   Did Mike have a reason to be as mad as he was about Loretta having slept with Don?

6.   Should Loretta have turned down Keith's invitation to Oregon? * I started to make her affair with her therapist, David but I changed my mind.

CHAPTER FOUR QUESTIONS:

1.   Do men really go through the lengths that Jamie went through in order to cheat? (separate house, phone, pager etc.,)

2.   Is it true that all women will allow their man to have at least one indiscretion and then forgive him?

3.   Is it true that women can forgive a one night stand more than they can forgive a full-blown relationship with another person?

4.   Don says that his past is the reason that he is such a dog. Is this a valid excuse?

5.   Was Mike justified in fighting with Don?

CHAPTER FIVE QUESTIONS:

1.   Who really initiated the affair between Jamie and Yvonne?

2.   Do women stop wearing lingerie later in relationships? How often do women dress up for men like Mia did for Jamie?

3.   Should Jamie have gone to Oregon?

4.   Should Loretta have slept with Keith?

5.   Should Jamie have slept with Yvonne?

6.   Does size matter?

CHAPTER SIX QUESTIONS:

1.   Should Loretta's assistant have opened the door to Loretta's office for Mike?

2. What do you think of the parking lot scene in Oregon? Should Loretta and Jamie have just gone their separate ways?

3. Should Loretta have met Jamie at his hotel lobby?

4. Was Jamie's breakup with Yvonne too easy?

5. Do men lie in relationships out of fear or to spare a woman's feelings?

6. Was Loretta wrong for discussing she and Michael's problems with Jamie?

CHAPTER SEVEN QUESTIONS:

1. Should Jamie have told Mia about his affair in Oregon when he first had the chance?

2. Did Loretta take Mike back too quick or did she take too long?

3. Should Loretta have given a *relationship* with Keith a chance? Did she lead him on? Did she use him for sex?

4. When Mia asked Loretta if she thought Jamie had been fooling around in Oregon, should Loretta have told her about Yvonne?

5. Is there really such a thing as women's intuition?

6. Was Wanda wrong for sleeping with Carl Allen?

CHAPTER EIGHT QUESTIONS:

1. Should Jamie have told Mia about the baby?

2. How should he have told her?

3. Was it worse by waiting two years to tell Mia?

4. Was Jamie wrong in considering putting his son up for adoption?

5. What do you think about adoption in general?

CHAPTER NINE QUESTIONS:

1. Do women typically dislike their mates friends?

2. Was Mia justified in calling Yvonne?

3. Was Yvonne justified in her way of thinking?

4. Yvonne knowingly went after another woman's man, is this common among today's black women?

5. Should Mia have divorced Jamie?

6. If this book is rewritten, what would you like to see done differently?

0-595-31323-X

Printed in the United States
25224LVS00003B/163

9 780595 313235